FIRE ON
BREAKNECK MOUNTAIN

A Sheriff Jordan Tynes
Modern Western Mystery

Book 4

GREGORY C. RANDALL

WINDSOR HILL
PUBLISHING

www.gregorycrandall.info
www.windsorhillpublishing.com

Printed in the United States of America

Published by
Windsor Hill Publishing
Walnut Creek, California 94596

Paperback ISBN: 979-8-9907508-5-2
Ebook ISBN: 979-8-9907508-6-9

Cover Design: Gregory C. Randall

FIRE ON
BREAKNECK MOUNTAIN

OTHER TITLES BY
GREGORY C. RANDALL

NONFICTION
America's Original GI Town: Park Forest, Illinois

FICTION
THE ALEX POLONIA THRILLERS
Venice Black
Saigon Red
St. Petersburg White

THE SHARON O'MARA CHRONICLES
Land Swap For Death
Containers For Death
Toulouse For Death
12th Man For Death
Diamonds For Death
Limerick For Death

THE TONY ALFANO MYSTERIES
Chicago Swing
Chicago Jazz
Chicago Fix
Chicago Boogie Woogie
Chicago Back Beat

THE MAX ADLER WORLD WAR II THRILLERS
This Face of Evil
Pawns in an Ancient Game

THE DEPUTY JORDAN TYNES MYSTERIES
One Yellow Dog
The Killings in Paradise Valley
Blood in the Yellowstone

White Rabbit
The Cherry Pickers
The Marigold Gang, The Mystery of the Four Bodies in the
Freezer
Four Women Named July
Wars Amongst Lovers
Sector 73

DEDICATION
This novel is dedicated to law enforcement
personnel throughout the United States
working tirelessly to rid the country of the
terrible scourge of drugs.

Chapter 1

Spring in Park County, Montana, had been dry, driest in years. That hazy morning, as the rising sun cast the long shadow of the Crazy Mountains across the Shields River Valley, the air smelled of buffalo grass and sage. Sheriff Jordan Tynes paralleled the river on Highway 89; she drove at speed, and her light bar flashed, no siren—it was not a matter of life and death. From the stands of cottonwoods along the river, clouds of fluff floated across the road, her yellow Jeep Sahara swirling them into snow-like clouds. She mostly closed her open window, trying to reduce her sneezing. The town of Clyde Park was four miles behind her, and the road was clear three miles ahead and back. She turned right on a dirt road and drove into the foothills that spread out from the mountains.

She slid to a stop on the dirt road behind Deputy Wells Courtwright's black F-150 Police Responder; dust enveloped the Jeep. She clicked off her light bar; Courtwright's light bar was enough. She didn't know what to expect; the radio described the crime scene as horrific. The initial reports used malevolent words: *evil*, *vicious*, *brutal*, *bloody*, *inhumane*, and *sicko*. Courtwright leaned against the Responder, smoking a cigar. She accepted his habit ten years earlier in Iraq when Courtwright was her sergeant. Smoking this early in the morning only added to her dread.

"You stay," she said to Maggie. The yellow Carolina dog was her constant companion. "I'll be right there." She pointed to Courtwright and climbed out. "Good morning, Sergeant."

"Hardly that, Jordan," Courtwright answered. "Certainly, not a goddamn good thing in there." He pointed to a swayback wood barn, half hidden behind the house, a hundred feet from where they parked. A few side planks were missing; dry grassland behind the building was visible. On the horizon, backlit with the coming of the sun, the Crazy Mountains materialized out of the dust and fog. "I saw it in Iraq, and I've seen it here. Never fails to scare the bejesus out of me. I fear for our future; I really do."

"We've been killing each other since Cain and Able; you called the coroner?" she asked as she adjusted her gun belt.

"Not yet. Them fellas not going anywhere." He pointed again to the barn. "I want your take on the savagery before I make the call. There's a woman in the back seat of my truck; she's the one who called it in." He pointed to the shadow visible through the rear window. "Her name is Shirley Gray Moon; Crow. We will get to her in a while. That's her truck." He pointed toward the house. "Says she lives there with her boyfriend."

Courtwright crooked his head toward a weather-worn two-story clapboard house fifty feet away in the shade of a massive half-dead cottonwood that leaned into the ridge of the structure. A Toyota Tundra with peeling blue paint sat beside the house; its driver-side flank displayed a deep furrow of a not-so-near miss.

"How bad?" she asked as she pulled a pair of blue nitrile gloves from her pocket.

"Remember that house we took in Al Amarah, the one with the—"

Before he could finish his sentence, she raised her hands. "I get it. How long?"

"More than a day, at most two—the blood has dried on the floor. The bodies, well, can't say." He also pulled a pair of blue gloves from his jacket pocket and tugged them on.

"That bad?"

"Worse."

A Park County Sheriff Interceptor Utility vehicle stopped behind them on the gravel behind the Jeep. Deputy Bob Claymore dismounted and strode to the pair.

"Good morning," Claymore said.

"Don't start, Bob. According to Wells, it is about to get worse," Jordan said. "Stay here and watch Wells's truck; a material witness is in the back seat. She may have second thoughts and bolt. Keep her here."

"Got it, boss," Claymore said.

Jordan and Courtwright crossed the dead lawn, passed the Toyota and the house, and approached the barn. The haze hung around the foundation and across the open field beyond. Jordan guessed the barn was older than the house, maybe from the late 1800s, making it at least a century and a quarter old. She wondered what held it up. The right door of the double doors was open, and the blackness beyond hid everything.

"Set it up for me," Jordan asked as she prepared herself.

"Shirley Gray Moon made the 911 call at 4:00 a.m. I confirmed it with her. She said she hadn't seen her boyfriend for a couple of days; she thought he was at the rez visiting his folks—she added, with some venom, that she also believed he was drugged out somewhere and would be back when he needed money."

Courtwright placed the remainder of his cigar in a tin box he'd taken from his pocket and slipped it back. Jordan appreciated his forensic thoroughness.

"She'd been in Billings to see her folks for a few days," Courtwright continued. "The boyfriend's name is Jesse Wing Foot Hoyle, also Crow. She has a pit bull. She says when she pulled in this morning, it was about four—the dog bolted from the truck and went straight to the barn. She followed the dog and found them."

"Them?" Jordan said, staring at the black interior.

"There's two—Jesse Wing Foot and, according to Shirley, his best friend, another Crow, Pete Black Hand. Shall we?" Courtwright waved her in.

It took ten seconds for her eyes to adjust to the dark interior. She pulled out her flashlight and washed the light across the dirt floor. The smell of death challenged her senses; the body does strange things after it dies; it is like it wants to rid itself of everything. At first, all she saw were two X-shaped forms suspended from the overhead beam that crossed the center of the barn. As her vision improved, the scene didn't. Two men, naked, were suspended by their arms from the beam, their hands bound with hemp rope wrapped around the beam. Their legs were spread and secured with rope to another beam on the floor used as an anchor. Both bodies had dozens of crisscrossing cuts, none deep enough to kill yet deep enough to bleed profusely. Blood pools lay at the points directly under the bloody legs of the dead men. Red bandanas were jammed into their mouths.

"I've heard about this in Mexico: cartel work," Courtwright offered. "It is used to extract information and to make an example."

Jordan, prepared by Wells's reference to what they had seen in Iraq during their Montana National Guard tour, took a deep breath and steadied herself. She remembered a house where they'd been sent to find a village leader. It was a simple request to negotiate a temporary location to park their vehicles; then again, nothing was simple in Iraq. Outside the house, a woman was crying; she was comforted by two other women. When she saw the American soldiers, Jordan was sure she was going to be struck dead by one of the women. Inside, they found the beheaded and butchered remains of the village leader. They parked outside the village, hoping to spare the village more object lessons.

"You okay, Sheriff?"

"I'm good—always stunned by what a man can do to another for whatever reason. In Iraq, it was religion and politics. Here? You think drugs?"

"A good place to start."

"How long, would you guess?"

"Don't like to guess—you know that. But the marbling of the skin, no rigor, flies, the smell—I'm going with three days at the most; the evenings have been cool. The coroner?"

"Yes, call him. Let's get this going. Whoever cut these fellas up might still be around."

Shirley Gray Moon, smoking a cigarette, leaned against the Responder's back door. The face of her pit bull was glued to the inside glass, watching her.

"Is he okay?" Jordan asked.

"As long as you don't mess with me—she's very protective. Other than that, she's a pussycat."

Gray Moon said it would be better to keep them together. She did not want a cop to shoot her Daisy for acting all protective-like. Courtwright had put the woman and the dog in the back seat.

Jordan had Gray Moon give her story again. Jordan took notes in a small spiral notebook. Considering what she'd just seen, she was surprised the woman hadn't gone into shock or even shut down. Jordan admitted that the woman was tough.

An hour later, a black Ford Expedition with PARK COUNTY CORONER painted on the door pulled in behind Jordan's Jeep. A bald, medium-sized man stepped out of the vehicle. The back of his black windbreaker read CORONER in bold yellow letters. Jordan crossed the gravel to meet him.

"Morning, Myles."

"Sheriff. Nice morning, now that the fog's burned off. Where to?"

"The barn, there in the back. Deputy Courtwright will give you a hand," Jordan said.

"Thanks," Myles Goodman said, looking at the Black officer. "That bad?"

"You will need Wells's help," she said. "Deputy

Claymore is here if you need more help."

"Follow me, Myles," Courtwright said.

Jordan turned back to Gray Moon. "Shirley, let's go over this again; what happened this morning?"

"I've told my fucking story two times; why another?" She threw her arms up, and the dog in Wells's vehicle began barking.

"Shut the fuck up, Daisy," Gray Moon yelled.

"You might remember something new."

Three well-crushed cigarette butts lay on the gravel at the woman's feet. Gray Moon looked about thirty, with a warm complexion and dark eyes set in a classic and pretty young Indian woman's face. Her black hair was in braids. She wore a loose gray and brown flannel shirt, blue jeans, well-worn cowboy boots, and no jewelry.

She dropped her cigarette and stepped on it. "I told the son of a bitch to walk away from all this shit, go back to the rez; it was safe there. Leave Pete to whatever the hell they were doing—get out." She waved her hand at the barn.

"That's Pete Black Hand?"

"Yeah, Pete Black Hand, Jesse's buddy. I never trusted that asshole. Pete had the connections; he's the one who put the meth lab together, taught Jesse how to cook that shit—and he's the one that introduced the guys from Mexico. They're the ones who brought the pills. 'You can make more money,' those spics said. Look where it got them—strung up like sides of beef."

"When did you last see them alive?" Jordan asked.

"Three days ago, morning, before I left to see my folks. They said a guy was coming, a new supplier, would pay them more. The guy was Chinese. Shit, they hardly got anything for the pills they were selling. It was a seventy-thirty split; these new guys from Seattle said they could have the territory—exclusive, cut would be fifty-fifty." Gray Moon staggered, put her hand on the side of the truck to steady herself—and then ran a finger under her nose.

"Are you high, Shirley? What did you take?"

"Something to take the edge off; I'm okay." She sniffed loudly, leaned back, and looked up into the sky. "What a shit show."

"Seattle? Do you know who?"

"No. A Chinese guy was all that they said. Here we are out in the middle of fucking nowhere, and we got the Mexicans and the Chinese fighting over fucking nickel and dime bags of shit and selling that shit to kids, tourists, and Indians. I told him to get away from all this. And look where it got him. Jesus Christ."

"The Chinese did that?"

"No. I know who the hell did that. No one should die like that. It's sick."

"Who?"

"Some guy from the cartel, the Culiacan Cartel— the CC, it's called. The guy has people around here, some in Billings and around the college in Bozeman. Jesse said the Mexican was coming for his piece. Scared Jesse—and Jesse don't scare. Mike said his name was *El Martillo*—whatever that means. I told Jesse to go and hide on the rez. He said not to worry; they would be okay. Yeah, look at the sons of bitches now." She lit another cigarette.

A white pickup truck pulled onto the driveway. Two big men climbed out, both Indians. Shirley's dog inside the car started barking.

"Who are they?" Jordan asked.

"Shut the fuck up, Daisy." She banged on the window again and turned to Jordan. "The man on the left is Isaac Hoyle, and the other is Abraham Hoyle. They're Jesse's brothers."

"How did they find out?"

"I called them."

The men marched to Jordan and Gray Moon. Jordan did not like the look on their faces.

"You fellas need something?" Jordan asked.

"Where's our brother? She said someone killed him," Isaac said, pointing to Shirley.

"The coroner's taking care of him; you stay here until he is done. One of the dead men is your brother?"

"I'm Isaac Hoyle; this is Abe. Our brother is Jesse Wing Foot. Who the hell are you?"

"Park County Sheriff Tynes. Look around—are you guys dense or something?"

"Abe, the cops are here. Big whoop," Isaac said.

"We'll find who did this," Abe said.

"Yeah, right, tough guy. The killer is back in Mexico by now," Shirley said.

Isaac turned to the woman. "Where the hell were you, bitch? You know that fool didn't have a lick of sense, and Pete just dragged him around. You could have stopped him."

"If I were here, I'd be dead, too."

"I don't fucking care," Abraham said. "Drugs, meth, and all that shit got them killed. Sheriff, what are you gonna do?"

Wells Courtwright walked up from the barn. He was six inches taller and fifty pounds heavier than the brothers. He stood there with his thumbs in his gun belt. The sheriff made introductions.

"I heard they got a Black man in the sheriff's office," Isaac said, looking at Courtwright. "First, a woman, then a Black—when do you get a Redman on the payroll?" He turned to Courtwright. "You're a big feller. You play football?"

"Florida State, till my knee gave me trouble. You play?"

Abraham laughed. "Him? Bro played for MSU. He's the fastest Indian wide receiver in the school's history. Sixteen touchdowns over three years."

"You're *that* Isaac Hoyle. Damn." Courtwright put his hand out.

"Jesus Christ, you guys are sick," Gray Moon said. "Your brother's back there hanging like a butchered bear, and you go and get all boys' clubby—you are all fuckers." She stumbled away.

"I have things to do, fellas. Go home."

"We are staying here until we can see our brother to make sure he's properly cared for," Isacc said.

"Then stay out of the way. When the coroner okays it, you can see him. He will be taken to the county morgue in Livingston. Deputy Courtwright will let you know."

The two men walked back to their vehicle; they watched in silence.

Courtwright held up a small rectangular chrome box.

"What did you find?" Jordan asked.

"A door camera. Bob found it outside, mounted on the porch; it's connected to a cell phone he found in the house. Whoever killed them didn't do a good job of cleaning up."

"Or wanted to ensure the locals knew who and what went on. Nothing brings fear and obedience faster than an object lesson."

Chapter 2

The crime scene took most of the day to clear. Even before the bodies were lowered from the barn's beam and taken to the morgue in Livingston, Jordan's people began a thorough search of the house, the barn, and the vehicles. They checked Shirley Gray Moon's alibi and confirmed she was a hundred miles away visiting her folks in Billings—not that anyone thought the one-hundred-pound woman could string up the two men in the barn. A dark blue Dodge Ram pickup truck was parked behind the barn; Courtwright guessed it to be eight years old. Gray Moon said it was Jesse's; MDT confirmed the license and registration. Tire tracks for a smaller vehicle were found in the dust of the driveway between the house and the barn. They were photographed, and plaster casts made—old school. Jordan hoped they would eventually match the tracks with a vehicle's tires—if ever found. Gray Moon told them about the door camera, one of the popular brands available at Walmart; it was synced with a cell phone found in the house; the phone was Jesse Hoyle's. She knew his password; they couldn't use Jesse's face. The retrieved video caught a white Toyota Camry driving past the front of the house toward the barn at 11:15 a.m. two days earlier. After the coroner placed the bodies in his wagon, Courtwright talked with the Hoyle brothers, and seemingly placated, the brothers left. They didn't say a word to Jordan.

On a hunch, Deputy Claymore drove ten minutes to Clyde Park on Highway 89 and asked the gas station owner if he had security cameras. They did, and a review of the videos revealed that at 5:32 p.m. (that same afternoon the murders took place), a white Toyota Camry pulled into the station and filled up. Ken, the gas station owner, remembered the fellow: Latino, middle age, big smile, clean, crisp shirt, black jeans, expensive ostrich boots, and a fine Stetson, friendly, paid in cash. Claymore emailed the video file to the office. Ken added that the man asked about the best way south to Jackson Hole, Wyoming. He told him that driving through the national park was the quickest and the shortest. A line of tourist traffic might be at the north entrance, but it was still worth the shortcut. If not, he'd have to go through Bozeman and around through the West Gate. Ken also remembered that the driver took a plastic bag from his car and threw it in the trash bin—and no, the trash had not been collected. Claymore found the bag; inside were bloody clothes, garbage bags, blood-covered blue gloves, chunks of rope, and a knife. The video also showed the Camry's license plate number. After calls to the Utah DMV, it was discovered to be an Avis rental, picked up at the Casper, Wyoming, airport three days earlier. Claymore talked to the Avis representative; the renter was Hector Lopez, who had an Arizona driver's license secured with an American Express Platinum credit card. The address on the license proved fake; the American Express card was real and secured to a National City, California, bank.

At 5:00 p.m. (after matching the blood types on the clothes to the bodies in the barn), an APB was posted for a white Camry Avis rental with a description and photo of the man who was now a suspect in the murder investigation. He was to be considered armed and dangerous. The rental agency was trying to get a location through its GPS on the car's whereabouts.

Jordan called her contact at Yellowstone National Park, Park Ranger Jim Phillips.

"You believe this guy headed here and not to Canada?" Ranger Phillips said. "I'd have gone north if I had a two-day lead."

"He flew into Casper, or at least he rented the car there," Jordan said. "We are checking on incoming passengers. Can you check the north entrance cameras and see if a white Camry passed through? It would have been two days ago, late in the day or early the next, assuming he went straight there and not east or west."

"Or north to Canada."

"Or north. Can you look? I know it's a lot—middle of the busy season."

"Always busy; however, since the pandemic, everyone wants to come to Yellowstone. A couple of thousand cars go through that gate in a day. I'll have one of the interns scan the videos. You have the particulars?"

"I'll send you what we have: a photo of the car and a license number."

"Thanks—at least it's not an SUV; half the vehicles are SUVs."

"Thanks, Jim."

* * *

That afternoon, back in her Livingston office, Jordan called a contact she had with the Helena DEA and asked about anyone using the moniker *El Martillo* and connections to drug trafficking in the region. Drugs had been trouble for a long time in Montana. Fifteen years ago, it was grass, then dope, then PCP, then meth. Now, it was the worst of all of them: fentanyl—cheap to produce, easy to smuggle (unlike bulky bundles of marijuana or cocaine), and not hard to find distributors, like Wing Foot and Black Hand, who would work for the few dollars they could scrape off of each drug sale. The precursors, the chemicals needed to make the pills, were manufactured in China and sent to Mexico, where the fentanyl pills were manufactured. They were sent north by truck, mail, or carried in the pockets of illegal migrants. Thousands of Americans have died from the illegal drug during the last few years, and Montana was no exception. It was pervasive throughout the state and the Native reservations. It was the number three killer behind heart disease and firearms—and its pervasiveness was growing. All her people carried naloxone (NARCAN) in their vehicles and were trained in the use of the medicine that almost instantly reverses the effects of a drug overdose. Sadly, her people had experience using it. The one thing NARCAN didn't do was fix stupidity.

Jordan had finally won the election for sheriff in the fall of 2020, the pandemic year. Four years later, another election was coming up. The years went by fast, faster than she imagined. She made good on many of her campaign promises: first, reorganizing and increasing the security of the evidence locker and chain of custody issues; second, upgrades to the computer system and its interaction with the deputy sheriff's vehicles and state systems; and lastly, three new hires. Two rookies were working their way through the system, learning the procedures and the territory. Sandy Bullock and Terry Morgan graduated from the Montana State University School of Criminology in 2022. The third, Deputy Wells Adam Courtwright, a 2003 Florida State graduate, fell in love with Montana during a horse-buying trip with his father and moved to Kalispell. Soon after arriving, he joined the Montana National Guard and was part of the celebrated 163rd Cavalry Regiment, located near Bozeman. It was in Iraq, during the regiment's deployment, that Jordan met him; he was her sergeant during the tour. In 2008, he joined the Kalispell Police Department. After thirteen years and slow advancement, Wells decided to look for greener pastures—he applied for the open position in the Park County Sheriff's office. Jordan was pleased that Wells had joined; she especially liked his wife, Diana Courtwright.

Through the window of her office, Jordan looked out onto D Street. For a June day, the weather was warm. She turned to a knock on the doorframe. In the corner, Maggie was sitting on her bed and woofed at the knock.

"Oh, shush, dog. I heard. What's up, Candy?"

"There's a call for you on line three. It's Jim Phillips," Deputy Candy Middleton, the office manager, answered.

"Thanks. Hi, Jim, any help?"

"You should go to the casino; we were big-time lucky. We identified the Camry at the North Gate at 9:35 a.m. the following morning, the day after you thought he'd go through. Once we had him, we picked the vehicle up at four points through the park. He stopped once at the Fishing Bridge General Store. Then he headed east on Highway 14 and through the East Entrance at 12:45 p.m. After that, no idea. Cody, Wyoming, is fifty miles further on."

"How far to Casper?"

"From the East Entrance, maybe three hundred miles. My thought was that he spent the night in Cody, where there are hotels that take cash. Then, he finished the trip to Casper the next day. But that's my guess. The fellow could be anywhere, and you did say the guy asked about Jackson. Maybe he doubled back."

"Or was intentionally misleading."

"Whatever route he took, he has a two-day start and could be in Mexico by now."

"Yeah, I know. We will focus east of the park. I'll let the Wyoming Highway Patrol know. Maybe our APB will come up with something. Thanks for your help; I owe you."

"Glad to help, Jordan."

She knew Phillips was right, and the guy could be anywhere. He hadn't returned the rental to Avis at the Casper airport, but then again, he could drop it anywhere: Cheyenne, Denver, even Rapid City. Claymore said he'd asked the Casper rental office to let him know if it was dropped anywhere in their system, but still no GPS connection. She noted what Phillips said and was about to call Candy. When she looked up from her notepad, Candy was standing there. This time, Maggie was getting an ear rub. "Get this to Bob, have him update the APB, and pass on the information to Wyoming; he knows who to call." Candy took the paper and then remained at the door. "And who now?"

"ATF Special Agent Michael Cardona," Candy said with a Cheshire grin.

Jordan rolled her eyes. "What line?"

"No line. He's in the lobby. Says he was in town, heard about the murders, and has some information."

Jordan hesitated; this was the last complication she needed today. "Okay, show him in."

Still smiling, Candy walked down the hallway toward the office entry, liberally called the lobby.

Five years earlier, Michael Cardona had been involved with the Park County Sheriff's office in a complicated mess dealing with illegal gun sales, drug dealers, cults, and some nasty people from New Orleans, all of which Jordan, her team, and Cardona shut down. A promoted Cardona was still in the Helena ATF office. He was also her occasional date and, for a year, a boyfriend. She was the one who put the brakes on; being sheriff was more than a full-time job.

Cardona was handsome (movie-star handsome), intelligent, a Naval Academy graduate, multilingual, and the Resident Agent in Charge of the Alcohol, Tobacco, and Firearms office in Helena II IO Field Office. He stood at the door in a lightweight suede field coat and brown Stetson. She was amazed at how quickly he dropped the Midwest look and adopted and adapted to Montana. He even gave up his penchant for Porsches and now drove a black Ram 1500 Limited.

"Afternoon, Sheriff."

"Michael," Jordan said, hugging the man. Maggie pushed herself between them. "I'm busier than all get-out, Mike. What can I do for you?"

He held up a manilla folder. "One nasty fellow named Diego Suarez, *El Martillo*—the hammer. You called DEA, they called me, and we have a record of the guy going back almost ten years."

Candy stood in the door holding two cups. "Cof-fee?"

"Thanks; sit," Jordan said.

Candy put the cups on the desk, looked back and forth at the two, then left.

"That woman is driving me crazy," Jordan said. "It's like she has a secret and will tell no one."

Cardona looked at Jordan and slightly shrugged. "I wonder what it is?" He paused. "Anyway, here's what we have." He pulled out printed pages and photos and slid one of the photos across the desk. "This is Diego Suarez. He is one of Culiacan Cartel's—CC for short—enforcers. We have linked him to at least fifteen executions on our side of the border, and God only knows what he's done in Mexico. They all involved drug dealers who decided to look for better deals, and most found their heads bashed in with cheap hammers—as such the moniker *El Martillo*, 'the hammer.' Once you sign on with CC, you are employed forever—there is no retirement program."

"You believe that this is our guy? These fellows were cut up, almost skinned."

"Multitalented. Yes, he goes by a few aliases—Hector Lopez being one, and Jose Menendez being another. There are thousands of Hector Lopezes and Jose Menendezes, but when Suarez's name popped up, we did a cross-check, and a guy by the name of Hector Lopez arrived five days ago in Phoenix from Mazatlán by way of Mexico City and flew on to Casper. We think he's your guy."

"Hardly looks like a psycho killer," Jordan said, tapping the photo. "Quiet eyes, almost handsome; he reminds me of you."

"Funny, I prefer a Glock over a Craftsman hammer. I was told that he cut these fellas bad."

"Hundreds of cuts—they slowly bled to death. He had to know he had the time. Would have taken hours."

She compared the ATF photo to the facial shot Claymore pulled from the gas station video. The face was the same.

"Damn, any idea where he is?"

"The Yellowstone rangers had him leaving the park and heading east yesterday morning. We have an APB out; we will amend it and see what happens."

Chapter 3

Jordan placed her sidearm in the lockbox in the hall closet and hung her gun belt and leather jacket on one of the pegs. Maggie had already headed into the living room. The television was on, and she heard a ball game.

"Hi, Pop," she said, walking into the room. Victor Tynes sat in his recliner, a glass of Coca-Cola on the side table. "Mariners?"

"Hi, honey. Yes, they are playing the Angels. No score; it just started. We heard about the killings. You okay?" he said.

"Give me a little time, Pop. It has been a long day. I smell stuffed peppers."

"No fooling you," Louise Tynes said, standing at the kitchen door wiping her hands on a towel. "Dinner in fifteen. You go wash up."

Jordan had moved back in with her folks six years earlier when her father had his stroke. Louise needed all her help, and they couldn't afford full-time home care.

Jordan, then a three-year veteran of the Park County Sheriff's office, helped when she could. Then, all hell broke loose when her boss, the sheriff, and two fellow deputies were murdered. She was asked and accepted the job of acting sheriff. Then, a year later, during a rancorous election campaign, she lost the election to her opponent, who died before he would have been indicted for multiple murders. She was reappointed, and at the next election cycle, she ran unopposed and won.

"How are you doing, Pop?" Jordan said as she leaned in and kissed her father.

"Excellent. This is the best I've felt in five years. We are even thinking about another cruise, maybe Hawaii."

"That's good. You two can tell me all about it. I'll change for dinner." Jordan walked down the hall to her bedroom, and Maggie followed.

It was time for her to consider moving out and getting a place again. Pop was doing well. Mom had finally retired from the county clerk's office, and both were in good health. On the other hand, as the saying goes, she needed to find a life—all work and no play. And Michael Cardona's surprise today, even if helpful, only reinforced her complete lack of a personal life. After their office conversation, he'd asked her to dinner, and she declined, again using her family as the excuse. She had become a coward when it came to climbing out of her rut—inertia had become her middle name.

"Your sister is coming down this weekend. Will you be around?" Louise asked when they sat down for dinner.

"I expect so. Are the babies coming, too? I haven't seen them in months."

"Yes, they are dropping them off. She and Ted are taking a long weekend, heading into the park to camp."

"A long weekend, now that's a concept I dream about."

"When was the last time you took any time off, a real vacation?" Victor said.

Jordan thought for a long time. "Maybe never, Pop. I think it was my second year as a deputy. I spent a week driving to and from Yosemite; that was nice."

"You need to get out, get away," Louise said. "Fly somewhere, do something exotic, maybe go to Paris or Rome. How about that ATF fellow? I like him. Have him go with you."

"Rome? You think that will help, and with Mike Cardona?"

"Maybe it will get you out of this funk; he may be the one to do it."

"He stopped by the office today. He had information on the investigation into the double murder."

"See?" Louise said. "He likes you; he could have emailed or called. Bringing it to you, that says a lot."

Jordan agreed, but this conversation was beyond what she wanted to deal with now, especially with her folks. This killer, Diego Suarez, was her entire focus. He had not only killed two young men, but he'd also destroyed the stability of the county. Summer was tough enough with a million tourists driving through; she didn't need the Mexicans or Chinese coming in and causing trouble—deadly drug trouble.

An hour later, Jordan and her father watched the Mariners take the lead in the bottom of the eighth, three singles in a row. She enjoyed these moments, but they were few. Yes, she wanted to get out and find a place; indeed, with her salary, she could do that, but it didn't compare to the time spent with her mother and father watching baseball. Maybe they all would take a long weekend and take in a game in Seattle. It was a long road trip; they had done it before. Her phone buzzed.

"Hi, Candy, what's up?"

"Just took a call from Sheriff Matt Cumber with the Natrona County, Wyoming, sheriff's office—that's where Casper is located. You need to call him. He says he has a Mexican national named Jose Menendez in his jail. He matches the alias posted with the APB. This might be our guy."

"The break we need. Text me the sheriff's number. Thanks, Candy. I'll see you in the morning."

"Something to do with the killings?" Victor said.

"Yes, if he's the guy we've been looking for. He was caught in Wyoming. I'll be back in a minute. Don't let the Angels score."

Unlike the previous couple of days, after a cool front moved through, the night was warm. Uncountable stars lit the sky, and the brilliant half-moon hung above the Absaroka's ragged edge of mountains to the south. High above, in an old Douglas fir, a great horned owl hooted—a premonition? Maggie woofed the second time the owl hooted its forlorn riff.

"Good girl—you keep that bird in the tree. Once, they were a bad omen. A hooting owl, an old Indian woman's tale, the sign of death." Maggie woofed again.

She punched in the number. "Sheriff Cumber? Park County Sheriff Jordan Tynes here. I understand that you may have my suspect in a double killing, Jose Menendez?"

"Good evening, Sheriff. Thanks for the quick call back. I was just about to head home. He and the car, a white Toyota Camry rental, fit the description in your APB."

"Any trouble? We pegged him as armed and dangerous."

"He was drunk and passed out in a trailer, so no gunfire or trouble. He's locked up nice and tight. We can hold him based on the warrant. Can we talk tomorrow morning? I have an event tonight that I'm already late for. Does that work for you?"

"Yes, it does, Sheriff; I'll call you in the morning. I'll send his photo and other information I received this afternoon from the feds; his real name is Diego Suarez. He is a very bad member of a Mexican cartel. And thanks, and I am thankful no one was hurt."

"So am I. I'm looking forward to your call. Send the information to this number, and I'll get it to those who need it."

Jordan called her deputies, Courtwright and Claymore, telling them about the Suarez arrest; Claymore had the night shift. She asked him to send copies of what they had to the Natrona sheriff's office. Then she called Cardona, told him about the arrest, and thanked him again for the information.

"Can I buy you breakfast tomorrow? I'm heading back to Helena for meetings. Breakfast at Dottie's?"

"Seven o'clock."

"Ouch—I'll be there."

Chapter 4

They had planned this wilderness hike since Christmas; it was a spur-of-the-moment idea then; beer was involved, and now it was real. The three fellas had known each other since freshman lacrosse at Montana State University. That was seven years ago. Since then, Gerard Hanson had married Abby Voight, Brandon Anderson had been seriously dating Sandy Tillerman for two years, and Dean Young had met Jillian Tombs when he had his knee x-rayed at the hospital in Bozeman (a touch football accident—beer was also involved). Jillian was an orthopedic nurse at the hospital. They all lived in or around Bozeman.

Gerard had hiked this trail in the Absaroka Mountains around Bridge Lake several times in high school and college: four days, two in, two out, in a loop around Bridge Lake just below Crow Mountain. The trailhead where they would leave their vehicles was at the Box Canyon pullout on Boulder Road.

Their rendezvous and jump-off point was the

Murray Hotel in Livingston, where they would spend the night. The six met for a late lunch at the hotel and then spent a few hours collecting their last provisions at Dan Bailey's fishing and outfitting shop. Gerard's checklist was double-checked.

At dinner that night, Jillian, the least experienced of the six, confessed to Abby in the bathroom that she was flat-out frightened.

"I'm scared. There's bears, snakes, mountain lions, even wolves," she said.

"Jill, it's a piece of cake," Abby said. "There are a couple of steep trails, but the circuit is just eight miles a day. I've climbed these mountains for years. I've only seen one bear, and he was a mile away. I have never seen a rattlesnake or a mountain lion. Once, I heard some wolves howling, but they've learned to stay away from humans. Lots of people climb these mountains, thousands every year. Did you ever hear of anyone going one-on-one with a bear or a lion?"

"No, but things happen."

"Yes, lots can happen. We will take our time; we won't rush or do anything stupid; it is stupid that will hurt you, not a wolf attack. Besides, the bigger threat is sunburn," Abby added. "Wear lots of sunblock and a hat. Even mosquitoes are a bigger pain. Girl, you will do fine."

Peer pressure does strange things; Jillian liked Dean Young. He was funny, athletic, and handsome, a perfect package. She was lucky that he hobbled into her waiting room four months earlier, which puzzled her. Strangely, he had no girlfriends she knew about. They struck up a friendship that turned serious—if climbing into bed on the fourth date is serious. He was good, she enjoyed the sex, and while he was no prude, she saw that he was tentative and even shy. Again, something more appealing than the macho cowboys she had dated since high school. But spending almost a week with five people she hardly knew spooked her. Jillian Tombs had hiked, worked out in the gym to relieve tensions, and even jogged, so the grind of almost twenty miles climbing mountains didn't frighten her. It was the unknown; she hated surprises, especially surprises that might kill you.

The Hansons were attractive in an unexpected, perfect couple sort of way. They had been married for almost four years. They dated through college at MSU and married the week after graduation. His father owned the Chevrolet dealership in Bozeman; Gerard worked there as a manager. Abby taught high school math and science. They had no children.

Brandon Anderson was a framer working on a construction crew. He had the week off while foundations were poured for a new project his employer was building. He hoped to become an architect but wanted practical experience first. Sandy Tillerman finished Gallatin College with a degree in culinary arts and told everyone, often in detail, how she would own a restaurant one day. She grew up in Billings and had camped and fished all over Montana with her family. After college, she moved to Bozeman, where she met Brandon.

Whatever nagged Jillian, she couldn't put a finger on it. It was a feeling, maybe a premonition—though, she'd say she didn't believe in those things if asked. That evening, as she lay in bed in a room she shared with Dean, she reviewed all the details. Gerard was thorough and ensured that everything was organized and there was food for six days. "Just in case," he said. That didn't worry her. The packs weighed about fifty pounds; the men carried the tents, sleeping bags, cookware, clothes, and toiletries. The women's packs went about thirty pounds, mostly dried food, sleeping pads, extra clothes, toiletries, and the ever-useful pee-rag. All carried first aid kits and a couple of hundred feet of rope. Everything carried in would be carried out. There were lots of Ziplock bags. Clipped on the outside of the backpacks were bear-spray canisters.

Lying there, Dean rolled on his side, gently slid his hand over her tummy, and slowly moved it up.

"Dean, I'm not in the mood; let's save it for after the hike. I'll make it up to you, I promise." The hand slowly slid away, and she felt a soft kiss on her cheek.

"That's a deal."

* * *

They left early, just as the sun broke the eastern horizon; the drive to the Box Canyon trailhead on Boulder Road took almost an hour. With the hotel's permission, they left Jillian's Ford Escape parked behind the hotel and loaded everything else into Gerard's Chevrolet Tahoe and Brandon's Jeep Cherokee. Jillian and Dean went with the Hansons. When they arrived, the sun had crested the east ridge and had just reached the gravel pullout. Two horse trailers were parked in the pullout.

"It looks like there's a pack trip here," Gerard said, studying the trucks and the door logo. "This has become a popular place to kick off, and that's a well-known outfitter. The fresh tracks point east; we're going west. Everyone gear up and get comfortable. The first leg is easy, and the trail's not rough. We'll get into it this afternoon."

Gerard was right. Jillian took to the easy portion of the trail and set a comfortable pace. It paralleled a shallow creek down from Crow Mountain; lunch was dense food bars, a handful of nuts, and fresh water they carried in. They would begin using the water purifiers the next day.

The trail was wide and well-used. Abby dropped back to Jillian's side.

"You doing better? I was worried about you," Abby said.

"It was just a few minutes of panic. I'm good. This air is cleaning out the lungs and getting the heart pumping; nothing better. Thanks for not saying anything."

"We girls need our secrets from these fellas. Watch your step."

Jillian carefully dodged a pile of mule shit. "Thanks. You and Gerard have been married four years?"

"Yes, four years, just after graduation. Jumped in up to our necks, as they say. We've always liked each other, and it seemed logical, even inevitable. And we are doing okay. I've always liked Dean and have known him and Brandon for a long time. Three fellas couldn't be tighter."

Sandy was the shortest and the fittest. She took point to set the pace; then came Gerard and Dean, Jillian and Abby, and then Brandon. The pace was leisurely and enjoyable. At four o'clock, Gerard checked his GPS against his paper map. "Let's find a spot to set up camp. We set a good pace today and need rest for tomorrow's push. As we discussed, each couple is responsible for their tent and bedding. I'll get the food together, and we'll take turns cooking over the next couple of days. The weather should hold, but no campfire—it is too dry. The weather says the wind might pick up." Nearby were dozens of dead pine trees killed by bark beetles and fungus.

As if his words were prophetic, a breeze swept up from the canyon below and blew over them. The tall pines and firs creaked and moaned, then the wind died. The hair on the back of Jillian's neck stiffened.

"What was that?" she asked, alarmed.

"Happens up here; temperature changes—cool canyons and warm mountainsides. Was just a thermal, no big deal," Abby said with a weak smile, the hairs still standing on Jillian's neck.

Dinner was fresh cut-up chicken cubes mixed into seasoned rice and, for dessert, a chocolate chip cookie. Their drink was fruit punch flavoring mixed with the last of their water. They turned in when the sun dropped below the western range of mountains. Twice, Jillian woke to rustling outside the tent; she swore she heard sniffing. The food bags were suspended twenty feet up in a nearby pine, and a bell connected to the wire cable. The bell never rang.

* * *

In another campsite, five miles northeast of the campers and on the north flank of Breakneck Mountain, a campfire ring sat cold and seemingly harmless. The well-used site had accommodated a group of overnight campers from Billings during the past weekend. The seven, all friends from college, did a commendable job cleaning the campsite, taking out their trash, and extinguishing the campfire and the embers. Their leader even tickled his fingers through the campfire muck to ensure it was out cold. For three days, the campfire sat dormant.

The pressure wave that blew through the Absarokas that evening and raised the hairs on Jillian Tombs's neck washed northward through the mountains. It was the lead pressure change of the dry front slipping down from Canada. It and the front were nothing to be concerned with. Gerard had studied the weather report, and everything pointed to a warm, dry, and slightly breezy few days. Perfect for climbing the mountains.

Surrounding the deserted Breakneck Mountain campsite stood a grove of limber pine trees, killed by pine bark beetles and fungus two years earlier. The largest, almost fifty feet tall and on the grove's perimeter, leaned into the heavy breeze, then cracked at its base and unceremoniously dropped through the campsite clearing to the ground. Three or four feet to the left or right of the campfire, and nothing would have changed. However, the dead tree fell directly onto the cold fire and drove dead branches bristling with dried needles deep into the rocks that made the fire ring. A branch, tinder dry, found a hot pocket of charcoal left unextinguished, and during the next hour and encouraged by occasional puffs of wind, ignited the dried needles and raised the campfire from the dead. In seconds, the hundred-year-old pine was set ablaze with a gust of wind.

The fire rapidly burned horizontally and upward through the dead limbs and needles until it cleared the campsite and found more fuel in the woody debris under another dead limber pine. There, it burned the tree's lower branches until, as darkness arrived, another gust of canyon air pushed through the campground, setting the adjacent trees afire.

Five acres were burning by 6:00 a.m. the following morning, and the narrow smoke column was over three thousand feet tall. A private pilot flying from Denver to Helena spotted the smoke plume at about 11:00 a.m. and radioed the sighting to the Montana State Fire Marshal's office.

Three hours later, when the first state aircraft was up to develop a situation report, the fire was two hundred acres and quickly moving southwest. The winds from the Canadian front had reached the northern part of the state.

After the initial assessment, the State of Montana's Department of Natural Resources and Conservation took over and quickly involved numerous federal agencies: USDA's Forest Service, the Department of the Interior's Bureau of Indian Affairs, the Bureau of Land Management, Fish and Wildlife Service, and on standby, the National Park Service. In the case of the newly named Breakneck Fire, the extent of the federal agencies was yet to be determined. What was determined—considering the incoming weather—was that an all-out assault would be launched. As dusk settled on the Absaroka Mountains and the initial day of the Breakneck Fire, the first L3Harris Company FVR-90 drone was airborne and mapping the exact delineation of the wildfire's boundaries and direction.

A day and a half into their hike and camped near Bridge Lake, the six hikers caught the first smells of smoke at nine o'clock on that second night. At daybreak, they saw the column of smoke beyond the ridgelines to the northeast. Gerard guessed it climbed to twenty thousand feet.

"I'm calling it, gang. We are heading back," Gerard

said. "Last place we need to be is here waiting for that son of a bitch."

No one argued.

Chapter 5

Diego Suarez sat on the thin mattress in the Natrona County lockup, nursing a hangover and pissed at himself for being so stupid. His breakfast platter of scrambled eggs, cottage cheese, and a slice of apple sat uneaten; half the water bottle was gone. He wanted an aspirin. He was alone; at least they hadn't put him in with the other drunks two cells over. The stench of vomit was unbearable. The police had taken his expensive tooled leather belt with its silver buckle, his wallet, some change he'd accumulated, and a custom-made pocketknife. He assumed that his hat, leather jacket, and a small bag with his change of clothes remained in the trailer. Somewhere he had seriously fucked up. How they knew he was in the trailer behind his associate's house, for the moment, baffled him.

The night before, in his motel room in Cody, his first call using one of the store-bought burner phones was to his boss, *El General*, in Culiacan. Suarez told him about resolving their problem with the two traitors to the CC. His boss told him to get out as fast as possible. So far, there had been no public news or police reports about the bodies. *El General* asked if he needed help, and Suarez told him no. He was good; there was no chance he was followed or identified. His second call was to Luis Gambuzza. Gambuzza was an old friend from his days growing up in the slums of Mazatlán. Gambuzza had gone north fifteen years earlier to establish the CC drug network in the Rockies. They chose Casper as the center of the distribution. The two men had worked their way up through the ranks of soldiers in the Culiacan Cartel. They had a lot of blood on their hands. Gambuzza was surprised and pleased to welcome his old friend and offered Suarez a trailer behind the house to use as needed. Suarez told him it would just be a day, two at most, before he would fly out from Casper to Denver, then on to Mazatlán. Gambuzza gave him the address. His last call was to a girlfriend in Culiacan; she said she missed him and would pick him up at the airport when he returned.

Someone had turned him in. After arriving in Casper, he ate an exceptional dinner of Sinaloan favorites he remembered from childhood, all cooked by Señora Gambuzza. Then, after he and Luis finished a bottle of El Tesoro Tequila, he passed out in the trailer. At 2:00 a.m., he was rudely awakened by the crash of the trailer's door, a flash-bang grenade, and, while disoriented, an AR15 stuck in his face. Now, twenty hours later, he was positive the traitor was his old friend—a man who was now dead to him.

Suarez was an enforcer for the cartel, a job few wanted. He hadn't kept count of the killings; they had to be done to maintain order and authority. For the soldiers and workers in the cartel, the temptations were great, the money significant, and with all the chaos and competition for the American markets, some took chances. First, it was marijuana and cocaine, then heroin, and now fentanyl. Dozens of Mexican and Columbian cartels fought for the veins and nostrils of the Americans. Others wanted in, their taste wetted by the billions of dollars sent south in the drug trade. Competition was not tolerated; heads on sticks proved their seriousness. Suarez was also a loner, and until now, he believed, a ghost to the authorities in the United States and Mexico. Gambuzza and his family would pay.

The airline tickets, his passport, and other identifications were for Jose Menendez, age thirty-nine. As far as he knew, no one other than Gambuzza and *El General* knew his real name or occupation. The business cards he carried were for the Compañía de Pescado Fresco del Pacífico, Mazatlán—a frozen fish distributor. He hated fish; he only ate steak.

"You awake, Menendez?" a deputy in a brown sheriff's uniform demanded. "You should eat. You never know when you might get another chance."

"Not hungry," he answered.

"Hell, you speak English. We weren't sure."

"Why the fuck do I care what you think? Why am I here? I did nothing."

"Because a lot of shit is coming your way, Menendez. There's an APB out for your ass. Somebody in Montana wants you, and we will, most likely, pass you on."

"I haven't done anything."

"Says you. They say you're a sadistic, murdering psycho who butchered a couple of Indians. Me? No opinion, yet."

"I was on vacation in Yellowstone. The trailer was a rental, Vrbo. What the hell is this, a shakedown? You got something against Mexicans?"

"The sheriff will work it all out. Sit tight, don't let the bedbugs bite."

"Asshole."

Suarez began to think this through. The deputy said Montana, which meant they had found the bodies. He was hoping to be in Mexico when that inevitability developed. Extradition—how would that be accomplished? It would be a long drive. He knew; he'd just made the trip. A lot could happen between Casper, Wyoming, and Livingston, Montana.

* * *

Breakfast with Michael Cardona was a pleasant diversion from all the news dumped on Jordan during the last twenty-four hours. Mike was pleased to hear about Suarez sitting in a Natrona County jail. The better alternative, he told Jordan, was hell.

"He'll get there sooner than later," Mike said, scratching behind Maggie's ears. She'd taken a position under the table. "Are you going to get the son of a bitch? I'll see what we can do on the federal side."

"Right now, all is good," Jordan said as she carefully spooned a piece of ice in her hot coffee. "I'll work out something with the sheriff in Natrona. It's a good bet he doesn't want the guy in his custody too long. The cartels have a history dealing with prisoners."

"And their jailers, too. I get it. How're your mom and dad?"

They spent the next half hour catching up on family issues, mutual friends, and the general status of law and order in Montana. Jordan understood why he'd adopted the state and preferred it to the politics that had embroiled everything in his past assignments. It was refreshing.

After breakfast, Jordan walked the four blocks from the restaurant back to the office, Maggie at her side. The Carolina dog was one of America's only native dog breeds. She had been her loyal companion and even lifesaver for five years. The two were inseparable. The breed went back ten thousand years and arrived with the first people to cross to North America from Asia after the retreat of the last Ice Age. The breed bonds strongly to one person, and the sad truth was that Maggie's first owner had been murdered, and Maggie stood by the body for days until it was discovered. When Jordan first met Maggie, a bond formed, one that had only strengthened.

She spent an hour on the phone with Natrona County Sheriff Matt Cumber. Photos and paperwork had been emailed and faxed back and forth between Casper and Livingston. The Toyota Camry had been impounded and searched for evidence (blood and other materials) to confirm that it was at the scene. Anything found by Natrona County would be sent on.

No additional knives used in the Montana killings had been found. Blood on the knife found in the gas station trash bag was being tested to confirm its use in the killings.

The clothes discovered in the trash bin were sent on for DNA and further analysis. She hoped they would find DNA on the clothing from both the victims and this guy, Menendez. She knew from the information Mike had given her that Menendez was Diego Suarez.

Nonetheless, she needed to confirm everything. Jordan was surprised by the discovery of the clothes so close to the murders. Suarez had hours to dispose of the clothes and could have dropped them in a trash container in Yellowstone, even Cody. Nonetheless, he dumped them not five miles from the scene where even a dumber guy would have looked for cameras. She knew the bad guys made mistakes; these baffled her.

During their conversation, Sheriff Cumber said, "The sooner this guy is gone, the better. I have an overcrowded jail, cases stacked a mile high, and if this guy is who you think he is, I want him out of here. Make him your problem; I've got enough of my own."

"Roger that, Sheriff," she answered.

The Park County attorney pushed hard for a quick extradition. These legal processes could go on for months if the man in Casper fought the extradition, which could still happen. Jordan wanted Suarez back before he realized he had rights—such as they were. There was already noise coming from the Crow reservation—the two fellas at the murder scene wanted justice for their brother. Somehow, the news of the arrest had made it through the system.

Sheriff Cumber had no problem with someone coming to pick up Menendez. He wanted it all to be on the up-and-up, with no blowback. The county attorney told Jordan that there would be a resolution this afternoon. She was figuring out the best way to move the man back to Montana.

Park County bustled in summer; she saw it in the Lewiston restaurants and bars. It was now nearing the Fourth of July, the height of the tourist season. Ranger Phillips said the entry count into the park had not been higher. "This post-COVID-19 need to get away certainly includes Yellowstone Park. The place is overflowing; there's talk about limiting the entries." He was also pleased to hear about Suarez's arrest.

That information told her driving was not the best way. It was almost four hundred miles from Livingston to Casper, which meant at least eight hours driving each way, plus an overnight before heading back. It would require at least two deputies, one to drive and the other to guard Suarez. She called the killer by that name, not Menendez. There were two routes: one through the clogged park, or east through Billings, then south through Sheridan to Casper—either one, four hundred miles, each way. The overtime and costs of room and meals would wreck her monthly budget. Standing in the parking lot behind the office, the mechanical hum of an airplane circling over the town before landing at Livingston's small airport caused her to look up.

Chapter 6

Deputy Wells Courtwright sat across the desk from Jordan, and Deputy Bob Claymore was next to him. Deputy Candy Middleton leaned against the door-frame; all told her this was not a good idea.

"Sheriff, Wells and I can be back in twenty-four hours, done and back," Claymore said. "We will switch off driving. The perp will be handcuffed and wearing leg irons. What can go wrong?"

"Maybe get hijacked?" Jordan said. "These guys play for keeps. I don't know the Casper sheriff or his people. The Hoyle brothers knew about this, so the word is out. The cartel may send a team to take their man back."

"Only in movies," Courtwright said. "Can't think of one instance."

"And I don't want to be the first. I'm proposing an in and out, less than six hours. I called Josiah Potts; he offered his Cessna and pilot. Mr. Potts was one of my biggest backers and offered the use of the plane at cost: pilot's wages and gas. He says it takes an hour and a half each way—on-the-ground time puts the trip at six hours, max. I can leave tomorrow morning and be back by four o'clock. What's not to like?"

"Who are you taking with you?" Bob Claymore said.

"Maggie." Jordan looked at the dog. She perked her head up at her name.

"Your dog? Really?" Courtwright said.

"Really. Suarez will be in cuffs and chains; I'm not worrying about him bailing out. It will be just an hour and a half in transit; the greatest exposure will be on the ground in Casper and here. That's your job to secure the trip from the airport to the jail."

"I think we can handle six miles from here to the airport," Bob added. "How experienced is the pilot?"

"Pilot is Jimmy Belvedere; he says he has almost ten thousand hours. He has been flying the Cessna 206 since Potts bought it four years ago. He flew a couple of summers in Alaska for an air service before joining Mr. Potts. He has been flying hunters and tourists for the last three years to help defray the airplane's costs. Potts bought the plane to take him and his family to and from Scottsdale and his second home. Jimmy is a good kid. I met him during the campaign."

"I get the time issue and the personnel demands; I'm still unhappy about it," Bob said. "Take one of us. The plane holds what, six people?"

"Jimmy is concerned about weight and the need for altitude to fly direct and over the Absarokas. A couple of hundred pounds has an impact, and you guys aren't lightweights."

"Poor excuse, but I get it. So tomorrow?" Wells

asked.

"The Park County attorney has no problem with this pickup, nor does Sheriff Cumber. We are taking off at nine."

"There's a wildfire on the north side of the Absarokas," Candy added. "Started two days ago, moving southwest. Over three thousand acres, according to DNRC."

"Jimmy knows about it. We will stay well to the west; he says we will fly Paradise Valley, then southeasterly over Yellowstone to Casper. We won't be within thirty miles of the fire. We will take the same route back."

"Still don't like it," Candy said. "Suppose the guy goes crazy and tries to hijack the plane?"

"I will open the door and throw him out," Jordan answered.

Everyone looked at each other, not sure if she was joking.

"We will be fine. Push hard on the evidence gathered at the murder scene. Get the DNA from the clothes done. The coroner's report?"

"Preliminary is expected later today," Wells said. "Myles is finishing up. He said the bodies were a mess. The preliminary report is death by exsanguination."

"Slow death by a thousand cuts," Bob said. "That's just wrong."

"I saw them," Jordan said. "I know their condition. That's why I want the guy here, not in a jail cell out of our control. I'm more worried about a full-scale drug war between cartels in our county and Gallatin County. Bozeman police say Chinese triads are now involved in the drug dealing in Gallatin. It is coming in from Seattle and Vancouver. I don't need that here."

"It's the university; there's no reason for them to come here," Wells added.

"I don't care where; I don't want it here. We need information, and maybe this Diego Suarez can fill in the blanks."

"An international assassin and killer helping us?" Wells said. "I'll believe it when I see it."

* * *

"You okay, Dad?" Jordan asked at breakfast the next morning.

"I'm good; not every day is a hundred percenter," Victor Tynes said. "A little tired, slight headache, and didn't sleep well—but what else is new? I took a couple of Tylenol."

"I'll take care of him," Louise said. "You will be back for dinner?"

"Yes, the whole operation should not take more than six hours. I'll be back by four or four thirty. They are prepared in Wyoming for my arrival—in and out."

"That plane safe?" Victor asked.

"Of course. The pilot says she's a workhorse, tough as nails. Thoroughly inspected and overhauled recently. Do not worry."

"Every day, when you walk out that door, I worry, honey," Louise said. "Every day. What do you want for dinner? The weather is nice; how about cheeseburgers on the grill?"

"Perfect." She stood, slipped on her coat, and retrieved her service weapon. Maggie walked behind her every step, following the familiar practice they had developed over the years.

Louise held out a canvas shopping bag. "Treats for

Maggie, six bottles of water, some energy and chocolate bars. Never travel without treats."

Jordan looked in the bag. "And M&M's. Wonderful."

They met Bob Claymore at Mission Field Airport on the east side of Livingston. He was talking to a big man with a beard and a dark gray Stetson. He wore a gray jacket with an embroidered patch on the chest that read POTTS AIR. Over it was an image of the Cessna.

"Sheriff Tynes, this is Jimmy Belvedere," Bob said, turning to his boss. "I've known Jimmy maybe twenty years—since he was a kid. All he's wanted to do was fly."

"I met Jimmy during the campaign," Jordan said, shaking Belvedere's hand. "This is Maggie; she's going with us. That's not a problem, is it?"

"Not at all," Jimmy said. "There's room behind the seats. The aircraft normally holds two in front, then two rows of two. I pulled out the back two seats—less weight. There are some blankets she can lay on."

Jordan walked around the plane with the pilot.

"Pontoons? You think we might need to make a water landing?" Jordan asked.

"I rig it with pontoons for the summer," Jimmy said. "I fly into a dozen lakes with fishermen and hikers who want to escape other fishermen. I can drop into the smaller and more isolated lakes; they love it—real back-to-nature stuff. The plane can hold a lot of gear with two or three people. The pontoons add to the adventure. Ever fly one of these?"

"Not a Cessna 206, but I've maybe twenty hours in a Cessna 150. When I got home from Iraq, I thought I might try flying. But life got in the way, and there was also a serious lack of money. I tabled it, but maybe someday I'll get back to it. I've always enjoyed the majesty, the freedom. The world looks very different three miles up."

"I love it. The flight plan is filed—we are in the air in fifteen minutes."

Thirty minutes later, after passing down Paradise Valley, Belvedere eased the plane southeast to cut over a piece of Yellowstone National Park before heading southeast to Casper. They flew at fourteen thousand feet, and the nearest mountains topped at eleven thousand feet.

"There's that wildfire my assistant told me about. Any problems?" Jordan asked, pointing to the column of smoke rising to the east above the mountains.

"They've called it the Breakneck Mountain Fire, burning southwesterly. No, we should be fine. It's more than thirty miles away."

The smoke rose in an almost vertical white column. At the top, the plume bent and headed southwest. The lower winds pushed the ground smoke toward the national park.

"That column must be twenty thousand feet—not a good sign," Jimmy added. "When we are on the ground in Casper, I'll see what I can learn."

Jordan reached into her coat and retrieved her phone—no signal bars.

"There's bad coverage on this side of the mountains, Sheriff. We'll be down in about forty-five minutes. There's good coverage in Casper. Do you need for me to contact someone on the radio?"

"No, Jimmy. I'm good."

The views were spectacular; they saw enough of

Yellowstone Park to remind Jordan she hadn't been to the park's eastern side for years. Then they flew over the central heart of Wyoming, a seemingly endless stretch of washes, canyons, buttes, and open grasslands. For a hundred miles, there were no towns or significant settlements.

When they passed over the rim of the aptly named geologic feature the Red Wall, Belvedere said, "There's a lot of history along that red escarpment. The Hole in the Wall Gang, Butch Cassidy and Sundance Kid, the Johnson County War, brutal winters, even some of the Indians from the Custer massacre hid out along that rugged piece of Wyoming."

After crossing the Powder River, he began their slow descent into Natrona County Airport.

Chapter 7

Jillian Tombs carefully wrapped Brandon Anderson's left ankle with gauze and tape. Earlier that second night, she made sure he soaked his foot in the cold water of the creek that washed down the steep hillside next to their camp. There was minimal swelling.

"His foot is not broken, but it is a good sprain. It will hurt like hell," Jillian said. "I'll wrap it as tight as I can. When you get home, it needs an X-ray to be sure."

"Thanks, Doc, I've had worse," he joked. "Most likely why that damn ankle twisted. It has always been wonky. I'll take some Tylenol."

"It was the Idaho match, senior year, I remember," Dean said. "That fool tripped you, and you caught a spike. Lucky it wasn't broken then."

"All I need now is a rock to twist it, then it will break. Old age is a bitch."

"Klutz," Sandy said with a laugh. "At least we won't have to carry you down the mountain."

"We could leave him here for the wolves," Dean

said. "Survival of the fittest."

"Funny guy," Brandon said.

Gerard had made a big push, possibly contributing to Brandon's injury. He was concerned about the fire. But they couldn't fly over the mountain, and the trail demanded respect. At six that night, after Brandon twisted his ankle, Gerard agreed to set up camp before it got dark. It would give Brandon's foot time to rest.

"I figure we can make the trucks early the day after tomorrow," Gerard said. "According to the GPS, we still have about ten miles, and I don't want to push it with Brandon's ankle."

Thin smoke now drifted through the canyons, and the glow of the fire became more visible as the sky in the east darkened.

"According to the maps, the fire is twenty miles away—tomorrow will be dodgy; maybe the smoke will get worse," Gerard said.

"Can it move that far in a day?" Jillian asked.

"I've heard they can if the wind gets going. I'm sure we are fine."

Abby and Sandy were heating water on their small camp stoves.

"Beef stew and biscuits, hot chocolate, and the rest of the cookies," Abby said. The smell of the smoke masked the aromas.

"I could eat all of it; I'm famished," Dean said.

"You will get your share, Dean Young, not a spoonful more. I'll be watching," Sandy said. "Eat a couple of energy bars; there's plenty."

Their campsite was perched on a ledge looking eastward, a couple hundred feet above one of the tributaries feeding Boulder Creek. Dozens of these creeks cut through canyons and valleys extending outward from the Crow Mountain watershed.

"It's all downhill tomorrow," Gerard said. "It's a lot easier than today. Brandon, can you handle it?"

"Of course I can. No way you will leave me here as bear food." He looked at Dean. "Or wolf food, either."

"Speaking of which . . ." Abby gasped. She pointed to the ridge across the canyon. The silhouettes of a bear and two cubs walking through the dry grass were visible.

"Oh fuck," Jillian said.

"They are a long way away, don't worry. That sow has seen a lot of campers, maybe even tangled with some. Bear spray leaves an impression."

"Ever been sprayed?" Brandon asked.

"Once, during a demonstration—freshman year," Jillian admitted.

"You? A demonstrator?" Sandy said.

"It was about a pipeline; I can't remember which one. A couple of cowboys thought it would be fun to spray the crowd. The police didn't stop them. I don't want that again—it burned like a fucking fire was in your eyes—couldn't see decently for a week. But I did kick one of them in the balls. This girl doesn't take shit from anybody."

"I can attest to that," Dean said.

After dinner, they sat around one of the lanterns that had replaced a campfire. Gerard explained the next morning's trail; he wanted everyone up early and to get a good rest.

"I have an announcement and news," Abby said. "Our folks know, but we haven't told anyone else. Gerry and I are having a baby. It is due at Christmas; this is our last big adventure before it becomes inconvenient."

"That's wonderful," Sandy said. "Congratulations."

"Thanks. It has been difficult, but we've wanted a family, and finally, nature took its course and obliged us."

"I'd offer to buy a round, but all I got is filtered water," Brandon said, holding up his water canister.

"There will be plenty of time later. We just wanted to share."

"Thank you; it's amazing," Jillian said. "A Christmas baby—how cool is that?"

The breeze blowing up from the canyon stiffened and became constant. With it, there was the intense smell of burnt pine and grass.

"Fires have distinct smells," Brandon said. "The wood smoke and the grass, yet they promote primal fear when mixed. We can't escape our genetic memories."

"Fight or flee," Abby said.

"That sow was taking her cubs west; she knew what was coming," Brandon said.

"Flee is good for me," Jillian said. "Is there a chance we can make it out tomorrow, Gerard?"

"Not certain we can. We are hiking toward the fire; if we make good time, maybe. When I was a Boy Scout, I learned the first rule of hiking and camping: Do not walk toward the forest fire."

* * *

Within twenty-four hours of discovering the wildfire, the Breakneck Mountain Fire GHQ was set up on Highway 298 about eight miles north of the fire and twenty miles south of Big Timber and Interstate 90.

The initial drone assessments had defined the current boundaries and expansion rate. Two L3Harris FVR-90 drones, painted in red and white, sat on the road near the GHQ. One, called Alpha, had just returned from the initial reconnaissance of the fire and was being refueled. The second drone, Baker, would be up in an hour. The drone team would maintain a continual presence over the wildfire, day and night.

The FVR-90 was a fixed-wing drone with a fourteen-foot wingspan that could remain aloft for over eight hours. It had four vertical and horizontal control rotors and a single 2-stroke engine that drove the propellor to provide thrust. GPS-enabled, it carried an array of sensors and infrared cameras. At night, it could spot a two-inch-square hot spot on the side of a mountain through the smoke.

The wildfire continued to spread. Winds from the north drove the flames over ridgelines and deep into canyons, causing their own weather with downdrafts and updrafts. By the third day, two hundred firefighters worked the perimeter; another team assembled for an effort from the east.

Throughout the Absaroka Mountain range and south into Yellowstone National Park, the pine bark beetle and blister rust killed millions of trees, and combined with the drought, the mountains became a tinderbox.

The drone crew chief, Al Hardt, stood back as drone Baker tooled up. From the controlling trailer, his partner, Bob Vega, signaled a thumbs-up. Baker slowly rose from the asphalt road to about ten feet, rotated 360 degrees, and after Al's final visual check, Bob took over, and the drone climbed to three hundred feet and headed south to the Absarokas. The initial operational plan was to skirt the western and southern edges of the fire so that data collected would be sent to the trailer to pass on the fire's exact location and speed of advance. It would be airborne until approximately 8:00 p.m.; then Alpha would be sent aloft. Al checked his watch; it was 12:15 p.m.

Chapter 8

Jimmy Belvedere taxied the Cessna to the Casper International Airport Transient Pilots Area, designated with a yellow box painted on the tarmac. Jordan and Maggie exited and, after allowing Maggie to do her business, crossed the taxiway and headed to the gate Jimmy pointed to. A white, four-door Chevy Silverado with a gold band and SHERIFF painted on the door side panel sat just outside the fence. A big barrel-chested man leaned against the back of the truck; a buff-colored Stratton Border Patrol straw hat shielded his eyes. His summer-weight sheriff's blouse and heavy gun belt impressed Jordan. She chuckled, thinking this is what a Wyoming sheriff should look like. She was half his size.

"Sheriff Cumber, Sheriff Tynes, a pleasure to meet you," Jordan said, extending her hand.

Cumber took it and smiled. "And this lady, what is your name?"

"She's Maggie; we are inseparable. She's had my

back more than a few times. Thanks for picking me up. I would have expected one of your deputies."

"Like you, I have the most flexible schedule. My people are working; this transfer work suits me fine."

"I understand. That's why I'm doing the pickup. Can you give me a minute while I make a few calls?"

"No problem. At least it's not a hundred degrees. The place can be a furnace."

Jordan looked at her phone; it read 11:15. They had made good time, just about two hours. She also had five calls, all from her mother. They started at 9:55; she called.

"Thank God," Louise Tynes said. "Where are you? I've been trying to reach you for more than an hour."

"Mom, slow down. I'm in Casper; you know I was flying down to pick up a suspect. What's the matter?"

"It's your father; he had another stroke. One moment, he was fine; we were talking, and then he started to talk gibberish, and his face twisted and sagged. I knew immediately. I called 911—they were here in minutes. We are in the hospital, and he's in intensive care. God, I wish you were here."

"Just take a deep breath, Mom; slow down. Did you call Robert and LeeAnn?"

"Yes, there's nothing your brother and sister can do, at least right now. LeeAnn will be here this weekend with the kids, you remember. Casper. I thought you were going to Bozeman."

"No, Mother, Casper. I flew down. I'm here to pick up a felon. How is Dad doing?"

"He's awake, but it's bad like the last one. They've loaded him with blood thinners and that plasminogen they gave him last time. Honey, it's bad, really bad.

When can you be here?"

"I'm on the ground for an hour. I will be home by three or four at the latest. That's all I can do. Tell Dad I love him, and I'll see you this afternoon."

"Hurry, honey, I love you."

"I love you, too, Mom." She slipped the phone into her pocket, took a deep breath, and studied the blue Wyoming heaven above. She closed her eyes briefly, then pursed her lips, let out a long sigh, and turned to Sheriff Cumber. The expression on her face told him all was not right.

"Everything okay? You look like you've been punched."

"My dad, he's had a stroke this morning, his second in five years. He's in the hospital, and I'm three hundred miles away."

"Someone to watch over him?"

"My mom, but she can be overwhelmed. I need to get back," Jordan said.

"We can hold the guy; that's not a problem. You can get him later in the week; maybe you can send some of your guys."

"I'm here; he's ready; we can be back up in an hour. Let's get him, and then I'll be out of your hair."

"Anything I can do, just ask. The office is ten minutes away, and your guy is ready in a holding cell. I have an idea. How about we bring him here? That work for you?"

"That would be great."

Sheriff Cumber climbed into his rig and tapped his phone. After a minute, he returned to Jordan, who was on her phone.

"We are good, Bob," Jordan said. "We will be back

in the air in thirty minutes; we should be in Livingston by three o'clock. I need to get to the hospital; my Dad had another stroke. I'll call as soon as we have coverage." She looked at the plane; Jimmy was standing next to it. He opened both his hands in a standard "what's happening" fashion. She signaled him to come to her.

"My fellas are bringing him out. This will save you at least a half hour, maybe more," Cumber said. "With all we have on our plates, you sure as hell don't need this. I heard about the trouble you had a few years back, the crooked police chief, the election—what a thing."

"All good now," Jordan said. Jimmy came to the gate. "Sheriff, Jimmy Belvedere, my pilot. Jimmy, Sheriff Cumber."

"Sir, it's a pleasure." Jimmy stayed on the airport side of the gate. If he went through, he would have to go through security in the adjacent airport office.

"Jimmy, they are bringing the suspect here. My dad has had a stroke, so we need to get back to Livingston as soon as possible. My deputies will meet us at the airport and take the guy. I'll head directly to the hospital."

"Got it, Sheriff. When you are ready, I'm ready. I had the tank topped off. The front from Canada is moving in; it's a dry one but with some push. It might add twenty minutes, but I'll get us there."

While they waited, Jordan called her office. Candy asked if she'd talked to her mother; Jordan told her she had.

"I'm so sorry, Sheriff. Is there anything I can do?" Candy said.

"We are leaving in fifteen minutes. Tell Wells, please. I will see you this afternoon."

Thirty minutes later, another Natrona sheriff's vehicle pulled into the parking area. Two deputy sheriffs exited, opened the rear door of the Ford Interceptor, and, with some effort, pulled a man from the back seat. His hands were secured with handcuffs, and his legs were shackled with leg irons. One of the deputies carried an envelope that Jordan assumed were the man's personal effects.

The man was Latino and clean-shaven, though he did sport a five-day beard. He was maybe six feet tall, had dark eyes, a close haircut, and no obvious tattoos, which Jordan had learned was not a standard trait among cartel people. He was wearing an orange jumpsuit and tennis shoes.

"What the hell is this?" the man yelled in English. "I want to know what's happening; I did nothing. You are deporting me? I'm an American from San Diego. I'm a tourist."

"You are not being deported, Suarez," Jordan said. "You are going back to Montana; you are under arrest."

"Who the hell is Suarez? My name is Menendez, Jose Menendez. I live in San Diego. What the fuck is going on?"

The two deputies stood to each side of Suarez; Jordan handed the sheriff her handcuffs, and he passed them to a deputy, who replaced the ones Suarez wore with her cuffs. This time, his hands were behind his back.

"I'll send the leg irons back; that work, Sheriff?" Jordan said.

"No problem," Cumber answered.

Jordan turned to Suarez. "You have the right to remain silent. Anything you say can and will be used against you in a court of law. You have the right to an attorney. If you cannot afford a lawyer, one will be provided for you. Do you understand the rights I have just read to you? With these rights in mind, do you wish to speak to me?"

Suarez smiled, looked at the other officers, and said, "Fuck you."

Fifteen minutes later, they had secured Suarez in the seat directly behind the pilot, his hands still behind him. His seat belt was snugged tight, all accompanied by liberal bitching on the part of the suspect. Jordan asked if he wanted water; he repeated his earlier rebuke.

Jordan thanked Sheriff Cumber and his people. The deputy handed her the manila envelope.

"At least the son of a bitch won't jump out and escape," Cumber joked.

"There's that. Thanks for all your help. I'll keep you informed about what happens."

"Be careful. I've dealt with the cartel. No one is meaner, and that's the truth. We've had mix-ups with these guys, and they do not play by the rules."

Jordan looked at Suarez. He ignored them like he couldn't care what they thought.

Ten minutes later, they were airborne and heading northwest. They had been on the ground for one hour, and her phone read 12:15. The transfer went better than she had hoped. She looked back at Suarez; he was stone-cold silent and refused to look at her. Maggie had curled up on a stack of blankets immediately behind Suarez, where the last row of seats had been. With luck and a minimal headwind, they would be in Livingston by 2:30.

The drone of the engine lulled Jordan and tempted her to sleep. She tried everything to stay awake, pinching herself, talking to Jimmy over the headphones, even turning to watch Suarez. His eyes were closed, but she was certain the monster was not asleep. Initially, he complained about his hands cuffed behind him, and she told him to shut up. They would be on the ground in an hour. Maggie moved to a spot where she could see Jordan and Jimmy. Every time Jordan turned to look, the dog was alert and watching.

"You take up skydivers?" Jordan asked.

"A few times during the year. There's a big convention in Billings; the boss lets me make a few extra bucks by taking jumpers up. I can make a hundred a head. The doors have quick-release pins. It's a good way to blow out the dust from the cabin, I'll tell you that. Once we're settled in, there is no problem. This is a tough airplane and fun to fly. Do you want to take the controls for a few minutes?"

Jordan took the yoke and slowly moved the plane to the left and right, then slightly up and down.

"Smooth."

"She is that, and we are flying light. I've had four big guys and a week's worth of hunting gear on board. She still handled it well."

She handed the controls back to Jimmy.

They flew over the Red Wall and turned a few degrees west to pass twenty miles west of Cody. The far northern horizon was a dirty gray-brown.

"That's the Breakneck Mountain Fire, Sheriff," Jimmy said. "The winds have kicked up and pushed it south. To save some time, I will cut it close around the smoke plume."

"Don't do it on my account. You take the safest route," she answered.

"We will be fine, and we're a couple of thousand feet above the plume. We will be good."

The smoke plume rose high and angry. The center of the column was now bent, forming a dangerous-looking, tornado-like hook.

"There's a second column," Jimmy said. "It is turning into a nasty fire. I'll slip more to the west. We will be fine."

They continued northwestward, the engine roaring unrelentingly. Jordan looked at Jimmy, who was intense and watchful. His head turned on a 180-degree swivel.

She looked forward, and through the prop's spinning haze, there was something, a dot, something was approaching. "What the hell . . ."

Before she could finish, something hard, like a hammer, slammed into the fuselage at more than two hundred miles an hour. Jimmy's side of the windscreen exploded, throwing glass everywhere. Through this open wound, the wind screamed louder than anything she heard. Jimmy was bloody; as the plane pitched, his body slammed forward into the controls and then back into the seat. Almost blind, she tried to wipe away the blood and glass from her eyes; the left side of the airplane was ripped open. The side window in the pilot's door was missing. There was no noise from the prop. The engine raced uncontrollably. Her mind throbbed. They hit something—a bird? No, more than that, it had to be another plane. She turned; Suarez's face was bloody. Maybe the blood was Jimmy's. The plane began to turn nose-down and dive. She realized the prop was gone, sheared off by what hit them. With no propulsion, they were a busted glider, a brick with wings. She shook Jimmy; he was out cold, or maybe worse—his head wobbled loosely from side to side; she couldn't tell. She grabbed the yoke in front of her and tried to even the forward tilt that was beginning to spin them into the mountains. With no power, she was at the mercy of the air and gravity. Below, the brown haze from the wildfire smoke filled the valleys between the mountains. The altimeter was spinning erratically; they were falling. She slowly raised the nose, and the airplane responded. It began to glide—maybe she could find a spot on the side of a mountain to land. Someplace flat where, God willing, she could land this chunk of aluminum and walk away. Everywhere ahead and below looked like the ragged granite walls of hell. White flashes of snow stuck between sharp-edged peaks ripped past, and ahead, more mountaintops filled her side of the undamaged part of the windscreen. She continually wiped her eyes; tears washed her face. Then Maggie's nose jammed itself under her arm. "Good girl. We won't die. I swear to you—we won't die."

To the left, a long, brilliant white snowfield rested along a mountain's ridgeline. Time was running out. That might work. She'd try to land; it was better than the snowless fields littered with rocks and boulders. She adjusted the yoke and, using the flaps, attempted to drop the plane on the upper end of the snowfield. A thick cloud of smoke blew up from the canyon and completely obscured the snow; it also pushed the plane up, then the plane dropped. She had no visibility as she fell. When the pontoons hit the snow, the smoke cleared, and all she saw was a blinding white table of ice, not snow. Maybe luck would hold. Then, the right pontoon hooked on a boulder and was ripped away; the right wing dipped, caught the ice, and snapped. The Cessna spun 360 degrees, and the other pontoon broke away. Now, sliding on the fuselage, the screaming of aluminum on ice filled her ears. With its wing brace damaged by the impact of whatever hit them, the left wing snapped, and the wing tore from the main carcass of the busted airplane. Fuel sprayed across the ice field as the wing slid uncontrolled to the edge, then flew off the mountain. Then, the body rolled over and over as the kinetic energy of the machine was dumped by friction and the scouring of the aluminum body. Torn from its mounts, the engine tumbled away like a busted bowling ball and joined the left wing over the cliff. The tail and rear stabilizers broke away. The central portion of the fuselage settled on its belly and continued to slide slowly down the mountain. To the right was a thousand-foot drop. Ahead were the first evergreen trees. Then, mercifully, the crying of aluminum on ice quieted and stopped. Inside the busted, dented, and ravaged hulk of the once elegant airplane, three people, who by any right should be dead, sat strapped and unconscious in their seats.

Chapter 9

"What the hell just happened?" Bob Vega asked as he scanned the monitors mounted on the interior panel of the drone control trailer. The monitors were gray and white interference noise; there were no images or data. One second, they were filled with crystal-clear images of the Absaroka Mountains, plumes of smoke, overlays of terrain, and data. The next second, nothing.

"Signal loss," Al Hardt said as he flicked switches and scanned across the instruments.

"Well, yeah, I can see that! But why? You are the tech guy. What caused it?" Vega asked.

"Catastrophic failure. Maybe it crashed?"

"We've had bird hits; they didn't blow up the drone—there was some damage, but not this. This failure is more than slamming into a buzzard or eagle."

"I told you never to mention the eagle, never. That was unfortunate," Hardt said.

"That was an accident, like those windmills, a casualty of war."

"Cute. It doesn't solve our problem, Bob. Time."

"The LOS was 1:15:25. The drone's location at that time was 45° 18' 05.90" N, 110° 10' 49.00" W. The elevation was 3,850 meters. Nothing is there; the mountains in the area are five hundred meters lower—it had to be a bird. There is no reason for another plane to be up there, none. There's smoke and updrafts. There are no other DNR aircraft up at the moment."

"Contact the Highway Patrol; see if they have anyone up."

They checked and rechecked every feed, but they found nothing. The Highway Patrol and the DNRC fire boss had no planes up.

"What's going on? Did you lose one of my birds?" the fire boss yelled over the phone.

"We are not sure, sir," Hardt said. "Right now, it is just a signal loss."

"Where was the loss?"

They gave him the location. Vega said, "There is thick smoke over the area, and the ground is impossible to see. Shall we contact the Air Operations Supervisor?"

"No, you've done enough. I'll contact them and find out what they can send up—if anything. I don't want to lose a pilot chasing after a drone; I have a fire to fight, and the situation is not improving. Can you send up the other one?"

"Baker was up; we can have Alpha ready in thirty minutes."

"Good, we will deal with the drone later. I want to know what's happening with my fire."

* * *

Deputy Wells Courtwright looked at his watch again.

It was 3:05. Jordan had called just as they took off from Casper and said they would be in Livingston by 2:30 to 2:45. He was parked next to Jordan's yellow Jeep. On the opposite side, in their Ford Interceptor, sat Deputies Bob Claymore and Corporal Jean Smith. They were there to take Suarez into custody and lock him up. The sheriff said she would head directly to the hospital. Courtwright climbed out of his truck and entered the Yellowstone Air Service office. The man at the counter, Terry Thompson, was the airport's general manager.

"Did you receive any transmission from Jimmy Belvedere? He flew into Casper and is returning with Sheriff Tynes?" Wells asked. "They were supposed to be down by two thirty. They are forty minutes late."

"That is Josiah Potts's Cessna 206, right, Deputy?" Thompson said.

"Yes, sir."

"I've nothing so far. The wind has picked up, and they may take a wider track around the fire."

"When does it become critical?" Wells asked.

"When did he take off?" Thompson asked as he pulled up information on his computer.

"I took the call at twelve fifteen. They were leaving Casper."

Thompson looked at his watch. "The plane can stay up for about five hours; that would make it overdo at about five, but I know Jimmy. He wouldn't take any chances. I will prepare the SAR; I wouldn't say I like this. I'll also call Josiah; maybe he's heard something."

"Could they have landed somewhere else?" Wells asked.

"There are maybe five possible airports in the area.

Yellowstone, Bozeman, and Ennis are the most logical, but hell, Deputy, if they could make those, they could get here. What concerns me is the fire. I said Jimmy was cautious, but he might have tried to cut some time. If there was a serious problem, he could land on one of the roads around here. He has the skills."

"Then he'd be here or would have contacted us."

"Yes, unless he ran into trouble. I'll start an Alert Notice and contact the Air Route Traffic Control Center; it is better to be safe than sorry."

Wells walked back to his truck; Bob and Jean were waiting.

"What's happening?" Bob asked. "They were supposed to be here by now."

"Terry is beginning to set up a possible SAR. I don't like this."

"Search and Rescue, damn. There is a lot of country out there," she said, looking south up into the Absaroka Mountains.

At three thirty, the three deputies walked back into the service center. Thompson's expression was not good.

"We have nothing; there have been no communications since he left Casper. All was okay then. His return flight plan mirrored his original flight plan. Mr. Potts told me that the plane had an older model ELT on board."

"ELT?" Smith asked.

"Emergency Locator Transmitter. These mountains can mask the transmitted signal. The older models can be picked up by overhead aircraft, which will be hours away. If he had the newer ELT, if it's activated, it's picked up by satellite. This late in the day, it won't be until tomorrow before aircraft can get up."

"And the wildfire smoke and haze will make it difficult if they are near it."

"Yes, it won't help."

Claymore and Smith returned to their vehicles to make phone calls and send notifications. Claymore also called Casper and talked to Sheriff Cumber, but he could add nothing more to what they already knew.

Wells waited in the airport office. At four thirty, Thompson filed an official SAR. All SARs for inland missing aircraft go through the Air Force Rescue Coordination Center (AFRCC) at Tyndall Air Force Base in Florida. The National SAR Plan was immediately activated. Local airports were searched to locate the craft, and a communications scan was started. As expected, no ELT transmitter signals had been received from the unit.

At five, Josiah Potts arrived at Mission Field. He was concerned and pissed that he hadn't put in the most up-to-date ELT on the plane.

"I'm such an idiot," Potts said. "We fly people all over, and I completely forgot about the update."

"Mr. Potts, your Cessna is officially overdue. It's been five hours," Thompson said.

"I know; I've already contacted some buddies; they will be up at first light. This will all be coordinated by the feds and the Air Force."

Wells and Josiah were sitting in the lobby waiting for news when Thompson handed Josiah a note.

"It seems we aren't the only missing aircraft," Thompson said. "This afternoon, about the same time our people disappeared, the DNRC and the fire boss at the GHQ for the Breakneck Mountain Fire reported that one of their drones might be down. The LOS was 1:15:25. The drone was near Mt. Douglas in the center of the Absarokas. It closely matches the flight plan filed by Belvedere. The drone was at 3,850 meters when it disappeared."

"You think that they collided?" Josiah asked.

"I have no idea. That elevation seems low. Doesn't the Cessna fly higher?"

"Of course, its max ceiling is almost sixteen thousand feet. Maybe the smoke pushed him lower; it's possible. But hell, the chance of these two hitting each other is damn near impossible. Did they have a number? Did they have the longitude and latitude?"

"Yes, to the millisecond."

"Good, at least we have a place to start."

Chapter 10

As Jordan woke, the front windscreen was gray; the ghosts of tall firs appeared and disappeared through the smoke that washed up and over the ridge. The crash knocked her cold, and she slowly tried to grab at the reality that hung just out of reach. Haze drifted in and out of her line of sight. She couldn't tell if it was an illusion. She looked at the others, still miraculously strapped into their seats. She looked for the dog and felt a weight on her arm. Maggie, the dog, sat looking at her, a paw on her arm. She inhaled and felt a sharp pain on the right side of her chest; she guessed she'd broken a rib or two.

"At least you're okay," she said and ran her hand over the hound's head. There was no blood, but she had to have tumbled through the cabin.

Smoke was everywhere; it was from the wildfire. A breeze pushed the smoke in billowing clouds across the ice field and into the trees beyond. And it was cold. She guessed they were at least at nine thousand feet, maybe higher. Her watch read 1:45; she'd been out maybe fifteen minutes, and the others were still unconscious. She remembered that the impact from whatever it was came at 1:15; she'd just looked at her phone for bars. She wanted to call her mother, but no service.

She rechecked herself, bruised with a slight bump on her head from the crash, and found that her hands and legs were good. No bleeding, just the sore chest. *Any landing you can walk away from is a good one, right?* She looked around; all was disaster. There were no wings, tail, or pontoons, just a fuselage that could hardly be called an airplane. And they were lucky the carcass rolled to a stop on its undercarriage. They could be hanging upside down like a gutted deer. Suarez was the first to moan, actually more of a guttural *¿Qué carajo?* Blood covered the front of the orange jumpsuit.

Yes. *What the fuck!* was appropriate, Jordan thought. "You okay, Suarez?"

"I'm alive. What happened?" Suarez said.

"We hit something, or something hit us; we are on the ground and lucky to be alive."

Suarez looked out the window to his left. The window was gone, and shattered glass covered his lap and hair. His hands were still cuffed behind him. "My shoulder hurts like hell. We gotta get out; there will be a fire."

"No fire. The fuel was in the wings, and they are somewhere back up the mountain—and you are going nowhere." She snapped her seat belt and carefully leaned over to check Jimmy. His pulse was strong, but there was a gash above his left temple. He slowly opened his fluttering eyes.

"You okay, Sheriff?" he mumbled.

"I'm good. It's you I'm worried about. Is there a first aid kit?"

"It's in the tail storage compartment; there's also an emergency bag. We need to call—" Jimmy's head rolled to the side, and he passed out again.

"Lot of good that kid is," Suarez said.

"Shut the hell up." She looked to the back of the plane where the tail end used to be; it was now a hole that looked back up the mountain. She carefully navigated around the glass covering the floor and found one bottle of water her mother had put in a bag that morning. She spied two others under the seat. She opened it, took a long swallow, retrieved the others, and asked if Suarez wanted a slug. He nodded; she held it to his lips as he drank. She could do nothing with Jimmy until he was awake. She didn't want him to choke. She held the bottle for Maggie, who expertly finished the first water bottle.

"Look, Suarez, I will retrieve the first aid and emergency kits. If you want to try to escape, go for it. Just know that we are on top of a mountain. It's cold out there, and tonight will be below freezing, and you will still be in cuffs and leggings. I'll be back."

Suarez didn't say anything. She could see the wheels in his brain clicking. He may be a killer, but not a stupid one. She was sure he'd be here when she got back. She pushed open her door and slid out onto the ice. The daily warming and cold nights had turned the snow into a thick layer of ice. She exited and looked back up the slope; the afternoon glare was intense, and clouds of smoke drifted up from the canyon and over the field. Beyond were parts of the airplane. The pontoons somehow had slid down the slope and were jammed against nearby boulders, and the tail section lay on its side, one stabilizer pointed up. That was her target, and it sat maybe two hundred feet up the ice.

All she had was the thin nylon jacket she'd put on this morning over her uniform, good cowboy boots—certainly not the kind to climb ice—and her Stetson. She still had her pistol. From the outside, she opened the cabin's double doors; Maggie jumped out but gave a little whine. She would look at the dog when she got back. She took the blankets from the rear and wrapped one over Suarez and the other over Jimmy. It was the best she could do. Outside, she slowly worked her way up the ice, Maggie at her side. In the dog's case, four wheels were better than her Lucchese Ropers. She stopped to catch her breath; vapor caught in the breeze; looking back, she saw that Suarez hadn't tried to escape—yet.

At the amputated tail, she found the door to the storage unit; it still held. She popped it open. Inside was a red bag about two feet long and one-foot square, with handles and a carry strap. She pulled it out. Behind was another bag, red and white, and in bold letters FIRST AID. Behind that was an orange electronic device mounted to the airframe. The label read ELT, Emergency Locator Transmitter, 121.5 MHz. A sensor light next to the switch flashed. She would ask Jimmy about this.

She slipped the bag and first aid kit over her shoulder and carefully slid back to the plane. As she looked around the mountaintop, she began to shake, and an adrenaline rush washed over her—there was no way on God's earth they should have survived. The smoke from the fire obscured the views to the west and north.

She guessed the temperature to be about forty degrees, and her phone had no bars. She shut it off to preserve the battery.

Back at the airplane, she opened the survival kit; it contained thirty high-calorie food bars, water purification bags and tabs, two flashlights, chemical body warmers, emergency blankets, two bundles of nylon rope, a small tent, a compass, a multi-use tool, heavy gloves, and other miscellaneous gear. The food might last a week; she knew Jimmy didn't have a week. She took the small shovel tool, broke up chunks of ice, and put them in the bags with half a dozen of the body warmers; at least there was water.

"Can I get my hands back? My arms are dead," Suarez said.

"I'll think about it," she answered.

"How can I eat or piss?"

"You are the killer. Comes with the territory."

"Cute. What killer? I'm from San—"

"San Diego, yeah, sure. I've got all your paperwork and have you ID'd by the feds as Diego Suarez. Culiacan Cartel member, executioner, and killer. I'm going with my guys."

Jimmy inhaled a deep breath from the front seat and said, "You two are giving me a headache." He laughed.

"How are you doing?" Jordan asked.

"I hurt like hell—there should be some Tylenol in the kit. Can you get me a couple? My arms must be broken; I can't move them, and Jesus, they hurt."

Jordan dug through the first aid kit and found Tylenol packages. Holding one of the water bottles, she helped Jimmy take the pills.

"Won't be much, but it will help. I saw an ELT in the tail. Do you think it's working?"

"It should be; it's an older model but still works, and the batteries are reasonably fresh. But it won't be until tomorrow before somebody is up."

"I know, standard SAR procedures. The smoke is getting thicker. Tonight will be cold; that front is moving in. Hopefully no rain, but well below freezing. What do you think, Jimmy?"

Jimmy had passed out again. She checked his eyes with the small flashlight; they dilated, and everything pointed to a concussion. He needed help now, not a few days from now. They must make it through one night, but in two or three nights up here, they could freeze to death.

"He dead?" Suarez asked. There was no sympathy behind the question.

"No, a concussion. We are here for the night. Maybe someone will find us, but we are climbing off this rock in the morning."

"There's no chance of that. He's no help. I'm chained up, and you can't manage all of it yourself."

"I'm thinking of leaving you here; come back for you later. That's what I'm working on."

"You are a cop. Aren't there some ethics involved?"

"You telling me about ethics? That arrogance deserves to be left tied up here on the mountain. Here's what I'm going to do. I'm unlocking your cuffs; you will put your hands in front of you, and I will secure them. I'm also wrapping a couple of loops of a length of rope around your midsection and tying it behind the seat. You will stay put."

"I gotta pee."

"Then you will stand after I cuff you, and you can piss out the window."

"No decency?"

"Suarez, this dog is well trained, and I can tell when she does not like certain people—people like you. It doesn't take much to set her off."

Maggie sat behind Jordan, watching Suarez as the handcuffs were switched to the front. He did his business and then sat. She tied him in and gave him two food bars for being a good boy. He said something in Spanish she would translate later.

Jimmy regained consciousness, drank water, closed his eyes, and slept. She then spread two emergency blankets over him to keep him warm. She then ate two of the bars and finished another bottle of water. The ice in the bags had melted using the chemical warming sticks.

The time on her watch was 6:48. They would hunker down in the fuselage, and then, in the morning, she would find a way to get them off the mountain. She resecured the rope around Suarez; surprisingly, he didn't protest. She also knew not to trust him. She leaned back against the plane's body and pulled one of the blankets over her. She relied on Maggie to help her get a night's sleep; she would need it for the next day.

Chapter 11

Sandy Tillerman looked up into the gray-blue early afternoon sky; clouds of smoke drifted westward, the smells frightening and primeval. "I heard a plane, then nothing. Strange."

"The mountains bounce sound all over," Gerard said. "Hard to tell from which direction they start. There are few commercial routes over these mountains. And you must stay more than two thousand feet above the tallest peaks. I agree; I thought I heard something. The smoke makes it hard to see anything."

"Strange, then it went silent."

"Went behind a mountain, probably," Abby added.

They had stopped for a thirty-minute break. According to Gerard, they were just five miles from the vehicles. It was one thirty in the afternoon; they had been on the trail since seven thirty. Abby broke out the energy bars. They all drank from their replenished canteens.

"Five miles to go, but we have to climb that low

ridge before we drop to the other side," Gerard said. "I'm not pushing it."

"The smoke is thicker, and it's getting hard to breathe, and my ankle hurts to high fucking heaven," Dean said. He sat on a downed tree trunk and began to unwrap a bar.

"Can't help it, Dean. Do you want me to fashion you a crutch?" Brandon offered. "That might help."

"Maybe a walking stick." Dean then asked Gerard, "Can we make it tonight?"

"I'll know when we reach the ridge. I don't know where the fire is; the smoke is the shits. Hopefully, the wind will shift. I don't want to detour, but we will soon find out."

"And if the fire is there?" Sandy asked.

"Then we have big problems. All we can do is push. But I won't climb down the mountain at night; it's too dangerous. Anyone of us could stumble and twist something—or worse."

They sat with their thoughts until Gerard stood and said, "Saddle up."

Dean's ankle required that his pack be split between the campers. Jillian had rechecked his ankle but did not retape or tighten the binding. The boot helped with the swelling; her more significant concern was that it was broken, and she had to wait until they were off the mountain to find out. The hike on the trail was surreal; the haze and smoke drifted through the dead pines, and there was no wind or even a breeze, just the omnipresent gray that flattened the shadows. High above, the sun was just a bright spot in the sky; it provided no warmth.

They forded a small creek coursing down the

mountain from a higher-up spring. As they rounded a massive boulder taller than the men, they came face-to-face with a black bear who was as surprised to see them as they were her. The bear was a sow because two cubs stood next to her.

"Well, this is fucked," Gerard said. "Get bear sprays ready."

Jillian looked at Gerard. In his hand, instead of a can of bear spray, he held a .45 caliber Smith & Wesson pistol.

"Where the hell did you get that?" she whispered.

"I've had it the whole time; I never go into the mountains without a pistol. It is for times like this; I want to be prepared."

"Is it a grizzly?" Abby whispered.

"No, she's smaller, but with cubs just as ornery," Gerard said. "All of you, start yelling. Dean, get that whistle out and start blowing. Make a hell of a racket. I don't want to shoot the girl. It will make her mad."

"No shit," Brandon said. "Please, no shooting the pissed-off mama bear."

They started screaming and yelling. The bear, startled at the six's appearance, stood upright, looked around, turned tail, and started back up the trail. The two cubs, first curious, bolted after the sow. In a minute, they were gone.

"Will she be back?" Abby asked.

"I doubt it; she's more afraid of us than we are of her."

"Bullshit. I'm scared enough for all of us," Jillian said between yells.

"They can move fast. Holy crap," Brandon said.

"That's why you don't run; she can run twice as

fast as you."

"We could leave Dean. While she's dealing with him, we could have escaped," Sandy said and laughed.

"That's very funny. Let's keep moving. My foot is better now. Much better," Dean said. "Besides, I can outrun you with even one good leg—especially when a bear is chasing me."

For the next two hours, they climbed to the ridge. There, they found what they didn't want to see. The fire was now just a few miles away, and the smoke was thick and almost suffocating. Flames reached upward more than a hundred feet, twisted and curled in a wall of orange and red.

"Now what?" Jillian said. "Do we turn around?"

At that moment, the wind shifted, becoming stronger and at their backs. The heavy smoke cleared but remained omnipresent, and the flames shifted.

"That front is coming; it's pushing it away—for now," Brandon said. He looked at Dean. The sweat on the man's face said it all. "Dean is done. We need to stop, Gerard. Can we find a clearing open and safe enough to stop?"

The ridgetop was clear of trees, both alive and dead. They stood in a hundred-foot clearing with only sage and large lichen-covered boulders. If necessary, they would use it as a refuge.

"Can we set up here, at least until morning?" Abby asked.

The night was coming. The most challenging part of the trail was below them, and going forward could prove deadly in the darkness.

"There's a spot over there surrounded by rocks and boulders," Gerard said. "We'll set up camp there; it's not the best, but it's better than being in the middle of the trees."

"I'll get dinner together. There are still a few bags of beef stew. Sandy, can you help?"

Sandy stood on a large rock and looked at the wild-fire. She was shaking. "I want to go on—get to the fucking trucks and get the hell out of here. You said it was just a few miles. Staying up here is suicide. I don't want to burn to death."

Abby took Sandy's arm. "Help me make dinner; that will take your mind off it."

"No, I want to go. Get out of here." She pushed Abby's arm away. "Now."

"Sandy, please take a deep breath," Brandon said. "We need to stay here; at first light, we'll be rested. We'll make the final push. We'll be at the trucks by ten, then out of here. You have to trust us; we all understand, but climbing down this mountain in the dark, as Gerard said, is not the right way."

"I didn't want to come on this bullshit hike—you made me, Brandon," Sandy declared. "You said it would be easy—this isn't fucking easy. We are all going to die."

Dean hobbled over to the woman, took her arm, and drew her down. "Please help Abby; I can't go any further until I rest; I can barely walk. I need your help and strength. Okay, Sandy? Please."

It was the way that Dean said it that calmed Sandy's panic. They all felt the fear and the terror, but they must remain calm. They knew it.

Dinner helped. The surge of warm food in their bellies in the cold of the night eased their minds.

"I have a surprise," Jillian said as she rummaged

through her pack. She pulled a bottle of peach schnapps from the bag. "I was saving this until we reached the trucks—something to toast the adventure. Right now is better. Hold out your cups."

Abby extended her cup to Jillian. "You sure, Abby?" Jillian said.

"Absolutely. It will be my last drink of alcohol for six months; it might as well be here."

Chapter 12

Maggie's nose pushed against Jordan's face, startling her awake. Daylight washed the top of the mountain; the smoke was thin, the sky brilliant. Around the interior of the fuselage, chaos reigned. Suarez had pulled the blanket over his head. Jimmy was still in his seat. She checked his pulse; he was alive. The beating was strong and even. He opened his eyes.

"Still here, thanks to you; got an energy bar?" Jimmy mumbled. "And thirsty."

"Will do." Jordan went to Suarez and pulled away the blanket. The man's cold eyes glowered at her. "Morning, sunshine," she said.

"Fuck you."

"Excellent, we all survived. Eat these." She handed him a couple of bars. "Now we get off this damn mountain."

She gathered and stuffed the supplies into the emergency bag, rigging the straps to fit her shoulders. Then, she placed the bag outside the airplane.

"Suarez, I will need your assistance. You can help if you want, or I can leave you here. We need to get Jimmy out of the plane. We will use one of the doors as a sled, put Jimmy on it, and then drag him off the mountain. I have a good idea of where we are; there's a road at the bottom. We will wait for help there. Up here, we will freeze. It is already colder than last night. Do you understand?"

"The fire, we are heading into the fire," Suarez said, using his handcuffed hands as pointers.

She heard fear. Good. She could work with that. She unshackled his leg irons, not his hands, and untied the rope restraint. She unbuckled Jimmy from his seat, bound his arms as best as she could with Ace bandages from the first aid kit, and, between them, managed to get the man out. The pilot's pain was visibly intense. He said nothing. She pulled the pins from one of the double doors and dropped the panel on the ice. Five minutes later, Jimmy, wrapped in one of the blankets, was secured to the aluminum door. She tied lengths of rope to the improvised sled and slipped the makeshift pack over her shoulders. She also filled the bottles and bags with the melted ice water.

"You ready, Diego?"

The familiarity surprised the killer. He stared at the sheriff and then the dog. Maggie's eyes never left the man.

"Put these on; you will need them," she said, holding a pair of leather gloves from the kit. She then looked at the tree line. "That way." She pointed. "Pull the sled when you need to and use gravity when you can."

An hour later, they cleared the ice field and were

in the trees following a game trail. As a hunter, she knew the trail would be easier than trying to forge a new one. The door slid easily over the spring grass and bracken ferns. Suarez said nothing; most of the time, he just pulled or allowed the sled to slide on its own. She walked behind the two men; Maggie occasionally took the point. They stopped to rest and ate more bars. The surge of energy helped. She was banged up; she guessed some internal bruising, maybe broken ribs, but there was nothing she could do. At least she wasn't peeing or spitting blood. Right now, it was life or death. And the smoke intensified as they moved lower down the mountain. Their travel was measured in feet per minute, not miles per hour.

She guessed they were about halfway at noon and would make the road by evening. From the right, a herd of deer walked quickly across the trail and into the woods, the smoke and fire driving them toward safety. The sight startled the Mexican, who stopped and looked at Jordan but again said nothing.

"Do you need to rest?" she asked.

"I'm good. The sooner we are off this fucking mountain, the better."

She wondered when he would make a move. It was in his nature; he's the killer who tied up his victims and tortured them; he's the one who slit throats and worse. She thought of the old story of the scorpion and the frog needing to cross the river; the frog agreed, believing he was safe, but the scorpion stung him anyway, and they both died. Her greatest concern was Jimmy and getting him to the hospital. If the son of a bitch tried anything, she would shoot him in the leg or worse. Maggie would be the only witness.

The trail was often steep, and it took both hands to hold the ropes to ensure that Jimmy didn't bust loose and slide down the mountain like a runaway toboggan. Jimmy was worse; he easily passed out no matter how much he tried to stay awake. He complained of a headache and once vomited; this was not good.

"The hombre is gonna die, Sheriff. Just leave him, we get to safety, then come back to get him. That's what I would do."

"You are a psycho. You would leave your mother here," Jordan said as she stood up from Jimmy.

"Not true. I love my mother. My father, now that's a different matter." Suarez laughed.

At four o'clock, they reached a wide ledge above a small creek; it wasn't Boulder Creek. But she was sure there was a pullout that hikers and trail riders used just over the next low ridge, but first, they had to cross the creek.

Jordan said, "There's a parking area just over that hill and a forest service cabin. It may have a phone."

To her surprise, Suarez volunteered. "I'll carry him over. You bring the sled."

They untied Jimmy from the door. Suarez, still cuffed, easily picked the man up and carefully waded across the creek; it wasn't a foot deep but rocky; the sled would have been impossible. A few minutes later, the men were across; Suarez gently laid the pilot on the short grass. He stood and waited. Maggie quickly crossed and stood next to Suarez. Jordan took hold of the ropes, clattered the door across the rocks, and dragged it through the creek until she reached the face of the creek's two-foot-high bank. Turning back to the door, she didn't see the tree branch Suarez swung and clubbed across the back of her head.

* * *

The vehicle parking was a hundred yards up the road. The smoke had settled in the valley and was the thickest they'd encountered. Above the hikers, on the far ridge, fire danced. They heard the massive jet plane through the haze before they saw it roar from west to east. A thick plume of orange fire retardant billowed from its belly. Chaos reigned.

Two gunshots echoed across the narrow valley. They froze.

"What the hell was that?" Jillian said.

"Gunshots, pistol," Gerard answered. "Maybe someone is asking for help?"

"We have to get out. The trucks are just up the road," Sandy yelled. "We need to get Dean to the hospital."

Another gunshot.

"We need to help," Gerard said. "It came from over that rise. We'll look, then head on to the trucks."

They changed direction and climbed the low hill. In a small clearing along a creek, a man stood. Two bodies lay on the ground; none moved. A ball of yellow fur lay on the ground next to the body near the creek.

"Yo! Do you need help?" Gerard yelled.

The man turned; a blanket wrapped his shoulders. He waved, almost panic-like.

"Can we help? What's the problem?" Dean yelled as he leaned on the rough crutch Brandon had made. They carefully worked their way down the gravel slope to the man.

"Plane crash, up the side of the mountain. We managed to get this far; the pilot, he's the one over there, was hurt badly. The woman hit her head when we crossed the creek. That's when that wolf attacked. I shot him." The man held up a Glock 17.

"It's not the kind of pistol one normally sees up here in the woods," Gerard said. "Jillian, can you take a look at the woman? I'll see about the guy."

"That's a strange outfit you're wearing," Abby said—she paused. "Gerard, stop right there. Something's not right."

Jillian reached the woman. "She's law enforcement, Gerard. She's wearing a sheriff's shirt. Her holster is empty." She put her hand on the shoulder of the sheriff, and she moved slightly.

When Gerard turned to the man, a pistol was pointed at him. "All of you, sit. No heroics," Suarez said. "I will shoot you. You—Gerard, right? Strip down; I want your clothes." The man turned to Jillian. "She alive?"

"Yes, a bump on the back of her head, some blood—she's alive. Is that guy dead?" She pointed to Jimmy.

"He's still alive but messed up in the head, and his arms are broken—from the plane crash. Come on, Gerard, hurry the fuck up."

"He's wearing an orange jumpsuit," Abby said. "He is her prisoner."

"Was her prisoner, lady. I need to get out of here before that fire gets here. You people, I don't fucking care. Stuff the clothes in one of those backpacks." Suarez pointed to Sandy. "You do it." Abby pushed the bag over. Gerard, now in his boxers, tossed her his clothes. "Boots, too. Everything."

Sandy opened the bag and pulled out camping equipment to make room. She found the handle of

Gerard's pistol. "Why the fuck are you doing this? Leave us alone," she yelled as she swung the heavy weapon up and toward the man.

"Don't do it, or you are dead," the man yelled. Jordan's pistol was aimed at her head. "Drop it. I mean it."

"Drop the gun, Sandy," Brandon said. "Just do it."

"Take his advice, Sandy," the man said. He swung the pistol to Abby and shot her in the leg. "You are next."

Abby screamed. Stunned, Sandy dropped the pistol.

"Sandy, my hero with the pistol, stand up and grab the bag. You are coming with me. Up, now."

Sandy stood; the pistol lay on the grass at her feet.

"Carefully pick up the gun, put it in the pack, and bring it to me."

Sandy's shoulders slumped. She carried the pack in her right hand. The man slowly backed up, careful with his footing.

"Sling the bag over your shoulder, *chica*. No one follows. If you do, she gets a bullet. Let's go, Sandy."

He walked backward, the pistol ready, until they reached the woods. Then they disappeared.

Jordan slowly sat up and touched the back of her head; a bloody, wet knot had formed. Then she saw Maggie. "Dear God," she said and crawled to the dog. She put her head against her chest; there was a heartbeat. A long red mark was across her left flank where the shot just missed. The branch, the one Suarez used on her, lay next to Maggie. Jordan assumed that Maggie attacked Suarez and was clubbed with the same chunk of timber. She reached for her pistol; it was missing.

"He took it. Are you okay?" a man's voice said.

Jordan looked around. "Where the hell did you all come from?" One woman was attending to another woman with a bloody leg.

"Who are you?" a man standing in his underwear asked.

"I'm Sheriff Jordan Tynes, Park County. We were transporting a prisoner, and our airplane crashed. We need to get our pilot to medical care. He was badly messed up in the crash." She looked around. "Where is Suarez? There was another man with us. Did you see him?"

"Yes, he had your gun. He shot Abby and took my girlfriend, Sandy," Brandon said, "and Gerard's clothes. They headed to those woods about fifteen minutes ago. They went that way." He pointed.

"Sheriff, I'm Jillian Tombs, a nurse." She left Abby and went to Jimmy. "He's not doing well—all the signs of severe concussion. When was this crash?"

"Yesterday afternoon. We were coming back from Casper. Something knocked us out of the air. It was a miracle we survived the landing."

"We need to move, or that fire will even out the miracle," Gerard said. He was on his knees next to his wife. Jillian was tightly wrapping gauze from the medical kit around the woman's wound. Her jeans were soaked in blood.

"He shot her?" Jordan asked.

"Yes, I had a gun," Gerard said. "Sandy pointed it at him, he shot Abby, and they left."

"And he took your gun?" Jordan asked Gerard.

"Yes. He has yours and mine. They headed to the pullout parking over the ridge there."

"Box Canyon pullout? The one near the small forest service building?"

"Yes, it's maybe a quarter mile away."

Waves of thick smoke washed through the canyon, and Jordan heard the pops and explosions of the fire above them. They saw no flames, but it was a matter of time, and time was not on their side.

Maggie rolled to her belly and slowly stood. The pain in her eyes broke Jordan's heart. Still groggy, she looked at the hikers surrounding her. One stood, another leaned on a crutch, and a man in white boxer briefs kneeled on the ground helping a woman with a bloody leg wound while the other woman went back to attend to Jimmy. They all looked at her for direction. It was a mess.

Chapter 13

Thirty minutes before sunrise, three privately owned airplanes sat on the Mission Field tarmac near the Yellowstone Service Center. A group of men and women stood inside, all holding paper coffee cups. They would be the first planes to fly the route in Jimmy Belvedere's flight plan. The theories behind the missing plane ran from losing his way in the smoke and crashing into a mountain to the remote possibility they may have hit a Montana DNRC wildfire management drone. The smoke was thick over the central and southern Absarokas. Seeing anything on the ground was impossible. Josiah Potts made sure everyone knew about the ELT; they would listen for the broadcast on 121.5 MHz, and catching that signal would help pinpoint the transmitter, even though the smoke may be hiding the crash.

While they waited for sunrise, a helicopter operated by Montana Energy landed near the airplanes; two men jumped out and walked into the lobby. One was the president of Montana Energy, Dwayne Pepper, and the other was the retired attorney general for Montana and close friend of Sheriff Tynes, Russell Pike. Everyone knew each other, and during times like this, everyone pitched in. Montana Energy, with the largest helicopter fleet in the state, offered up an aircraft and pilot during search missions. It didn't hurt that Pike and Peppers went back a couple of decades. All Pike did was ask.

The helicopter would be used as the primary rescue aircraft. The others would locate the plane on the ground and fix its location, and then the helicopter would follow in. All this assumed that Potts's ELT was functioning and there was enough visibility to make a rescue possible. If not, it would require hiking in, something no one wanted during a wildfire.

Six hours later, they had finished a series of coordinated grid searches. On the last pass, they picked up the signal from an ELT. No other planes were missing; the signal had to be the Cessna. Cross-referencing the signal, they pinpointed the location about three miles from the last location of the DNRC's FVR-90 drone. The smoke cleared enough over a mountaintop ice field for one of the pilots to spot wreckage: a wing, a pontoon, airplane pieces, and what looked like the fuselage.

The pilot of the power company helicopter and Russell Pike flew to the coordinates; their luck held. It was clear enough to make a landing. He sat the aircraft on the ice about fifty feet from the fuselage. Pike slowly walked to the body of the plane, afraid for what he'd find. Looking around, he couldn't imagine anyone surviving. The plane's identification numbers, painted on the fuselage, matched Josiah Potts's Cessna. Walking around the fuselage, he noticed footprints in the thin crust of ice, the missing door, and the torn and empty food bar wrappers. He called the SAR base on the satellite phone he carried.

"There are no bodies," Pike said. "They were here, and it looks like they left early this morning. There are bandages and energy wrappers. There's a trail of footprints and what appears to be sled marks leading to the fir trees on the western edge of the ice field."

"They bugged out?" came the obvious question.

"Looks like it. I can't go after them, but they are heading toward Boulder Creek. I can do nothing here; the fire is just a mile away. The canyons are filled with smoke, and seeing anything is impossible. We know they are alive; we're heading back."

"Roger that."

Pike stood on the edge of the ice field and watched the fire race up the side of the far canyon. Then, through the smoke, a red and white apparition rose. The massive DC-10 air tanker skimmed over the crest as orange fire retardant billowed from its belly. It climbed steeply, banked, and dumped its load across the mountain. Pike admired the skill and the courage it took to fly one of these giants.

The phone rang.

"Pike here, what's up?"

"The DNRC's second drone is up, sweeping the western side of the mountains. The infrared cameras can penetrate the smoke. What are they looking for?"

"Tell them it appears that three people made it out. They are heading down the mountain in a westerly descent from my location. If they spot anything, let me know. We are leaving the site and are heading back; we are thirty miles southeast of the airport and should be there in twenty minutes."

"Josiah wants to know the condition of his plane?"

"It is a two-hundred-yard-long debris field; the fact that anyone survived is a testament to the pilot's flying skills and the plane's construction. And probably a prayer or two on landing."

* * *

Gerard put on flip-flops, pajama bottoms, and a T-shirt from his bag. He would not wear Suarez's orange jumpsuit. Brandon pulled a thin sweatshirt from his pack and handed it to him. After a lengthy discussion, it was agreed that Jordan and Brandon would hike to the parking area and try to call for help. Jillian would remain and manage the patients, and Dean would help as much as possible. Gerard held his wife and watched the gray sky, hoping the firestorm stayed to the north until help arrived.

They found the trail left by Suarez and Sandy as they entered the woods. They followed it until the gravel banks of Boulder Creek; they carefully waded the swift water of the creek. Maggie wouldn't be left behind and, with some help from Brandon, made it across. Ten minutes later, they were in the parking area.

"Three days ago, there were two horse trailers here. They are gone. Could have used their help," Brandon said, looking around. "And that asshole took my Jeep, and the tires are flat on the Tahoe. What the hell did the guy do?"

Jordan, not wanting to panic Brandon more than he was, said he was a suspect in a shooting.

"A shooting? Is the guy a killer? What the hell will he do with Sandy?"

The wasplike buzz of an aircraft came from an overhead smoke cloud.

"What the hell is that? Sounds like a drone, not an airplane," Brandon said.

"Drone?" Jordan said. "Damn, that's what happened—a drone used by the wildfire fighters. Damn, has to be it."

"What are you talking about?"

"Our plane hit something; it nearly killed my pilot, and it forced us to crash on the mountain. The only thing up there had to be a drone used to spot fires."

"Well, that's fucked."

"Yes, it is. No radios, no cell service." She looked at her phone. "Chances are slim, but let's check out the forest service building; maybe there's a phone."

There wasn't.

In the gray haze, a helicopter's blades' *whomp-whomp-whomp* came from above. Then, as the smoke billowed up and spun away from the road, a helicopter's blue and white fuselage appeared and settled on the gravel. Dust mixed with the smoke, and then the rotor shut down. Russell Pike emerged and hugged Jordan.

"We got word from the DNRC," Pike said. "They spotted heat signatures on the ground in this area. We were heading in but took a chance. It is good to see you, Sheriff." She introduced Brandon Anderson and explained what was happening.

"We have five others over the hill there. Jimmy Belvedere is in bad shape, with broken arms and a concussion. Suarez shot one of the women in the leg; one of the hikers is a nurse; she's helping."

Pike looked at Maggie and took a knee. "She's in bad shape, and you don't look good either."

"I'll be fine."

From up the road, the sounds of sirens filled the canyon.

"The calvary," Pike said. "There's a hotshot crew working this side of the mountain; they got the word the same time we did. They sent two crews to get you out."

Two pumper trucks pulled up behind the helicopter. Eight men jumped off. Jordan told them about the injured. Twenty minutes later, they had carried out the battered and wounded and laid them on the road near the trucks. One of the crew was working with Jillian on the injured.

"The pilot will take out Jimmy, Abby, and you," Pike said. "There's an ambulance heading here to help with Dean and get the rest of you out of harm's way."

"I'm staying here," Jordan said.

"Not a chance," Pike said. "You are the sheriff; your dad needs you, and besides, you've got busted ribs and what else I don't know. The helicopter can only take four, so you go. We'll all get out on the trucks. And take Maggie as well. I love her but do not want to deal with her without you. I'll see you in a couple of hours."

Chapter 14

Jordan followed the two gurneys as they wheeled Jimmy Belvedere and Abby Hanson into Livingston Health Care and Hospital through the emergency doors. Maggie limped along next to her. She tried to carry the hound, but her chest hurt too much, and besides, Maggie wouldn't stand for it. The two injured were swiftly moved into adjacent emergency rooms, and she was ushered into a third. A nurse pulled Maggie's records (she had been a patient in this hospital before), and they gave the dog a light sedative to relax her. They would take X-rays and clean the wound. Jordan waved off assistance and went to look for her father.

She walked the second-floor hallway to a room in the far wing; she hadn't had time to call her mother while they flew in. Louise was sitting in a chair next to the hospital bed. Victor, looking comfortable and well, was the first to see her. He smiled crookedly; Louise looked up from reading a book, jumped from the chair, and hugged her daughter.

"I didn't know they found you; I was terrified," Louise said.

"I'm fine; I just got banged up. How are you doing, Pop? You look pretty good."

Victor tried to say, "I'm doing okay," but his words were garbled. Then, disappointment distorted his face.

"His speech took the biggest impact, honey. It was like before; the left side of the brain affected his right arm and leg the most. We were lucky; we got him here before too much damage." Louise, still holding Jordan in her arms, looked at her. "We are okay here; you need to be looked at. Your breathing is difficult; I hear it." Louise looked past Jordan to the door.

Michael Cardona stood in the doorway.

"It's good to see you again, Michael," Louise said. "Please take Jordan back to emergency. I know her; she's not right."

"Yes, Mrs. Tynes, I will do that." Cardona took two steps toward Jordan and caught her as she collapsed.

* * *

Jordan spent a restless night. It's never dark or quiet in a hospital, and Livingston was no different. Her collapse was due to hunger, stress, and exhaustion. The X-rays showed two busted ribs on the right side just below her right breast and some severe bruises on her hips and lower back; thankfully, her liver and spleen were good. However, her kidneys showed the stress of dehydration. The CT scan showed no internal bleeding. Doctor John Larkin, the hospital's top doctor and chief administrator, said she could go home the next day, but her father would remain a few days longer. He recommended time off before returning to duty. The hospital allowed Maggie to sleep in Jordan's room that night.

The next morning, she stopped by Jimmy's room, he had suffered two broken forearms, smashed by what turned out to be the DNRC drone that crashed into the Cessna. The cuts and abrasions would heal. However, he had a severe concussion, and a hematoma had pushed into the left side of his brain. They performed surgery to relieve the pressure and then put Jimmy into an induced coma to give his brain time to heal. They wouldn't know the complete extent of the damage for a few weeks. She went to Abby's room.

Abby Hanson was lucky, if being shot in the thigh by a psychopath was luck. The bullet missed arteries and bone. She lost a considerable amount of blood, but it was Jillian's quick work and tourniquet that saved her life. She was transferred to the Bozeman Hospital to be closer to her family. The baby was unaffected. Gerard was furious with himself for forcing this adventure on his friends.

Dean's injury was an aggravated Achilles tendon. It was not torn, so surgery would not be needed. He would wear a boot for at least a month.

Gerard's Tahoe, with its flat tires, was lost when the wildfire raced through the Boulder Creek parking area the next day. The winds picked up that night, forcing the hotshot crew, who helped the hikers escape the advancing flames, to abandon the valley. The firestorm consumed everything, including the forest service building.

Two weeks later, on the first clear day, Josiah Potts sent a crew to turn off and retrieve the ELT. Later, he would try to recover the aircraft debris, but it would be costly.

To everyone's relief, Sandy Tillerman was now also in the hospital; her boyfriend, Brandon, was sitting next to her when Jordan stopped to see how she was doing. She had been found in the back seat of Brandon's Jeep parked in the Livingston Albertsons parking lot. She was tied, gagged, and bruised when Deputy Bob Claymore made a sweep through the parking lot late the same night that Suarez and Sandy escaped the wildfire. Another vehicle, a 2001 brown Chevy pickup, was reported missing from the parking lot by an Albertsons employee.

* * *

Three days later, Jordan, her chest wrapped in tape to protect her broken ribs, entered her office and sat. She was furious, and sitting at home didn't help to ease her temper. Suarez had disappeared; they found the brown pickup stolen from the Albertsons lot on a back road ten miles north of Livingston. She was ready for his attempt to escape but failed, which she relived repeatedly. She called in the information on Suarez while she flew to the hospital in the helicopter. Her people did everything to find the killer, but he slipped through the blockade. Deputy Claymore pulled security tapes from the store; Suarez was identified purchasing three prepaid cell phones and using cash that Gerard confirmed was in his wallet. Other videos showed him hotwire the brown pickup and leave. Jordan was positive he called for help; his people must have met him where he dropped the truck. There was nothing in the Jeep that could help them. At least he hadn't killed Sandy Tillerman.

Candy Middleton stood at the door, scratching Maggie's head. "You have company. Do you want to see them? It's the feds."

"Great, just what I need. Please get me a coffee and show them in."

Michael Cardona and two men strolled into her office. Mike had spent evenings at the Tynes house while she recovered; he brought flowers. She did not recognize the others and did not stand. Candy remained at the door.

"Sheriff Tynes," Mike said, "this is DEA Special Agent Will Brewster and FBI Special Agent Luke Morris; they are from their respective Helena offices."

"That's a lot of special agents," Jordan said, shaking hands. "Candy, please have Bob and John join us."

When everyone settled, she asked, "What can I do for you, fellas?"

Chapter 15

Special Agent Mike Cardona asked, "First, how is your father? I told Will and Luke about what happened, the airplane, Suarez, the escape, and, more importantly, your father."

"He's good, all considered. They expect a full recovery. He's tough," Jordan added. "It's just rough on Mom and my brother and sister. We are trying to work out the logistics of care. They think he can go home Friday."

"Please give Louise a hug from me," Mike said.

"I will. What do you have there, Agent Brewster?"

DEA Special Agent Will Brewster slid a manila envelope across the desk.

"Fan mail?" Jordan asked.

"Hardly. It is the police report from Natrona Sheriff Matt Cumber. It concerns the prisoner transfer that went upside down last week."

"It wasn't that simple—more like crashed and burned. What am I looking at?"

"Sheriff Cumber says that they found two bodies in a house in Casper. It was the house in front of the trailer where your suspect, Diego Suarez, was apprehended. The male, Luis Gambuzza, was found hanging by his arms from a beam in their living room; he had been slashed a hundred times and bled to death. The other body was his wife, Arabella Gambuzza; she had been cut up and strangled. It was messy and brutal. Sheriff Cumber told me that Luis Gambuzza informed him about Suarez and where to find him."

"Well, damn," Jordan said. "Any collateral?"

"None found; they had two children, four and six. Luckily, they stayed with the mother's parents, who had come up legally from Mexico ten years ago. The grandparents were interviewed, and their papers are being reevaluated."

"I think Suarez did not return to Mexico," Jordan said. "He is still here settling scores."

"We are chasing every lead and confidential informant we have in the region," FBI Agent Morris said. "The murders of the Indians and the Gambuzzas did what they were supposed to—no one is talking. The word is out across four states."

"The cartel runs a massive organization across the West," Mike said. "We estimate that they do more than a billion dollars across the Rocky Mountains—that's a billion with a *b*."

"And there are a lot of zeros after that *b*," Bob Claymore offered. "It can buy a lot of silence."

"No one saw anything around the Gambuzza house?" Jordan asked.

"No, and no cameras, at least any we found. Suarez was there a day or two before he was arrested; he may have seen them and pulled them after the killings. The Natrona sheriff is chasing down Ring accounts; like everyone, he has limits to his staff. His primary challenge is to find the killer or killers."

"Killers?"

"He reports at least two additional pairs of footprints on the bloody floor. Suarez had help."

"I will call Cumber and offer what I can," Jordan said. "This did start here in Park County."

"Suarez is a psycho and sociopath and cold-blooded killer," Mike said. "He is who started this."

"And he is smart. I spent a day and a half with him. He is calculating and patient. Even when you know he's coming, he will strike when you are the most vulnerable. That's what happened to me. Why he didn't kill Jimmy and me, I don't know."

"And Maggie," Mike added.

The dog picked her head up from her bed and crooked it.

Jordan smiled and looked from the dog back to the agents. "The man has a weakness; I think it is his ego. He believes he is invincible; I saw that on his face as he sat in the airplane that night. Even chained, he was certain he would find a way out, so he waited. He could have escaped, and maybe he'd have made it. But he didn't; he waited until the time was right."

"We are setting up a task force," Mike said. "The three agencies and you. Livingston seems to be a drug transfer point north to Canada and south to Salt Lake, with Yellowstone Park in the middle. The drugs come in from Seattle and Chicago. Our confidential informants say there is a transfer spot somewhere in the area. The packages are broken down, repackaged, and sent on. That means there are workers and logistics involved. Jordan, your people know the territory. We have the budgets and the resources to support you."

"The girlfriend of one of the dead men said that the Chinese were also involved," Jordan added. "They were trying to use the Indians to turn on the Mexicans. The cartel got wind of it and killed them."

"We have been getting information from the Portland and Seattle field offices," Morris said, "about arrests involving Chinese gangs, all recent immigrants. They were selling fentanyl, meth, and cocaine. Unbelievably, shopping lists are online; they are using one of the delivery services to drop the drugs at the user's residences."

"We got lucky when one Chinese kid turned on his bosses," Brewster said. "He wants to stay in the US; he came to the States illegally. The evidence he provided gave us a look through the windows of the operation—scary stuff. The kid said that they intend to take over the cartel's territory. Push them out."

"A billion in revenue will do that," Deputy Claymore added.

"There are several ways we can go about this," Jordan said. "We can press our CIs and see what they know. We can canvass the area and see if anything pops up—warehouses and out-of-state license plates—which, unfortunately, are everywhere this time of year. Press the users and see what they know—sadly, we will also watch the high school. Sometimes, we get lucky. The last way is to set up a sting, draw them in, and make buys. They need to replace the Indians. Distribution is critical."

"I like the sting idea," Brewster said. "Who can do

this?"

"My people are too well known," Jordan said. "And besides, I need them on the roads this time of year. Can you bring in a couple of your agents from out of the area and set up a shop here in town? We can ask around the reservations, and the tribal police can help us there. The cartel has shown us they don't like competition; if it looks like someone is trying to take their business, it won't be long before they surface."

Two hours after the feds left, Candy again knocked on the door.

"What now?" Jordan said.

"You have visitors. It is the hikers who got mixed up in the Suarez mess. They want to thank you."

Jordan gave Candy a quizzical look. "I should be thanking them; show them in."

Four people came into the office. Jordan stood and pointed to a couple of chairs. One of the men, on crutches, sat while the others remained standing.

"We never formally met," Jordan began. "I'm Sheriff Jordan Tynes, and that is Maggie. We were escorting a murderer from Casper to Livingston when our plane crashed. I want to thank you for helping. You most likely saved our lives."

Jillian took a step forward and put out her hand. "I'm Jillian Tombs, this is Sandy Tillerman, that's Dean Young, and Brandon Anderson is sitting. Gerard and Abby Hanson are in Bozeman. The gunshot wound to Abby's leg has been stabilized; it was close, according to the doctor. An inch away was the femoral artery. She would have died."

"I'm so sorry that you got involved," Jordan said.

"But I thank all of you for your help."

"Honestly, Sheriff, I didn't want to go on this hike." She bent down and kissed Brandon. "And I've told Gerard it will be a long time before we go hiking again. Once around that mountain is enough. He lost his truck in the wildfire; it could have been worse."

"The reports are that the fire is still burning," Jordan said. "They have it thirty percent contained if you can truly contain one of these monsters. It may take a month more to put an end to it. We could use rain, but none is forecast until the end of the month."

"I was told your father had a stroke; we hope he is better," Jillian said.

"He is, and thank you. Are you heading back?"

"Yes, we have had enough of the wilderness, at least for this year."

"I understand. It is both beautiful and challenging."

"Who was that guy? I've never seen evil that close; it was palpable," Brandon said.

"He brutally killed two Indians who worked for him—drug dealers. He was caught in Casper, and I was bringing him back to the county to face charges when we crashed. Jimmy, the pilot, was badly injured but is improving. Time will tell. It was a serious brain injury."

"And has this killer been found?"

"No, but I will find him."

Chapter 16

For a week, it was federal agents here and federal agents there. It was driving Jordan and her staff crazy. Candy was involved in the coordination, but it was more like taking orders. They had ways of doing things Jordan knew would drive Candy up the wall. They started demanding notes in triplicate, dedicated phone lines, and office space (none of which they had). It was about the bureaucracy; Jordan hadn't heard one word from any of her confidential informants about pressure or contacts from the feds.

The first break came a week later; two high school boys were found unconscious in a red Ford Maverick parked in the school parking lot. NARCAN saved their lives; an hour later, they would have been dead. It was Wells Courtwright's quick action that saved them.

Jordan met Wells at the hospital. The boys shared a room. Both were wired up, and tubes for IV drips led from the pumps. Lance Collins's parents sat in chairs. Beth Collins sat next to Lance and held his hand. Robb

Collins stood when the sheriff entered. A nurse remained at the door behind them.

Lance, a toe-headed sixteen-year-old with a round, pleasant face, was propped up on a pillow. He smiled meekly at Jordan. Dan Singleton, a lanky redhead, also sixteen, lay on the adjacent bed; he timidly waved at Jordan and Wells.

"Robb and Beth Collins, Sheriff," Robb said, his hand out. "We can't tell you how happy we are about saving our boy and Dan. I don't know what we'd do if we lost him."

"I'm glad I was there," Wells said. "There's been too much of this happening in the county. The boys were lucky."

"And stupid," Beth said. "The Singletons, who we've known since the boys were in grade school, just left. I'm sorry you missed them. They are shocked and upset. Dan is their only child. Tanya, Dan's mother, wants to find the son of a bitch who sold them the drugs. They do not want this to happen to anyone else."

"That's why we're here; we have questions," Jordan said. "Do you mind?"

"No, we do not," Robb said. He looked at Lance. "You talk to these officers."

Lance nodded. Jordan looked at Dan, and he also nodded.

"Good," Jordan said. "The doctors said it was oxycodone that had been laced with fentanyl. Pills were found in Dan's pockets. Did you know what you were taking?"

Lance turned his head and said, "We were told they were uppers; we were just having fun. We'd done this before, no problems, just a nice high. No big deal."

"Jesus," Beth said. "No big deal? You've done this before?"

"Yes, Mom, a couple of times. Those were pills some of the guys shared. I don't know where they got them."

"You said this wasn't the first time?" Wells asked.

"No, it wasn't, Deputy," Dan offered. "The stuff has been going around the school; some guys get them. No one's been hurt."

"Till now. If I hadn't found you, you would be dead. Do you understand?"

Neither boy said anything. Jordan watched Beth's face; she saw fear. The fear a mother has when she learns her son could be in the morgue, not a hospital room.

"We need to stop this before someone else overdoses and dies," Jordan said. "Who sold you the drugs?"

The boys remained silent. From where they lay, they could not easily see each other. Dan tried to pull himself up; the nurse ran to the bed.

"You want to say something, Dan?"

"I don't want anyone to get in trouble," Dan said; the oxygen prong in his nose fell out. The nurse readjusted the plastic device.

"Trouble is what both of you have right now," Robb said. "Can they be arrested? Can they go to prison?"

"Sadly, stupidity isn't a crime," Jordan said. "But withholding evidence in a felony investigation is. If you are not forthcoming, the county attorney might decide that your silence is protecting drug dealers and killers. He could press charges and mess you guys up. Colleges are not keen on drug dealers and felons."

"Killers? What the hell do you mean?" Beth said. She rose and stood next to her husband and took his arm.

"The drugs are the same as found at a location where two men were brutally murdered a few weeks back. We know who is responsible; he is part of a Mexican cartel that controls the drug distribution here in Montana. Your noncompliance may mean you are protecting him and his gang. That makes you accomplices in everything they have done and will do. You are withholding important information."

"You don't mean that," Beth said.

"I mean every word, Mrs. Collins," Jordan said. "This man and his people are now responsible for four brutal murders that we are aware of. He controls the distribution; we need names."

"If he gives you the information, won't they try to kill them?" Robb said. Beth let out a cry and put her hand over her mouth.

"We can protect them. Their names will not be released; they are minors. But there are no absolutes in this. We need names and where you got the drugs. The sooner these men are found, the better."

Lance looked at his father. "I must tell them. If I don't, I'll be tossed from the baseball team. I won't be able to play football. You know the school's policies; it's zero tolerance. Can you keep our names out of this, Sheriff?"

"You are a smart fellow," Wells said. "Dan, are you on board? Prison is a nasty place."

* * *

Sitting directly across from Jordan at the steel table in the interview room sat a lanky, narrow-faced kid about eighteen. His long, oily hair hung to his shoulders, his skin was pale, and his cheeks were pockmarked. His arms were heavily tattooed with angular art, unreadable phrases, and gang symbols. The knuckles on his right hand read FUCK, and the left YOU! He wore a black Kurt Cobain T-shirt that needed a wash.

Jordan sighed, opened a blue folder, and flipped through the dozen typewritten pages stapled inside. Standing in the corner, Deputy Claymore leaned against the wall, watching. She looked up at the kid.

"I was not surprised when your name came up, Lucius. You have been a busy boy for someone so young," Jordan said. "When drugs are involved, I almost always find you or Clem Barnes. How you have managed to stay out of prison confounds me."

She carefully turned through the pages stapled inside a file.

Lucius Menke glared at Jordan, looked at Claymore, and flipped him off.

"Rude, that is just rude," Jordan said. "Do you have any idea why you are sitting here?"

"Gee, let me think. I got a parking ticket I haven't paid. That it?"

"Cute. No, it has to do with the Wing Foot and Black Hand murders. They are known associates of yours; your names were offered up as primary drug distributors to the under-twenty high school crowd. That's bad, very bad."

"Jesse and Mikey are dead? What the hell? You shoot 'em?"

"You didn't know. I find that surprising. No, it seems the Mexicans did that. It was the CC cartel, cut them up. It was bad. Very bloody." Jordan slid an envelope out from inside the folder and removed a large colored photograph. She showed it to Lucius. It was hard to believe, but the kid turned paler. He put his hand to his mouth.

"Don't you get sick in here, Menke," Bob said. "I will make you clean it up."

"That's sick, the Mexicans are sick, this whole thing is fucked and sick. I just sell some candy, a little dope, coke, meth, I'll cop to all that. Hell, if I make five hundred a week, I'm killing it. Hardly covers my food and gas money."

"Poor choice of words, but life is hard. Where is Diego Suarez?" Jordan asked.

Lucius crossed his arms across his chest; the face of Cobain was tattooed on his right forearm. "Suarez? Don't know a Suarez. He connected to this?"

"Lucius, I have your partner, Clem Barnes, waiting in another room. I will ask him the same questions. The first to help me help themselves. Selling drugs to kids—there is nothing worse or contemptible. I want to tie the two of you to a tree out in bear country, cover you with pig grease, and see what happens."

"You can't do that. There are laws that prevent that. There are rules. I know my rights."

"There are lots of laws—most you choose to ignore. Time is important –back to the subject of Diego Suarez, where is he?"

Lucius Menke sat at the table, quiet-like, for a while. What brain cells were left in his head were working overtime, comparing the odds. "Okay, I don't know the cartel's top guys; my guy is a runner from Billings named Ernie—no last name. There are a couple of others, all from Billings. Ernie would pass the stuff to

Jesse Wing Foot. I wondered why I hadn't seen Jesse."
He looked back at the photo. "Which one was Jesse?"

"He's on the right."

"Fuck me. That's' sick, really sick."

"Name."

Lucius looked up at Jordan, then at Deputy Claymore. "Are you arresting me? Charging me with what?"

"The list would fill a page."

"I want a lawyer; I don't like where this is going."

"And we don't like where it's been. Just a name or two, then we can discuss lawyers and charges, if any."

"Another name is Gus. When I see him, he usually has this other guy with him who calls him GG. GG calls the other guy, Moe. GG's a Mex, mid-thirties, beard, black eyes, like coal. Moe is about the same age, black hair in a ponytail, fancy boots tipped with silver, and a scar on his cheek here." Lucius made a slash on his right cheek. "I call this number and punch another number when the menu is read. The number changes all the time. I place my order. The price and location are texted to me. Been everywhere, from the Albertsons to a Big Timber pizza shop parking lot. Seldom the same place twice, always public, lots of people around. This van pulls up, the door opens, and the package is pitched to me. Only twice we met; that's when that guy called him GG. Both times, he warned me to stay quiet. One time, he threw a dead chicken through my window. They are sick."

There was a tap on the door, and Deputy Claymore opened it. FBI agent Luke Morris walked in. Jordan was annoyed; she did not stand.

"Who the fuck is he?" Lucius said. "A fed; I can smell them; they are like feral dogs."

"Woof, woof, Menke," Morris responded. Jordan remained annoyed. "I am here to make a deal. You interested?"

Lucius looked at Jordan. "Him. What is he? I want nothing to do with him."

"FBI. That's how far up the food chain we are, Lucius." Jordan turned around to Morris. "What does Clem Barnes want?"

"Full immunity, a place in Arizona, a new name, and a Chevy truck, black. He says he knows where Suarez is."

"That asshole don't know shit," Lucius said. "I do the deals. He is just a driver. Goes where I tell him. I handle everything, the orders, the pickups, the money. He works for me."

"That's not his story." Morris looked at Jordan. "A black truck. Silverado?"

"Seems you are sucking the hind tit," Bob said. "He bit; he's getting the deal."

Lucius slammed his hands on the table. "Clem don't know shit, I'm telling you."

The three looked at Lucius and waited. "Enlighten us," Jordan finally said.

* * *

Jordan stood behind Deputy Claymore as he locked the cell door, securing Lucius Menke. In the cell next door sat Clem Barnes. She watched the two drug dealers tear into each other.

"I didn't tell them nothing, Lucius, nothing," Barnes said.

"A fucking black Chevy truck—you would trade me for a truck? You are an idiot," Menke said.

"What the fuck are you talking about? I told them

nothing."

The light bulb went on. Menke spun around and glared at Jordan. "You bitch."

Jordan and Deputy Claymore walked the hallway to her office. Mike was alone in a chair.

"Where are your playmates, Mike?"

"Busy. I don't keep their calendars. Those two tweakers give you anything?"

"Enough. Fear is a good motivator. And their fear of Suarez is palpable," Bob said.

"He is still in the area, and it appears he's taken over the cartel's logistics," Jordan said. "They didn't know about the Indians, and that scared them. Suarez has at least four associates working an unknown number of distribution teams. Menke knew of two in Bozeman, two in Billings, and one on the Crow reservation south of Billings. He also believed there was one guy selling in the Yellowstone National Park campgrounds. They took over when we put Billy Black in prison five years ago. Black wasn't much, but it left a hole in sales, especially in the park. They took over and have been working it since the pandemic."

"Even drug dealers appreciate a vacuum and an opportunity—ah, capitalism," Mike said. "Can they be useful?"

"Possibly. I'm going to let them stew for the night. I'll see where they stand tomorrow."

Candy knocked on the door. "You have another visitor."

"Who?" Jordan said.

"Kyle Reeder."

Mike smiled.

"Don't you start. Kyle has his moments."

"I heard that," the man standing behind Candy said and squeezed past the office's gatekeeper.

Kyle Reeder was one of the new breed of twenty-first-century journalists: independent, high-tech, a blogger, and no boss other than his conscience. He also had one of central Montana's most listened-to podcasts. He used all the privileges that the press had asserted for the last 150 years, especially as to the secrecy of who his sources were. He'd cut his teeth working on the Montana State University newspaper, *The Exponent*, and later the *Bozeman Daily Journal*. Two decades earlier, the summer after 9/11, he hopped on a plane and did a yearlong stint in Kabul, Afghanistan, as a stringer for the AP. When the contract and money ran out, he returned to Montana and took up guiding and writing feature articles about the glorious wonders of Montana. He wrote blog posts on his website, the *Livingston Bugle*, and quickly pissed off a few self-important people and a couple of politicians. He liked the feeling and the feedback and then expanded his scope to include news and politics. He also listened to his scanner and the police and state troopers complaining about tourists, drunks, and the weather. He was what they called a pain in the ass. He also was right more than wrong.

"I'm glad you weren't killed in the plane crash," Reeder said. "That is quite a story."

"You got most of it right," Jordan said. "I haven't seen you for a while; where have you been?"

"I took two weeks to research national politics in New York City."

"That's a bad road to go down," Mike said.

Reeder glared at him but didn't rise to the bait.

"What can I do for you, Kyle?" Jordan said.

Reeder's look changed to a smile. "Special Agent Cardona, if you are here, something is in the works."

Kyle had dated Jordan for a time more than eight years earlier. Then Mike Cardona walked in out of a cold and freezing night suffering from amnesia, helped Jordan shut down a terrorist cadre of crazy women environmentalists and gun dealers, and changed the dynamics in both Jordan's social and professional life.

"It's nothing that concerns you, Kyle," Mike said.

Ignoring the remark, Kyle said, "Two brutally murdered Crow Indian drug dealers, drugs in the schools and sales to tourists, fentanyl, the detention of two known drug dealers, and an escaped cartel boss. I think there's a lot that concerns the people of Montana."

"As Mike said, this does not concern you," Jordan said.

Maggie had hobbled over to the reporter and nuzzled his leg; Kyle scratched her behind the ears. "At least someone is glad to see me. Is she okay? I heard she was shot."

"Grazed and lucky."

"I also heard that Jimmy Belvedere is out of the hospital. That's good. He is on my list to interview. I hope you don't mind."

"If I did, would it stop you?"

"No. He has a story to tell—an important part of this story."

"And that story is what?" Jordan asked; she was getting her back up over the direction of the conversation.

"Sheriff, I'm trying to piece this together. There's a very bad man out there poisoning our kids, and that man escaped from your custody. I know about the two high school boys."

"Leave them alone," Jordan said. "They and their families have been through too much for you to upset them. Show some restraint here, can you?"

"I will, but there will be a time. Can we declare a truce? Tell me what you can, and I'll help. Having more eyes and ears, the people can be a big help."

"Maybe he can help get the word out, a tip line," Mike said.

"Do not encourage him, Mike," Jordan said. "I don't have the staff to run a tip line. You know that."

"Maybe I can find the help," Mike said.

Chapter 17

Larry Hang Chow sat in the front passenger seat of the Range Rover and watched the Montana countryside slide by. He was still jet-lagged from his two-day ordeal of scheduled commercial flights from Hong Kong through Vancouver to Bozeman. At least the twenty-minute ride from the airport in Belgrade to the Chow Group distribution center in north Bozeman was short. He had called his associate in Bozeman from Vancouver after he took his seat on the Alaska flight.

"Have Jimmy Lee meet me at the terminal's pick-up area," Chow said. "I'm exhausted." He checked his Rolex. "I will be there at twelve thirty and need three hours of sleep before we meet with the crew. Have everyone ready."

"Yes, Commander Chow," the man on the phone answered.

Lawrence Hang Chow was the grandson of the sister of the Hong Kong triad's leader, George Hang

Chow. George Chow, now eighty-three years old, was the son of the triad's founder, Clarence Hang Chow, who reorganized the criminal operation after the defeat of the Japanese in 1945. In the chaos that reigned in British Hong Kong and China after the war, Clarence Chow, called Mountain Master, reinstituted the drug trade, the slavery trade, illegal immigration, and control of illegal imports in and out of Hong Kong. Eighty years later, the triad, now called the Chow Group, LTD., had its fingers in over twenty countries, all the continents except Antarctica, and were larger than most of the Fortune 500. If a number were placed on its operations, it would be well north of four hundred billion dollars in annual revenues. They had partners in the Chinese Communist Party and the People's Liberation Army. Four hundred billion dollars would buy a lot of influence and loyalty. Clarence was sent to stop what was becoming a serious problem: the growth of the Mexican cartels into their business operations in North America, especially in the northwest American states. His people in Seattle and Vancouver were aware of his visit, and they warned him against direct involvement. They would care for these interlopers; the family would not need to be directly involved.

Nevertheless, Hong Kong sent Lawrence to take charge and eliminate this threat. Fear had always been the force behind the Chow Group's management style, and object lessons were their primary control methods. Lawrence Chow was good at his work.

Larry Hang Chow knew that other divisions within the Group were involved in money laundering and raw material sales to the Mexicans. Still, when the Culiacan Cartel began to assert itself in the distribution and sales of narcotics, especially the newest and most prof-itable drug, fentanyl, he was ordered to put a stop to it. The potential for billions in sales and profits was more than enough reason to accept the assignment from his uncle, Triad Mountain Master George Hang Chow.

Larry Hang Chow napped soundly, and when he awoke, he stretched and performed his exercises and ablutions. He dressed in his management uniform: black suit, white shirt, and black tie. He joined his crew in the front room of the house. The house was the distribution center for the Chow Group in central Montana. Its location was disguised as a ranch house, hidden away from the prying eyes and ears of the local law enforcement agencies. To any neighbor taking a curious look, it was a standard one-story house with an outbuilding built sometime during the late 1990s. His people kept a low profile and were mostly out of sight while they methodically began picking the low fruit of local drug dealers. When they were informed of the brutal murders of two Indians they were close to sign-ing, they realized that the Mexicans had changed the game. They would not let this attack by the cartel go unanswered.

"Albert, what do we know about Diego Suarez?" Chow asked his crew.

Albert Sung was the local Chow Group captain, or Red Pole as he was titled. Sung had been born in Hong Kong and legally entered the United States two years earlier on a student visa to study agriculture at the University of Washington. He never attended class and disappeared a week after his arrival. He was now the head of drug sales and distribution for the Chow Group in Montana and Idaho. The universities in these states were his primary markets. He had tripled sales during the past year. The students, more than willing consumers, were unwitting contributors to the profits of the Chow Group and the Chinese government.

"Diego Suarez is an executioner sent north from Culiacan, Mexico, to ensure the loyalties of the local dealers," Sung said. "These two Indians were his first lessons. We understand he also eliminated one of their own in Casper two weeks ago, who had turned against the cartel. Many of our dealers have gone into hiding, at least for now. We are reaching out to them."

"Try harder. We need them. I want sales to increase. And Suarez?"

"He was arrested in Casper, Wyoming. During his return to Park County by the local sheriff, the plane they were on crashed. All survived, and Suarez later escaped. We are looking for him."

"And our local contact, what does he know?"

"Nothing."

"Nothing? That is not an acceptable answer, Mr. Sung. Our informant must know something."

"He informed us of the crash and escape; we have heard nothing more. He has been silent; he does not answer my inquiries."

"Unacceptable. We pay him to answer our calls. How important is this man?"

"Considering his position, very important. We will contact him and set up a meeting."

"I will be here for five days. Find him. I want to talk with him."

* * *

Jordan sat in a chair next to her father in his hospital room. Louise stood next to the hospital bed, holding her husband's hand. They had come to take Victor home; there was nothing more the hospital could do. After twelve days, his condition had improved enough that additional time in the hospital would serve no purpose. Home was the best medicine for his recovery, the doctor said.

"Are you ready?" Jordan asked.

Victor smiled. "I'm sorry, honey. Sorry about having to put you two through this. What about LeeAnn? I thought she was coming with the babies."

"She will come down to see you at home. They put off their trip for a few weeks. Mom agreed that this wasn't the best time."

"I wanted to see the babies; it has been months," Victor protested.

"We will work it out. First, let's get you home," Louise said.

That evening, after Victor was helped to bed, Louise and Jordan called her brother and sister and discussed the problems.

"We need to find help for Mom," Robert said. "I can help financially but can't carry the whole load."

"The babies have totally sucked every extra dollar Tim and I have. I can come down to help, but that's about it. Sorry, Jordan," LeeAnn said.

Tim Grayson and LeeAnn married four years earlier during the pandemic. They met using a dating app, their friendship blossomed online, and before the pandemic was over, they married. Two years later, to LeeAnn's surprise, the thirty-three-year-old woman had identical twin girls, Christina and Katherine.

"The girls are all you need to worry about; Dad is tough. He will pull through this," Jordan said.

"I can deal with most of this, and Jordan helps when she can," Louise said. "The neighbors have been friends for over twenty years, and you know all of them. If there's a problem, I'll ask for help. Honestly, it's the long-term care I'm worried about—costs not covered by Medicare and insurance. I have heard stories."

"Don't pay any attention to those stories; they just want to sell you stuff," Robert said. "I will talk to my financial guy and to HR here at Nike. I will get a good idea about what we can expect—make some plans. Okay?"

"That would help a lot, Robert," Jordan said.

"How's that Italian federal agent doing?" Robert asked.

"He's an American, not Italian," Jordan said. "And he works for the Bureau of Alcohol, Tobacco, and Firearms."

"And explosives. Mike added that when we met last Christmas—seems like a good guy. What's the 411, Sis?"

"You are such a Millennial," LeeAnn said. "It's none of your business, and Jordan's too busy with her day job. There's a lot of stuff going on."

"I am right here, guys," Jordan said. "We will talk later; thanks, Robert. Mom and I will let you know. LeeAnn, kiss the girls for us. I love you both, and I will see you soon."

"That was abrupt," Louise said with a smile. "Are they getting too close to home?"

"Don't start. Long day tomorrow. I'm going to bed. Think about the help. I'll also ask around. Come, Mags."

Jordan walked down the hall to her room, Maggie

leading the way.

Her sister was right; there was a lot going on. A more serious relationship would be nice, a diversion, an occasional dinner out, and an evening or two together. Two years earlier, she and Mike found the time, but the pressure she faced or allowed to intrude made it all seem like two ships in the night.

Maggie stuck her head in Jordan's lap like she could read her mind.

"Yes, Mags, I'm in the dumps. I, a macho Montana sheriff, am in the romantic abyss of loneliness and ennui, desperate for a man and afraid to find one. Maybe when this is all over, whatever this is, I'll make some time for myself."

She swore the dog nodded in approval.

* * *

A few nights later, Mike joined Jordan and Louise for dinner. Victor sat in his lounger and stuttered as he tried to talk, which Jordan saw as frustrating her father.

"Mike, it's good to have you around," Victor said. "I wish it were under better conditions."

"I'm just happy that the stroke wasn't bad. You look good."

"I feel like crap, but thank you, Mike."

Dinner was simple: venison burgers, potato salad, and peach cobbler.

"Louise, this is the best meal I've had in weeks. Thank you," Mike said.

"You are most welcome," Louise said. "Are you staying in town?"

Jordan shot Mike a look. She knew he would not tell them the real reason he was staying.

"For a few days, then back to Helena."

"Why do I think you are not telling us the real reason?" Victor said. "It's that killer—he's still around?"

"Dad, that is not anything you need to worry about. Mike is finishing up a few things, that's all," Jordan said.

"She keeps things close to her vest and tries not to bring her work home. But I know this woman. She is like a dog with a bone. She won't let go until it is finished."

"Dad, I do not want to talk about it. Your job is to get well, take Mom on another cruise, and enjoy retirement."

"See, Mike?" Victor took a deep breath and slowly let it out. "If you are here to put this son of a bitch down, good. Some people just need killing, and this animal is one of them."

Chapter 18

Jordan passed on the information she learned from the drug dealer Lucius Menke to the sheriff of Yellowstone County. Billings, the largest city in Montana and the county seat, has had its fair share of drug problems, and the sheriff thanked Jordan for the heads-up.

"Anything you need, just call," the Yellowstone sheriff said. "Glad to hear you are all right. Plane crashes are a bitch—I slid off a runway in a De Haviland Beaver when four of us went hunting, maybe ten years back. It busted me up; I'm lucky no one was killed. My wife set the law down; I drive everywhere now. She had a point with us having three kids under twelve."

"Thanks, Craig. We will talk soon.

He was right; flying was a speedy way to get where you want to go. But there are bold pilots and old pilots, but there are no old bold pilots, as the saying goes. It was exhilarating passing over the mountains; the feel of the plane in her hands and the sense of freedom was all there. And the odds of flying into a drone were zero now that she'd done it.

Her next call was to Sheriff Cliff Rodgers of Gallatin County. His history of drug dealing at the university went back a long time; then, it was pot and homegrown meth. This new onslaught was expected—not wanted, but expected. Fentanyl overdoses were on the rise, and like Park County, his deputies carried NARCAN. They'd lost two students in the last four months before school let out for the summer. The coming fall term concerned him.

"It's the respite before the storm, Jordan," Rodgers said. "We are preparing for the fall term and what's coming. That Mexican they arrested in Wyoming, is he as bad as the reports were after his escape?"

"Yes, Cliff, he is that evil. I'll keep you posted. If anything comes up, you will be the first to know."

"Thanks, Jordan."

She called her mother. Her father was resting. The tensions brought on by the stroke and the attendant frustrations continued to plague him. Some nights, he slept little, and other nights, he slept for twelve hours. It was as if his body didn't know how to heal itself.

"I feel so worthless," Victor said that morning before she left for work.

"You are not worthless; you are everything to us. LeeAnn is bringing the girls down this weekend. I want you rested; I know what the girls can do to you."

"They are wonderful—another generation here in Montana. I'll rest; I'll be ready."

She closed her eyes for a moment to relax. Then, she took a deep breath and slowly let it out. It was cleansing, she thought. However, it was short-lived.

"Special Agent Will Brewster is here to see you,"

Candy said.

"Did he say why?" Jordan asked.

"No, but he's all gussied up in a sharp suit and fancy tie. If I didn't know better, I'd say he was going to church."

"Well, show Mr. Gussie in. I don't want to interrupt his date with the Divine."

Brewster strolled in all-federal-agent-like and carrying attitude. Jordan was not an aficionado of suits, but Candy was right. This one looked nice—and expensive.

"Good morning, Sheriff. You look well, considering the last few weeks," Brewster said.

"Is that a compliment or an assessment? Mike said he was considering putting together a tip line on drug dealers and Suarez. You a part of that idea?"

"He mentioned something about it, but no. I don't have the budget," Brewster said, pulling a chair over to her desk and sitting.

"The DEA's budget is three billion dollars. I should think you could find a few thousand to run a tip line," Jordan said.

"My budget for Montana is a minuscule part of the budget. I'm stuck with other priorities. How about your buddy and the ATF?"

"Their budget is half of yours, and this is about drugs, not guns and explosives. The guys with the big dollars are the FBI. Maybe I will try and tap Agent Morris."

"That's just what we need, the FBI running rogue on all this. Always headhunting and glory-seeking," Brewster said.

"What does that mean? Aren't we all on the same

side? Stop the drugs, stop the deaths, save our communities?"

"That's the party line, Sheriff. The reason our budget is three billion is this shit is everywhere. There are corrupt governments in South America and China, all using this to attack America. They are not just domestic battles. The war is in the jungles of Mexico and the streets of Hong Kong."

"And the drug dealers are the governments in many places," Jordan said.

"You are catching on. Anyway, see what the FBI can do for you. I got nothing."

"You came here to tell me this? You could have texted me."

"Just a friendly visit, Sheriff."

Candy appeared at the door. "A big white Ford Explorer is blocking the crosswalk in front of the building. Is that vehicle yours, Special Agent Brewster? The fire department is towing it, and as a favor, I'm letting you know."

"Really? I was taking a minute, Deputy. Just passing on some information to your boss."

"It's the fire department, and they are picky. I'm relaying the info—you better skedaddle. If not, it will cost you a hundred dollars." She turned and walked away.

"Is she always like that?" Brewster said.

"She is in a good mood today; normally, she'd have stood in the doorway and watched the vehicle be towed. She's like that. So, what is the information?"

"My people in Seattle tell me the Chinese are upset over the Mexicans and their inroads in the region." Brewster stopped and waited.

"And?"

"Doesn't that help?"

"Help what? They are all drug dealers, and they do not give a damn about the people they are hurting and killing. What am I supposed to do? Maybe you and your people should deal with them—that *is* your job. I have the Fourth of July coming in a week, and a million people are heading to Yellowstone Park during the next month. Officially, I'd like all this to go away so I can deal with the crowds and the traffic."

Jordan looked out the window at the street. A tow truck had just arrived. A large man in an orange jumpsuit and a red beard walked around the Explorer.

"Special Agent Brewster, they are towing your ride."

Brewster looked out the window, said goodbye without meaning it, and rushed out. On the sidewalk, he flashed his credentials and yelled at the driver. Jordan had known Larry Bowen since high school. His towing service was dependable; she had used him often, and there was no more stubborn man in Park County. With a flourish of his arm and hand, she watched as Larry backed away and allowed Brewster to climb into his Explorer and drive away.

She turned and saw Wells standing at the door. "What was that about? We have trouble with the DEA?"

"No, not now, but soon. He came to tell me the Chinese drug dealers are coming."

"Just great. Now we have the Chinese screwing with us."

* * *

Two and a half weeks had passed since Isaac and Abraham Hoyle watched the Park County coroner and deputies carefully lower their brother to the ground from the barn beam he and Pete Black Hand had been hung from. They put the need for revenge aside while they prepared the men's funerals. The funerals were held on the Crow reservation in Crow Agency.

St. Charles Catholic Church had become, over the last fifty years, the center of religious growth of the Crow community. The Crow Nation was reinventing itself and blending its traditional and Catholic beliefs. Isaac and Abraham Hoyle were the community's leaders and warriors in their clan.

The reservation's young people were constantly challenged, and addictions to alcohol and drugs twisted their futures. Too many had died by drugs or their own hand. Now, it was murder, and murder was to be avenged.

Jesse Wing Foot and Pete Black Hand were buried in the clan plot in the Crow Agency cemetery after a funeral Mass at the church. The incense was sage, and the hymns were sung in the Crow language. As the brothers stood near the grave of their youngest brother, they rocked to the beat of the tribal songs played on drums and a bird bone flute. Their mother cried, and their father danced in traditional warrior dress with his sons. The Agency cemetery was the final resting place of those of the Crow Nation and was a source of pride.

The community was spread across the rolling countryside and had no traditional town center. It was split by Interstate 90. Three miles to the south and east was the Little Bighorn National Cemetery and Battlefield, a financial blessing and cultural curse. Their ancestors were allies of the US military and were employed as scouts. Some died in the battle. However, the battlefield was a victory for their enemies, the Lakota and the Cheyenne. A greater enemy was now causing pain and sorrow: drug dealers.

Their father joined them as Isaac and Abraham walked away from their brother's grave.

"On this sacred ground, I know what is in your hearts, my sons," Joseph Long Spear said. "Vengeance—it has been the way for our people since the first rising of the sun. But I will ask you to let your brother rest in peace. Your mother grieves; her heart is torn. There is an empty seat at the table, and it will forever remind her. I will not allow you to join him."

"This murder must be avenged," Isaac said. "As warriors, this is what must be done."

"This is the white man's problem. A true warrior knows which battles are worth fighting. This evil river carries all who jump in, but the drugs kill all—like the river that drowns us. Let the whites take care of this man. My sons, you both have families. You must care for them. If the white men can't fix this, then we will talk. Until then, your family needs you, not your brother."

Joseph Long Spear Hoyle walked away, the black- and gray-striped turkey feathers of his war bonnet trimmed with ermine skins and red wool ties bouncing with each step as the elderly leader walked to the drums still being played across the cemetery. He had spoken, and his sons would obey.

Chapter 19

Diego Suarez sat in the back seat of the dark blue Dodge Charger as the setting sun cast its last light on the Crazy Mountains to the north. It reminded him of sunsets from the porch of his hacienda in the Cuenca Mountains north of Culiacan. Of course, last winter's snow was still capping the Crazies, but then again, in Montana, there weren't endless days and nights of heat like Sinaloa. Two men sat in the front seat; two others sat next to him in the back seat. They had just passed through the small town of Big Timber on their drive west from Billings on Interstate 90 to Bozeman. The route would take them through Livingston. He thought of the sheriff and why he didn't shoot her that day. That was a mistake—but he owed her—she could have left him on the mountain. He smiled; there would be a next time, and then he'd pay the debt.

Two weeks earlier, Suarez, after escaping in one of the hikers' trucks with the woman gagged and tied on the floor of the back seat, drove into Livingston.

Time was of the essence before the sheriff and the police would be after him—or, more precisely, the stolen
Jeep. After parking in the lot, he casually walked into
Albertsons grocery store and went straight to the aisle
selling phones; he needed three. After selecting models
he knew, he grabbed a couple of energy bars from the
checkout racks and two cans of Coca-Cola from the
cooler. He paid with cash found in the wallet in the
back pocket of the man's clothes he now wore. The
woman at the checkout appeared tired and bored, so
he selected her. She mumbled something about having a nice day. He smiled and walked out; maybe she
would remember him or not. He looked at his watch
and then remembered it was in the personal property envelope still on the airplane or somewhere on the
side of the mountain. He liked that watch. He'd tak-
en it off one of his victims, a gold Rolex. He wasn't
sure how long he had before an APB would hound his
tracks. He scanned the parking lot and walked past the
stolen Jeep and the girl to the rear of the lot. There,
he found a 2001 muddy brown Chevy pickup. He assumed employees parked in the outer areas of the lot;
hopefully, it would give him additional time. The truck
wasn't locked. He expertly hotwired the ignition and
then casually drove out of the Albertsons parking lot.
Forty-five miles east on Interstate 90, he pulled off
the highway and into the one-street town of Greycliff.
There, hidden in a grove of cottonwoods along the
Yellowstone River, he ate the energy bars and made
two calls. The first was to his boss in Mexico, the second to a number he knew, and Mexico confirmed, in
Billings. Fifteen miles farther east, at the Reed Point
exit, he found a shady spot near a fishing access. Again,

hidden from the main road, he made a follow-up call to Billings, then took a nap. An hour later, a gray van with rust along the running boards stopped behind the truck. Suarez gripped the Glock and waited. Two men got out, men he had known since childhood, Jose Beccara and Juan Carrillo, both cartel soldiers.

After abandoning the stolen Chevy pickup at the fishing access, they drove to a double-wide trailer on the southeast side of Billings near the auto auction yard. During the ride, Suarez was brought up to speed on the APB broadcast for his initial arrest in Casper and the latest complications dealing with drug distribution in central Montana. He was safe in Billings; the house was a hundred miles from Park County. He tried to relax. However, the Hong Kong Chinese were making serious inroads into their Northwest market; he'd learned some of that from the Indians he'd left in the barn. The two men offered much to save their lives; it didn't matter. He would act before the Chinese became a bigger threat. In Billings, he slept ten hours, the first uninterrupted sleep he'd had in three days.

He rested at the trailer for two days with his men. Trina, a cartel soldier, lived with the men and made their meals. Luis Gambuzza's traitorous action of turning him to the local sheriff ate at him. He did not like doing what had to be done, but lessons must be taught, control maintained, and fear is always a great intimidator. After resting, they drove south on Interstate 25, murdered the Gambuzzas, and returned to the trailer. The total time was just under ten hours, including an hour for dinner in Sheridan.

That was ten days ago. It was strange that he had not heard of any news broadcasts about the Casper

killings; he assumed the police were keeping the information close. On this bright and clear Saturday morning, he and his men were headed to a Bozeman address
his boss had texted him. The house, an address hint-
ed to by the Indians, now confirmed by Mexico and a
Montana source, was the Chinese distribution center
near Montana State University. According to Culiacan,
it had been set up three months earlier. Nevertheless,
with a billion dollars at stake, the cartel wanted to make
an example to start a war they would win.

They drove into the heart of Bozeman on Main
Street, turned south through the university, and headed
toward the ranchlands beyond. They passed a residen-
tial complex of university buildings identified as student housing, a rich market. Rising sharply beyond the
ranchlands and filling the horizon stood the Gallatin
Mountains. Another mile south, they found their target: a house hidden from the road behind a hedgerow
of evergreen trees.

"*Prepararse*," he said in Spanish.

His soldiers acknowledged. Safeties clicked as the
men rechecked their weapons; all carried suppressed
AK-47s and automatic pistols. A single guard casually
confronted them as they turned off the road and onto
the driveway. Beccara, sitting in the front passenger
seat, shot the man, a Chinese, in the head. He dropped
before he could make the alarm. They drove fast to the
turnaround at the house. Three vehicles were parked
in front of the one-story ranch house. Suarez's crew
quickly and expertly exited the Charger; two men went
to the rear. He and his men crashed the front door
and, with practiced military precision, swept through
the house, killing the four men they found. Not one

defensive shot was fired. Suarez heard the muffled snaps from the rear of the house, two rifle shots. Two more down. They carefully and thoroughly searched the house and found no more living Chinese. Obviously, this was the current headquarters; all the bedrooms had been used, food was in the refrigerator, and the rice cooker was still warm.

An arsenal of pistols, AR15 rifles, and boxes of ammunition were stacked in a closet and on shelves; in one of the outbuildings, bundles of marijuana, plastic-wrapped packages of heroin and cocaine, and cardboard cartons full of bagged pills were found. Tables were set with weigh scales and boxes of two-inch-by-two-inch polyethylene baggies. It was a well-stocked distribution center. They removed the heroin, cocaine, and pills and placed them in the Charger. They also collected the weapons and, after removing two plastic fuel cans, put the weapons in the trunk next to the drugs. They had to force the trunk to lock.

Suarez searched the house, tapping walls and looking behind cheap Chinese art. He found what he was looking for in the kitchen: two account ledgers under a removable panel in one of the kitchen silverware drawers. A glance pissed him off; the information was in Chinese characters; some were addresses, a number followed by a character. He needed these translated. He would find an interpreter when they returned to Billings.

They lined the dead along the front of the house. Suarez took photos and any identifications they found on the bodies or in the house. He sent the photos to Mexico. He looked through the IDs and passports, and one jumped out: a name from his boss in Culiacan,

Lawrence Hang Chow. It was a Chinese passport; the address was in Hong Kong. He kept it as a souvenir.

Then, his men took the fuel cans and poured gasoline throughout the house and outbuildings; flares were tossed through the open doors. The operation from entry to exit took fifteen minutes. They left the buildings completely engulfed in flames.

Chapter 20

Jordan was tired. She'd spent the weekend with her father, helping him through another period of anxiety. She was also there to help her mother as much as she could. LeeAnn came down for the day, which warmed her father's heart, though he missed the grandchildren. Nonetheless, it was exhausting. In some ways, being at her desk in the office was a relief; it gave her a few moments to relax.

It became obvious that Victor's demeanor had changed since his second stroke. He was verbally aggressive and demanding, less patient, and had outbursts when he had trouble speaking. His language was loud and confusing. When he became confused, which was becoming more frequent, the one thing that helped calm him was Maggie putting her head in his lap and nuzzling him. He would pet her and then often fade into sleep. It was a remarkable transformation, but sadly, it was also short-lived.

LeeAnn's job was office manager at a Schwab office in Helena. Unfortunately, she couldn't do this back and forth to Livingston indefinitely. Her husband, Tim, would take care of the twins when she visited, but the pressure was intense. Everyone was feeling the stress.

Jordan's older brother, Robert, lived in Portland and worked for Nike in marketing. He had already flown in twice. Mary, his wife, understood; her mother also had issues, but the time commitment was tough on everyone in the Tynes family.

After one of the doctor's sessions, he carefully prepared them for the possibility that Victor was showing early signs of dementia. The words were knives that cut into both Jordan and Louise. LeeAnn wouldn't believe it and wanted another opinion, and Robert was silent.

One evening, after Victor was asleep, Jordan and her mother sat on the backyard patio.

Louise said, "Honey, we never thought it would end this way. Vic and I were tough, and our families were tough—we are Montanans. But this slow dance is dragging both of us down. You got a county to run; your brother and sister have their lives. I don't know what to do."

"We are here for you and Dad," Jordan said. "He will get better; I know it, Mom."

Louise, tears on her cheeks, took Jordan's hand. "I love you, honey, but that will not happen. The same thing happened to my grandfather. I was just a kid, but he slowly faded away. We will do what needs to be done. We have had a good life, three wonderful children, and now grandchildren. Vic and I will hang on to it as long as we can. But the future is in God's hands."

* * *

Candy knocked on Jordan's office door. "Agent Cardona is on the phone, line one," she said, smiling a smile that greatly annoyed Jordan.

"Hi, Mike," Jordan said as she glared at Candy. She told her to close the door.

"We have a big problem," Cardona said, passing over pleasantries. "It appears that Suarez has resurfaced."

"Damn. Where?"

"Bozeman. He's ignited a war between the cartel and the Chinese. He shot up their distribution center on the south side of town; they killed seven and burned the buildings. We assumed he took their drugs and money. He then laid them out like dead fish on the lawn for a photo. It was messy."

"Are you sure it was Suarez?"

"We are certain. Through the video footage the sheriff, with the FBI's help, collected from cameras in the neighborhood, we have a dark blue Dodge Charger entering Bozeman, going to the house, and leaving. The Charger was found burning on a back road in an industrial park near the airport in Belgrade. The car was reported stolen two days earlier from in front of a liquor store in Billings. Ballistics on the slugs removed from the bodies and shell casings that littered the house, and the rear yard had at least five separate weapons, all 7.62mm, most probably AK-47s, and automatic pistols. Neighbors reported no gunfire; we assume suppressed weapons."

"When?"

"Saturday afternoon. We asked the Gallatin County sheriff to keep this low-key for now."

"I know Cliff Rodgers; he'll be pissed about that.

There is nothing low-key about any of this."

"He's furious but will sit on it for one more day. Too many people know about the fire and the bodies. He has to have answers to questions. For now, he's saying this is under investigation, and a presser will be held soon."

"Suarez? You sure?"

"As I said, the Charger was stolen in Billings from in front of a liquor store where the owner, a college kid, left it running while he filled a shopping cart with beer. Twenty-four hours later, it was dumped in a warehouse district parking lot near the Belgrade airport; multiple security cameras from an adjacent storage facility caught the men exiting the car; there were five. One was identified as our guy, Suarez. Brazen son of a bitch. Someone was waiting for them in a gray panel van. They spent two minutes loading boxes and rifles into the van before lighting the Charger up. After that, they disappeared. We could not get a license plate read."

"Did you know about the Chinese?"

"ATF did not. However, our friend at the DEA says they knew they were in the area but not the specific location of their base or this house. Agent Brewster says they are close, but Suarez's informants were obviously better. As I said, it was messy."

"Now, Mr. Special Agent, what do we do?"

"Try and stop an all-out drug war. The Chinese will not let this go; Brewster tells me the DEA has someone deep in their Seattle operation. He says the information has already been sent back to Hong Kong, and they are planning retaliation. We have confirmed that one of the people in the house was the nephew of the head of the Hong Kong Triad. He was Lawrence Hang Chow. His uncle, George Hang Chow, is the head of the Chow Group, a known international gang of seriously bad people. We expect he will be sending in soldiers from Vancouver and Seattle."

"Great, just what we need. I thought that the Chinese were suppliers of the raw materials the cartels needed to manufacture fentanyl and meth—an opportunistic relationship. Why the killings?"

"Yes, it is, but bigger money drives this," Mike said. "For the last ten years, the Chinese have had multiple financial connections to the cartels. They are their money launderers, bankers, and even supply raw materials. The cartels have warehouses full of American hundred-dollar bills; it is just paper unless they can clean it and make it real by converting it to digital numbers in bank accounts. The cartels hand the money off to Chinese money brokers here in the States; the cartels get pesos or cryptocurrency in Mexico. The American dollars are then used to buy hard goods like electronics and computers, even phones, at serious discounts in China. These are shipped to Europe and South America and sold at retail prices; the difference is the profit the Chinese keep. There is a new twist, and we suspect that the Chinese are now buying land, American land."

"Land? That's not a fungible asset like gold or even a box of iPhones," Jordan said.

"They think long term—not months but years, even decades. Land, and in the right spot, is valuable to them. I would suggest that some condo deals in New York, Chicago, and Miami are because the sellers are desperate and don't mind hard cash."

"But land? Really?"

"There are millions of acres across the West; corporations buy up large ranches, and no one thinks twice. If they don't change the use, no one cares. But that asset is leveraged against a loan or other non-cash deal. Then, as fast as you can say *jackrabbit*, the money is clean."

"And that's why the killing. The Chinese want control of the trade and the dealers."

"Exactly," Mike said. "They are playing one Mexican cartel against the other. The Chow Group's operations in Seattle and Vancouver have grown substantially; they are taking on direct sales and distribution, and they do not like competition. They can launder their drug money, cut out the percentage they pay the cartels, and build a new empire here in the United States. The DEA has its hands full; it's like whack-a-mole—shut one down, another pops up. That's the real reason for the task force."

"So, the Mexicans did us a favor? Where do I send a card?" Jordan said.

"Perversely, yes. Sorry, there is no address yet. The FBI and DEA are worried. They hope to keep a lid on the story for a few days; they must sort out what's happening. But it is too big, too bloody, too public. That is also why the Casper killings are not all over the news; this has gotten serious."

"Eleven bodies, Lord knows how much cocaine and fentanyl in the counties, and a drug war—yes, this is now very, very messy."

Chapter 21

John Chan Wang clicked off his phone and set it on the table in his office, a well-secured room in his tenth-floor apartment overlooking Seattle's harbor. Two of his men, loyal lieutenants, sat nearby on a couch. They had driven down that morning from the Chow Group North American headquarters in Vancouver.

Wang had been a key soldier of the Chow Group since he was a teenager growing up in Hong Kong, where he ran numbers to the gambling grandmothers in the towers that fill Hong Kong. His father owed fealty to the Group and had been a loyal soldier of the Chow family for forty years. Lawrence Hang Chow did not deserve to be murdered in a ranch house in Bozeman, Montana, by the Mexicans. The kill orders had come directly from Clarence Hang Chow, second in command to the family boss, George Hang Chow. The Chow Group did not make elimination orders lightly; they understood that this would begin a war that neither drug cartel could afford to start or fail to respond to. And it would also draw in the US government.

Over the past ten years, the Chow Group had carefully and covertly expanded throughout the Northwest of the United States. They first focused on the universities in Seattle, Portland, and Moscow, Idaho. Many of their local distributors worked off debts incurred when they were secretly brought into the United States from Mainland China. These "immigrants" worked with forged work permits; now, some had citizenship and US passports. They all swore allegiance to the Chow family and understood what fealty required and the penalty for failure.

If John Wang knew what Mike Cardona had told Sheriff Tynes, he would have smiled. The feds knew a tenth of what they thought they knew about their operations. Money laundering was pervasive and global, but the best investment assets were in North America, Canada, and the United States. He had accumulated thousands of acres in British Columbia, Washington, Oregon, and Montana. Other Chow Group shell corporations owned dozens of Los Angeles and San Diego properties. Unlike the Midwest and South, those of Chinese ancestry did not stick out in Southern and Northern California.

The men on the couch, Oscar Lin Chi-Yung and Joe Zen Ma, had been in the United States for two years and had earned their relocation to the States through their brutality and loyalty.

"The Mexicans murdered Lawrence Hang Chow and six of our brothers three days ago in Bozeman," John Wang began. "We expected this move by the Culiacan Cartel, and we have talked about it. I did not believe they would make it so soon; it was stupid. Hong

Kong has ordered us to stop it now; do what is necessary and eliminate the threat."

The men looked at each other and smiled.

"We will need more men," Joe said. "Three is not enough."

"I have contacted five of our people; they will meet us at the distribution house in Butte. From there, we will use our contacts to set up a meeting to discuss our future with the Culiacan. It is a logical business move; they will expect it and see the necessity. At the appropriate time, we will eliminate them."

"They are not that stupid, John. They will suspect something. Most likely, they are planning a retaliatory strike," Oscar said.

"Hong Kong told the cartel that they will no longer receive the raw materials we control and are holding the cash they have until this is resolved. Their action was arrogant and unnecessary. We are also reducing the raw materials and supplies to the other cartels—they are not pleased. We have ordered them out of Montana as compensation."

"They won't do it," Joe said.

"Of course they won't," Wang answered. "That is why they will be eliminated."

* * *

John Wang landed with Oscar and Joe at Bert Mooney Airport in Butte in a private Citation jet owned by a shell company. It was usually parked at Seattle's King County Boeing Field. The driver of the Lincoln SUV was one of his people, Jonas Hu. He and Hu went back more than ten years. Hu was one of the first from Hong Kong to be inserted into the Northwest; his territory was western Montana, northern Idaho, and Wyoming.

Hu's cover was a Hunan restaurant he owned in Butte; his office was on the second floor. He'd opened another restaurant under the same name in Coeur d'Alene. The restaurant, Hunan Palace, had won local foodie awards. Hu took Wang's bag and stowed it in the back of the SUV. Oscar and Joe placed theirs as well.

"The others have arrived—they are at the house, Mr. Wang," Hu said. "We await your orders."

The safe house was on the west side of town, off a gravel road, nestled in a hollow that hid it from the dozen other homes and businesses it passed. A hidden eight-foot chain-link fence and gate enclosed the property. Behind the gate, blocking the driveway, sat a weathered Dodge van; one man sat in the front seat. The Lincoln approached but held back about one hundred feet. The man exited the van; he had an AK-47.

Hu punched a number on his phone and said something in Chinese. The man, phone to his ear, raised his rifle and pumped it twice. Hu clicked a button on the SUV's visor; the gate slowly opened.

The guard returned to the van and slowly moved it out of the way, then took a defensive position behind the truck and watched. Hu passed him and drove the gravel road toward a house surrounded by trees. The clapboard-sided single-story ranch house was built with concrete blocks, steel doors, and plexiglas-backed windows. For all its appearances, it did not look out of the ordinary compared to other houses in the neighborhood. Two steel ancillary buildings sat behind the main house.

"Just one man?" John Wang asked.

"There are two others in flanking positions; they are hidden. Both have sniper rifles and clear lines of sight across the property. It is difficult to surprise us."

"I hate surprises."

"So do I." Hu pulled into the open garage of one of the outbuildings. The door closed behind them.

"How secure are we?" John asked before he left the vehicle.

"As far as I know, we are unknown to the FBI, the local sheriff, and the Butte police. But our people tell me they are asking questions. I have another safe house in Bozeman; one man is there now. If we need to bug out, we can be there in less than ninety minutes."

"I intend to move quickly. Can we use this Bozeman house for our meeting?"

"Yes, but I caution against moving too quickly. They may ask for a more public location."

"I will make that decision, Mr. Hu."

Hu's cook prepared an excellent lunch, some of Wang's favorites. Word of his cultural and culinary preferences had reached Butte, Montana.

Nine men sat in the living room: Wang's Seattle crew, four brought in from Vancouver for this operation, and Hu and one of his men. The guard at the gate was not one of the men. Wang assumed that the other men still guarded the property. He also remembered the three vehicles in the garage, all large GMC SUVs.

John Wang turned to Hu. "Have you made contact with the Mexicans?"

"Yes, it is underway. Like us, they are layered, and the senior leaders avoid direct contact until necessary. I expect a call this afternoon. Word has reached them in Mexico about the cutoff of supplies and ingredients and the slowdown in money laundering. Two air transport flights were canceled. It has caught their attention."

"I should think so. The fools, what did they think would happen?" Wang said.

"Maybe they have alternatives," Hu's man suggested. "Other sources for the raw materials?"

"It is possible but irrelevant. I have been ordered to eliminate them, and that is the purpose of this meeting." Wang turned to Hu. "Your men?"

"These men are the best we have. All are excellent marksmen and fighters. Not one Mexican will leave that meeting."

"Excellent. What time is he expected?" Wang asked, looking at his watch.

"Now—he was told to be here at two. The gate will call when he arrives."

Almost on cue, Hu's phone buzzed. He read the text. "He's here."

"You men have lunch; Mr. Hu's cook is excellent," Wang said. "We will join you in an hour. Get some rest. I will let you know when we are operational; it may take a few days to prepare."

Wang and Hu walked to the front of the house and took seats in the living room. It looked as though IKEA had been the primary source of every piece of furniture. The walls were beige and bare. Wang lit a cigarette as they watched a white Ford Explorer stop in front of the house. Through the building's tinted and bulletproof windows, he studied the tall, angular white man exiting the driver's side; he was the only passenger. The driver wore sunglasses, a black polo shirt, gray slacks, black cowboy boots, and, perched high on his waist, a holstered Glock. He was painfully American. He removed the sunglasses and looked around, then at the window. He nodded.

"Let the man in, Mr. Hu," Wang said.

"I do not trust him," Hu said.

"I do not either, but he has been helpful, and we will show respect."

A moment later, DEA Special Agent Will Brewster stood in the room. "It is good to see you again, Mr. Wang. You are a long way from Seattle. I can truly use an iced tea. Is it possible that Mr. Hu here can rustle one up?"

Chapter 22

Jordan saw Mike Cardona standing along the bank of the Yellowstone River as she pulled in behind Mike's truck. There were a dozen other vehicles and trailers parked in the gravel turnaround. It was a good place to park and drop a driftboat to fish the river. Downriver, two fly fishermen knee-deep cast their lines. Above, a driftboat slowly worked its way across the river with the current. A fisherman stood in the bow, gracefully casting his line. The guide, oars at the ready, sat behind him. Mike waved and walked toward her; she let Maggie out, pointed to a picnic table, and held up a bag.

She laid out napkins, bottles of water, and two bundles wrapped with butcher paper. She then took out a bowl, filled it from a water bottle for Maggie, and placed it on the ground.

"I have turkey and Havarti, and ham and Swiss; your call," she said.

"Turkey."

"Good choice. Sit."

They used this spot mainly because the view was great, and they didn't have to deal with office snoops and gossip. Privacy was lost in the sheriff's office, and having a private meeting was impossible. They had met here often when they were dating and recently twice during these difficult times.

Nothing was said for a few minutes while they ate, each in their thoughts. It was like that amongst friends; sometimes silence was as good as conversation. There was activity on the river when the fisherman in the driftboat hooked a fish. They sat silently until the trout was netted, the obligatory photos were taken, high fives exchanged, and the fish was released. Upstream, another driftboat rounded the bend, adding to the endless parade of anglers.

"So, the Mexicans," she said, breaking the silence.

"Yes, Suarez and his thugs. Sheriff Rodgers has had it with those people," Mike said.

"Shooting up a house, killing seven, laying them out like trophies, and then setting everything on fire— *people* is too civilized a term; more like butchers and terrorists. And they should be treated as such. Arrest them and ship them to Guantanamo. They kill innocents, young people too naive to understand the crap they are swallowing. And they bring their political and economic shit here and cause pain. I should have thrown Suarez off the mountain."

"No good to look back. We will find him and do what needs to be done."

"I know, but the man is a rabid dog. And I know what needs to be done with a rabid dog." She paused and looked at Mike. "This is nice, but what's the reason for the meeting?"

"To spend a few minutes with you without all the bullshit, to enjoy the scenery, and inhale fresh air," he said, looking at her.

"I appreciate that; I really do. Thanks—there's something else."

"There's a fox in the henhouse."

Jordan paused and let the information sink in. "An informant? A rat? A snake?"

Mike smiled at the comparisons. "Worse. Someone is feeding information to the Mexicans and, it's hard to believe, to the Chinese as well. Someone is playing them against each other, and that intelligence is leading to murder and worse."

"Worse than murder?" Jordan said. "The massacre in Bozeman?"

"Yes, because that information is not getting to us. This informant knew about the Triad house, and who was there, then the Mexicans learned about it."

"The Mexicans could have their spies."

"Not likely. The Chinese are insular, so they keep everything close to the vest. Whoever it is, they trust."

"Considering the paranoia of these people, hard to believe they trust anyone."

"True, but they must have their reasons."

"Any idea who?"

"No, and I've been racking my brain. I have four people on my team. Brewster has three, and Morris and the FBI have at least five, which I know about. Morris has connections back to Washington—hell, the number of FBI people is maybe in the dozens. I've disliked the idea of the task force since the FBI proposed it. The request came through the governor's office. The FBI suggested they bring in the local yokels, as one of the FBI people said—to provide cover."

"So, I'm a local yokel—how nice. And from the FBI? That's rich coming from Washington, and disrespectful." Jordan laughed. "It was their idea for the tip line. How is that working? It's worthless. They see a problem and throw money at it. That money would take care of my 'wish' list twice over."

"The Chinese and the Mexicans have been two steps ahead of us," Mike continued. "We come in after the crap goes down and clean up the mess, and we are not any closer. When you got Suarez, it was luck. He screwed up, and one of his people turned him in. And he fixed that with a knife. It was a warning to others—his own soldiers. He's smart and cunning. Yes, a rabid dog."

Behind them, a dirty and rusted Chevy truck pulled in behind Jordan's yellow Sahara. Maggie crossed behind them and went on alert.

"You expect someone?" Mike asked as he stood and placed his hand on his Glock.

"Yes, I asked Wells Courtwright to join us. He's been checking out stuff under the radar. I've been trying to get inside the operations."

"Well, thanks for the heads-up," Mike said.

"A woman has to have her secrets," Jordan said.

Wells exited the truck. Maggie carefully approached the man, identified the deputy, and jogged over to him.

"Sheriff, Agent Cardona," Wells said.

Mike put his hand out. Wells took it and then slipped into the bench seat next to Jordan.

"Wells has been setting up buyers and distributors hoping to find the source of the drugs coming in. He has some news, I hope."

"Yes, I believe so," Courtwright said as he lit a cigar. "One of my dealers says that it's now a wide-open war, Mexican on Chinese and vice versa. No holds, no mercy, no quarter. The winner takes all. And we are caught in the middle."

"This informant, how does he know?" Mike asked.

"He's from the Blackfeet reservation up north and still has family there. He says the Chinese are continuing to funnel drugs in from Canada. There are more than fifty miles of frontage along the Canadian border, dozens of places where they come across, and no one cares. From there, it is moved south, where it runs into the Mexicans—people die; there're dozens of his people dead from fentanyl and meth. He's tired of it. He preferred the old days—homegrown grass and safe pills. Some of his friends have been murdered. He wants them all gone."

"A saint," Mike said.

"Hardly, but they are almost untouchable on the rez. From there, the shit is distributed to dealers across the Northwest. Earlier in the week, at least a dozen Chinese were seen crossing into the rez; he's certain they are joining up with some of the Triad already here."

"This is news, bad news," Mike said. "Sheriff Rodgers said he heard rumors, and I assume the Chinese want their pound of flesh."

"I'm okay with letting them kill each other and wait until the dust settles," Wells said. "Like you said, we clean up the mess."

"You know we can't do that, Wells. I can't let this happen, not in my county," Jordan said. She looked at Mike, a question on her face. Mike put his hands up and nodded. "Mike says a traitor is working with the Triad and the cartel. Passing on information and setting them up against each other."

Wells's face contorted as he chewed on the information. "A fed? That makes sense. The bad guys are limited. But if they have someone who finds things out, locations of shipments, distribution centers, like in Bozeman. Someone on the good guy side, so to speak?"

"Possibly, and I need to stop it," Mike said.

"If they are not Triad or cartel, how do you go about ferreting out this piece of shit?" Wells asked. "They must be in it for the money, and both sides have enough capital to buy the services of a hundred federal agents—assuming that is who we are talking about."

"Wouldn't be the first time, would it, Mike?" Jordan asked.

"Sadly, no, it wouldn't. I haven't the authority to audit federal agents and look at their accounts—no one does except the attorney general. And once it started, it would be impossible to hide. Whoever it is would shut their operation down and burn every bridge—maybe even disappear."

Jordan walked toward the river, Maggie at her side. Standing there, she watched another fisherman play a nice trout to the driftboat. The guide carefully slipped a net over the side and took the fish. She turned back to the men at the table.

"I have an idea."

Chapter 23

Imagining a train wreck around the bend, with her as engineer driving directly for it, Jordan wondered when all this would end. The feds and a half dozen other Montana jurisdictions wanted a piece of the action. Suarez was wreaking havoc and wantonly reshaping the illegal drug markets in Montana and Wyoming—and the bodies were piling up. Wells Courtwright and Bob Claymore sat across from her.

"This is nasty business," Bob said.

"An understatement, Bob," Jordan answered. "Ideas?"

"My sources are afraid," Wells said. "The word is out; some of the dealers have disappeared and are not answering my calls, and the two I talked with are scared shitless. The massacre of Chinese drug distributors got people thinking. Was it the competition, or is there a vigilante group taking out the big boys, and if so, are they next?"

"You dance with the devil, this is what you get," she

answered. "It is a good bet that distribution is down, but at what cost? I am tempted to leave it to the feds and let them handle this. They have the resources, and we have a lot on our plate. The summer is booming, and speeding tickets are up." She smiled.

"I know you," Wells said. "You won't let this rest."

"Damn straight I won't, the feds be damned. And in the end, it will fall on us. We get the leftovers, and it's our schools and our kids. I like the old ways, stringing up a few bad guys for the world to see—frontier justice. Bob, maybe you could find a nice tree somewhere downtown during your lunch hour?"

"God, I hope you are not serious," Bob answered.

"The rumor would be interesting." She smiled.

"Amen. The street prices are going up, a sign the market is tightening," Wells added. "We can use this. I told you about that Blackfoot dealer; maybe he can help? And a week ago, you talked about a sting; we can set up a new player—one of ours."

Jordan leaned back and thought about the idea. "Who do you have in mind?"

"Me," Wells answered. "I did undercover work in Kalispell; there it was the Chinese; they were pushing in from Spokane. We put a stop to it, but only for six months. They answered by flooding the market. It is a never-ending battle. I fit a profile they understood."

"Because you are Black."

"I am what I am." He laughed. "The stereotype works."

"I don't like it, but I understand. What do you suggest?" she asked.

"I'm new to the area. No one knows me or expects me. Let me make a few calls. From the information we have from those two dealers sitting in our jail, I will do some trading and see what I can promote."

"Have they been charged yet?"

"In the works. The county attorney is setting up the indictments," Bob said. "I'll talk with him. Those two aren't smart and face a minimum of ten years in prison. Their public defender can help set up a deal; we should try."

"See what you can do. We will talk later. I want this son of a bitch."

"And the reaction by the Chinese?" Bob said.

"It will be swift and brutal—and Suarez will not let that happen."

* * *

Jordan knew the tip line the feds set up would be a bust. It had been operational for a week, and nothing came of it besides a few crank calls and even more false leads. She estimated the cost was tens of thousands of dollars and countless wasted hours; she could have used that money for her budget. She also knew your name would be on a list when you rat on the Triads and cartels. A list a drug dealer did not want to be on. What impressed her was how quickly Wells's undercover operation showed results. He set up his base across Highway 89 from the Old Saloon bar in Emigrant. It was a beat-up double-wide set on high ground on the east side above the Yellowstone River. A friend owned it. He'd already made three direct contacts with local drug dealers who wanted no part of either the Chinese or the Mexicans; all said they would be interested in changing suppliers. He offered them products sourced in the United States from Chicago suppliers. "Be proud; buy American," he said. He'd talked again

with Cardona, who passed on names from his old undercover operations in Milwaukee and Chicago. Since
Cardona's cover had been blown years earlier—and he
barely escaped with his life before ending up in Montana—these Midwest contacts were, surprisingly, still
active. Courtwright did not use Cardona's real name;
he referenced the one Cardona gave him, and that
name belonged to a dead man. However, Wells learned,
the mob in Chicago had heard of the troubles brew-
ing between the Chinese and the Mexicans and saw
an opportunity. Courtwright's name, when undercover
in Kalispell, was Frank Lee Matthews, a mix of two
of America's most notorious drug kingpins from forty
years ago. Known as Franky Lee during those days in
Kalispell, the word got out quickly that he was back in
business and a reliable source of high-grade cocaine,
heroin, meth, and oxy. The response was immediate
and greedy.

Jordan, to her surprise, also heard from DEA Agent
Brewster. He said the Chinese had contacted the Culiacan Cartel for a summit meeting. No one knew where
it would take place, but she asked Wells to keep an ear
open. It was all cat and mouse; both sides of the drug
world needed intelligence to anticipate, trap, or avoid
the other. Greed worked both ways. Offer enough
money, and a man will turn on his grandmother. Jordan
was sure that the DEA, the FBI, and even the ATF had
cartel moles paid for by Central and South America,
Europe, and even the Far East. She was also certain the
feds had moles buried in the Triad and cartel families.
For some, it wasn't the money to turn on their families;
it was the promise of a gold-embossed blue American
passport if they survived and a new start with the wit-

ness protection program. Jordan and Wells kept each other at arm's length, never meeting and only talking on cell phones.

"Did the county attorney come through?" Wells asked.

"Yes, Menke and Barnes have agreed to help," Jordan said. "They may not be the brightest bulbs, but they understand what they face. When it was all laid out and a DEA attorney was sitting in, they boosted their self-interest a few degrees. You could almost see intelligence sneaking back into their feeble brains. They know their future, and it is not with the cartels. They also realized there was no place they could hide should they bolt. We own them."

"Good. I have an initial shipment coming in from Chicago later this week," Wells said. "I'll meet with Menke and Barnes and get the operation underway. I'm calling the business Puffer Fish."

"It doesn't need a name, Wells. Besides, Puffer Fish sounds weird."

"It's because when it blows itself up, it looks ten times bigger than it actually is."

"Adorable," Jordan said. "I suppose you want business cards?"

"That's an idea. Nothing says 'I'm in the drug business' more than business cards with an adorable puffed-up fish covered with sharp spines."

* * *

The early evening was pleasant, and there was the scent of impending summer rain. Jordan left the office and walked to the parking lot with Maggie. Leaning against her Jeep was Kyle Reeder, looking all woodsy in a gray-green checkered shirt, worn jeans, dusty boots, and a buff-colored and equally tatty cowboy hat. In his hand was his phone. Jordan was certain the record app was just a hovering finger away.

"Good evening, Sheriff, nice evening," Kyle said, straightening up. "How is Victor? I heard he's having a tough time."

"How did you hear that, Kyle?"

"I stopped at your house, hoping to catch you. Louise told me."

"I wish you wouldn't bother them; they are going through enough. I've gotten used to your annoying personality; they don't need it." Maggie pushed her face into Kyle's lowered right hand; he scratched her head.

"That wasn't my intention, sorry. Just pass on my good wishes and hope he gets better. I stopped by the house to talk to you; Louise said you were still here. Got a minute?"

"On or off the record?" Jordan asked. "And about what?"

"There are seven dead Chinese drug dealers and a burned-out house over in Bozeman. Nasty work, from what I've heard. All under wraps. That is a lot to keep from the people. They have a right to know that drug dealers are living and dying next to them. This isn't Chicago or Detroit. So, on or off the record is your choice tonight."

"Who told you? And besides, it was all going to be released tomorrow in a presser by Gallatin Sheriff Rodgers."

"The shoot-out was a week ago. Everyone in town could see the smoke from the fire, and the answers from the sheriff and the fire department were vague.

The TV stations are pulling at the leash, and I sure as hell won't wait much longer."

"Isn't Bozeman out of your territory? I thought you focused on Park County."

"You know as well as anyone my beat is where I am and where I want to be. Bozeman, Helena, Livingston, the I-90 corridor from Billings to Butte. There is more than enough news to fill my podcast. So, a house fire in Bozeman, dead Chinese, alleged Mexican killers, and, obviously, drugs. Jordan, what is happening?"

"Can't talk about it." She opened the driver's door, and Maggie pushed her way past Kyle's leg and into the passenger front seat.

"Do we have a drug war starting in Park County?" Kyle asked as he held the doorframe. "There has been an increase in fentanyl overdoses and deaths these last few months across the state. People are scared and pissed."

"Are you going to feed their anger, amp them up in your podcasts? We are doing what we need to do to stop this. That's all I can tell you."

"*We?* Are the feds involved?" Kyle paused. "Of course they are; who else could have afforded that tip line? How did that work out? And that guy Cardona, is he involved?"

"The tip line? Yes, as I expected. And I will not comment on the feds and their personnel. You need to talk with them."

"That bad—sorry. But you never know. It is that Suarez guy. He didn't head back to Mexico; he's still here and taking out the Chinese. Am I right?"

"The press conference will spell out what they know, and yes, the feds are involved. I am up to my neck in federal employees wearing guns. You must talk with Sheriff Cliff Rodgers; it's his show."

"Are you going to be there?"

"No, I wasn't asked." Jordan climbed in next to Maggie and pulled the door shut. Kyle extracted his fingers fast enough not to get them caught. The window was open about two inches.

"Not the best camaraderie between your office and the feds—they wouldn't shut you out."

"Who said they have?" She closed the window and smiled at the reporter.

Jordan backed out, pulled onto North C Street, and drove two blocks. She turned to the curb, put the Jeep in park, and looked at Maggie.

"Now, I have Kyle all worked up, Mags. What's a girl to do? There's a war going on. If he gets in too deep and asks too many questions, they have a brutal history of eliminating the problem. I couldn't deal with that."

Maggie crooked her head and stared at Jordan with dark, glistening eyes. Her ears pointed upward, capturing every remark.

Jordan knew the dog understood everything she said. "You are right. In for a penny, in for a pound. I wanted this job, I earned this job, and I won this job. It is my show. Damn those men."

She pulled away from the curb and headed to Dotties to pick up dinner. It would be a long night.

Chapter 24

"Turn here," Diego Suarez said in Spanish and pointed to the gravel road that headed south and disappeared into the foothills that extended outward from the Absarokas. To the south, the haze of the Breakneck Mountain Fire held in the passes and valleys. The air, still and dry, hung over the mountains.

Jose Beccara had exited I-90 fifteen miles behind them to the north. He drove the van as Suarez directed. In the back, sitting uncomfortably on the Chinese weapons and cartons of drugs, were Juan Carrillo, Gustavo Garza, Sergio Molina, and Trina Duarte. After a mile on the gravel road, they crossed over an old bridge and pulled up to a double-wide trailer that had seen a better century. A newish metal barn with double doors stood behind the trailer. The stark remains of a burned-out house sat off to the side of the barn. The entire complex was hidden under a thick grove of old-growth spruce and pine perched above a wide stream shaded by cottonwoods. White puffs of cotton from the trees drifted in the still air.

None of Suarez's men had been to this safe house. The cartel bought the property three years earlier through one of its straw corporations in Idaho. The address had been given to Suarez by his boss in Mexico. With the house and barn came four hundred acres and frontage on a decent trout stream fed by the snows in the Absarokas. Beccara parked the van in front of the barn, and the Mexicans climbed out. They walked around stretching and working out the kinks of the ride from Belgrade. Suarez unlocked and swung open the doors of the outbuilding. Inside sat a dark blue Dodge Challenger like the one Beccara stole in Billings and torched in Belgrade.

"Nice," Beccara said as he walked around the car.

"Good to have a backup," Suarez said. He took a set of keys and handed them to Beccara. "Back the Dodge out; there's a secured vault under the car. The red key will open the padlock hidden in the fake drainage grate. Move the guns and drugs into the vault, get what ammunition you need."

After backing the car out and opening the vault, the men found a dozen long guns, semiautomatic rifles, two RPG shoulder guns, a case of rockets, and an assortment of handguns and boxes of ammunition. There were two cases of military-grade flash grenades and M67 grenades.

"Bueno, boss," Beccara said.

"There's food in the house. Trina?"

"Si, I'll see what I can do," Trina said.

"Sergio, get us some beers. They are in the kitchen." Suarez tossed another set of keys to the man.

They spent an hour checking the weapons and

loading the rifles. As they walked to the house, Suarez's satellite phone buzzed. The four men looked at their boss; he told them to turn off their cell phones in case of tracking.

"Sat phone. We are inside the range of the towers on the interstate, but it's better to have this. Give me a minute." He answered as the others went into the house. "It's done."

"The word is out; the Chinese are pissed. It appears you killed one of the top family members. They are sending in a crew to find you," the voice on the phone said.

"As I expected. What else?"

"They are cutting the supply of raw materials. We have enough for six months. It will have an impact."

"Also expected. The sooner we finish the job, the better. There are other sources." Suarez looked south to the Absaroka Mountains; a plume of dark gray smoke climbed to the brilliant blue sky from somewhere beyond the front range of hills. The wildfire still burned in the mountains beyond.

"They want a meeting; the word came from Hong Kong. Do you want me to pass on your contact number?"

"Yes, use this number." Suarez gave the number of a burner phone. "Tell them I expect their call." The line went dead, and he walked to the house.

"What now, *jefe*?" Beccara asked. Trina opened cans of food and started to prepare dinner.

"We wait. They want a meeting to settle this. What they really want is to set a trap."

"They aren't creative. You expected this."

"Yes, we wait. There is food for two weeks, beer,

and good water from the well. Get some rest."

* * *

Jordan and Mike walked through the remains of the house in Bozeman. In front of the incinerated shell stood two burned-out vehicles. Twisted metal shapes that were once appliances filled one area of the house, and the brick remains of the fireplace defined the exterior wall of another room. A tangle of wires and copper pipes mingled with piles of plates, pots, and pans. An obscene gray dust of soot and ash covered everything.

"The bodies are in the county morgue; the sheriff and coroner found seven. All were found laid out here in front of the house like trophies," Mike said. "Identifications are tough, and we don't have dental records. Only one carried identification, Clarence Hang Chow. He's linked to the Hong Kong Chow Group, an international drug and slavery ring. A corporation in Coeur d'Alene owns the property; the FBI is checking on the owners. No identifications on the others yet. All were Chinese."

"Chinese? You said they might be connected to a Triad out of Vancouver, not Hong Kong," Jordan said as she carefully walked through the remains.

"Our working theory is that this was the distribution center the DEA has been looking for. There are signs of drugs and distribution paraphernalia in the outbuilding. Suarez did a good job. The DEA believes that their base is in Hong Kong and they move their shit through Vancouver and British Columbia."

"This is obscene. I want him," Jordan said.

"Get in line. The Chinese won't let this pass; it's war."

Jordan's phone chimed. She walked away from Cardona, past the three men in white hazmat suits who were carefully and methodically digging through the ashes.

"Hi, Candy. What's up?"

"You asked for an update on the Breakneck Mountain Fire. I talked to the DNR and the fire boss. It's still bad, and it is spreading further south. This weather front is pushing the fire, which doubled in size during the last four days."

"Damn, what else?"

"There is a weather front moving in from the south. It is going to bang up against that cold front from Canada. They expect lightning and thunderstorms as well as rain. Some heavy."

"That will help the firefighters."

"That's what they hope, but we expect flash flooding. Hopefully, not like that storm a few years back."

"When it rains, it pours."

"A joke?"

"Not really. I'm heading back; I'll be in this afternoon. When is this weather going to hit?"

"Tonight or tomorrow morning at the earliest."

"Have the swift water rescue fellows placed on alert. The Yellowstone River will likely be impacted. I want to be ready this time."

She slipped her phone back into her pocket and waved to Mike, who waved back. She pointed to her Jeep and let Maggie out to do her business. She had kept the dog in the Jeep because she didn't want her to wander through the debris. She watched Mike talk to the hazmat crew and then walk to her.

"I've got to get back. There's a big storm coming

in. Thanks for the tour," Jordan said.

"I'm here for the rest of the day, then back to Helena. All hands meeting tomorrow. I'll let you know what's up. They expect another presser tomorrow afternoon. Do you want to be there?"

"Thanks, no. Too much to do. So, it's war?"

"That's what we expect. The Chinese will not let this rest. Suarez stirred up a lot more than a hornet's nest."

"The Chinese will escalate. I spent two days with that SOB. He's a patient and deliberate psychopath. My guess is he will draw them in to eliminate them."

She drove to Livingston on I-90 through the Bozeman Pass. As she approached Livingston, the massive column of smoke from the Breakneck Mountain Fire rising from the Absarokas beyond Paradise Valley and Emigrant Peak cast a pall over the mountains. Behind her and scudding in from the west, clouds were building from the collision of the two fronts meeting over the Absarokas. Montana weather never creeps in; it comes with violence, explosions of thunder and lightning, and rain and snow measured in inches and feet.

Chapter 25

As Jordan sat with her folks in the living room that evening, her phone buzzed. She recognized the name James Phillips.

"I've got to take this, Mom." She stood and walked to her room.

"Hi, Jim. What's up?"

"A heads-up, Jordan," the Yellowstone park ranger said. "This storm is busting in the mountains of the park, hopefully not as bad as 2022, but still, there's a lot of rain. We are measuring it in inches, and it's warm. We expect the snow left in the lower elevations to melt and add to the total. I just wanted to let you know. It all goes into the Yellowstone River."

"And directly at us and Livingston like last time. Two big storms in two years. Probably mess up the Fourth of July festivities."

"Right. This storm is not very patriotic."

It wasn't easy to forget the June 2022 flash flood. That massive storm dumped enough rain to raise the

Yellowstone River by five or six feet. It came down the mountain in a furious torrent, washing out bridges and roads, destroying buildings along the banks, and flooding the low-lying land of Livingston. The flood's effects went down the river for hundreds of miles. It kept her staff busy for a week; thankfully, no one was lost. Recovery took most of the summer.

She called the office, and Candy answered.

"What are you doing there?" Jordan asked.

"I got the word on the storm and thought I'd coordinate. I started making calls for everyone to come in."

"Thanks, I'll be there in twenty minutes."

Her staff of deputies were the best, and this showed it. When she arrived at the office, five of her deputies were in the ready room, and Candy was pouring coffee.

"Where's Mags?" Candy asked, looking for Jordan's shadow.

"She's with the folks. Unsure what tonight and tomorrow will turn into; she's better there. The others?" she asked.

"On the road," Candy said. "They are setting up barricades and doing traffic management. Only residents living south of town toward Gardiner are allowed on Highway 89. They will keep lookie-loos and tourists off the road. The last report from the monitors shows that the flow is still below the last one, which is good. Nonetheless, it will be a mess."

"We can deal with that; I do not want swift water rescues. The guides and drifters?"

"Bob is making calls. They are canceling the Fourth of July parade and picnics for tomorrow and probably the rest of the week. The river will be unfishable;

there's that. Sunrise in in six hours, then we can see the impact."

Her deputies continued to call in—the water was rising fast. The Yellowstone River was pinched by a cut in the Gallatin and Absaroka Mountains just south of the town. The ridgelines on either side were two thousand feet high above the river. The flood would back up here and into Paradise Valley; this squeeze also slowed the impact of the flow. It was here where a large chunk of Highway 89 was washed out two years earlier, now repaired. They would learn how good the repairs were—but nothing would stop the torrent.

* * *

An hour before dawn, Jordan drove Highway 89 south toward Emigrant and stopped at Buffalo Mountain Lodge and Resort. The river coursed its way fifty feet below the lodge; the lodge had withstood the previous flood well, high and dry. Curt Coogan, the owner, met her in the parking lot. He was talking with Deputy Daniel Mecklenburg.

"How's the river?" she asked as she walked up to the men.

"Now that it's light enough to see, I would say the river is pissed," Meck said. "The forecast is for no more rain. Thank God for that."

"Hi, Sheriff," Curt said. "I can fill your thermos if you'd like."

"Thanks—any damage?" she asked.

"None, but your roadblocks are putting a crimp in my guest's travel plans," Curt said. "They can't get out and can't get in."

"Sorry about that. I don't want stranded folks like last time; such are the wilds of Montana."

"God's country—until she's peeved. I get it," Curt said. "This should blow through in a day. Russ said you had broken ribs; how are they doing—and Maggie?"

"Still hurt, but only when I breathe." She smiled. "And Maggie is doing well; that dog has more lives than a cat."

"That was something, Russ said when he saw the plane wreckage. He wasn't sure he wanted to land. I'm guessing you have a few lives left to count."

"God smiled on us."

Jordan mentally checked off the issues they had been dealing with since the crash. Bizarrely, the river and the flood seemed to pale to what she knew was coming her way.

"All good, Curt. Full house?" she asked.

"And then some. Between the guests and the condo residents, I've been dealing with constant complaints and bitching. When will it be clear, what's the effect on the fishing, will that forest fire reach us, will we be able to take a horse ride? The city folk haven't a clue. But we are handling it."

"Thanks, I don't envy you." She turned to her deputy. "Is most of the road clear?"

"All good, boss. I sent the two rookies toward Gardiner; the river was churning but staying within the banks. My contact in the park says that the rain has stopped, and the sun is rising to clear skies."

"Small favors—get what we can. Call me when you think the road might open."

"Copy that, boss."

Jordan's phone buzzed. "Well, damn," she said when she read the screen. "Give me a minute." She walked away.

"What can I do for you, Special Agent Brewster? I have my hands full."

"We need to meet. Seems some things are heating up. The Chinese are—"

"Look, Agent Brewster, I can't do anything right now," Jordan said, pissed. "I have a flooded downtown, closed roads, and stranded people all up and down the Yellowstone River. Anything to do with your troubles is your problem for the next few days."

"This is critical; I have to talk with you," Brewster said.

"It will have to wait, do you hear me? Call me in a few days." She clicked off the phone. "Asshole."

Deputy Mecklenburg walked over. "The feds?"

"A lucky guess."

"You said 'asshole.' You never swear except when it's the feds." He smiled. "We got a problem off Highway 89 where the Yellowstone River heads north out of Livingston. We have four young men who camped along the river. Yesterday, they hiked in from Convict Grade Road and Sheep Mountain Park and waded the river to an island. They hadn't heard about the coming storm or the flooding. Now they are stuck on a dry hillock surrounded by the river—and their spot is getting smaller."

"Great, maybe we should let them sit it out."

Meck paused, unsure about what his boss meant.

"Just kidding. Is Candy getting the swift water people together?"

"Yes. Bob Claymore and Jean Smith are meeting them."

"Call Candy, tell her I'm heading there—thirty minutes. I'll call Bob on my way—and we were doing so well. You take care, Curt. I'll try to open the roads as soon as possible."

"I know you will—stay dry."

"Funny guy," she said, pointing at the big man.

As the morning sun rose, she climbed into her Jeep and headed north. She stopped in Livingston and picked up Maggie. It would be a long holiday.

Chapter 26

The island with the stranded campers was one of a dozen created where the Yellowstone River braided and meandered. With the high water, it was impossible to determine the main channel flow. Every year, the smaller islands and sand banks appeared and disappeared during the spring snowmelt. After the storm of 2022, this section of the river had been dramatically twisted and rechanneled. Only one island, covered with trees and thick undergrowth, survived the seasonal realignment and the flood; it was directly across the channel from Sheep Mountain Park. The river was turbid and sounded angry.

Jordan parked behind the two sheriffs' vehicles. In front of the two units was the Search and Rescue Ford 4x4 with its trailer. One of the county vehicles was Deputy Claymore's rig; the other was Jean Smith's. The trailer was empty. She left Maggie in the Jeep.

"How are they doing?" Jordan asked as she handed her deputies cups of coffee.

"Safe and wet," Bob said. "The rescue fellas put in here; the access was the easiest. They then went upriver a few hundred yards to where they could access the campers."

"How did the fools get there?"

"The river was down," Bob said, continuing. "Last night, they waded across and set up their tents on the far side, out of sight of the highway. They didn't want their campfire seen."

"Those two pickups are theirs," Jean said, pointing to a blue Toyota Tundra and a red Maverick. "They hadn't heard about the storm or the notice to stay away from the river. Woke up this morning with six inches of water in their tents. They climbed to higher ground."

"That's when they called for help; the river was too fast to wade," Jean said. "Bob called off the helicopter; it wasn't worth the fuel or hassle."

"Thanks. Good call."

Bob's radio squawked. "Claymore here. Over."

"Got a problem, Bob. These idiots weren't here just drinking and fishing; they were doing drugs. I have two unconscious and in serious distress. The other two are freaking out."

"How old?"

"Sixteen and seventeen. We need ambulances and EMTs; I'm administering NARCAN. We will have them out and to you in twenty minutes. Over."

"Copy," Bob said and looked at Jordan. She mouthed an obscenity. "Making the calls. Over."

The hospital was ten minutes away. When the EMTs arrived, the swift water rescue crew and their two rubber inflatables were swinging up to the high-water mark of the gravel boat ramp in the park. The EMTs and rescue crews quickly carried the two unconscious boys from the boat and took their vitals.

"They are in bad shape, Sheriff," the lead EMT said. "Overdosed. We administered NARCAN to both. But they are bad, real bad."

The other two boys stood apart, and Deputies Claymore and Smith flanked them.

Jordan turned to them. "What did they take?" It was then she recognized one of the boys. "What the hell is wrong with you, Lance Collins? One overdose wasn't enough? That night in the hospital wasn't enough? Good God, what is wrong with you?" Then she realized what was happening.

"You're dealing, and you got them the drugs—what was it?"

Collins just stared at the gurney and his friends. "Oxy. It was good shit—that's what they said."

"I'd guess fentanyl-boosted, Sheriff," the EMT said. Both showed positive responses. They would be going to the hospital in five minutes.

Jordan stood to the side as the two boys were loaded into the van. She told Deputy Claymore to hold the other two for questioning. This time, she would not let the parents dictate the outcome.

"You fellas are in deep, deep shit," Jordan said. "For you, Lance, this is much more than a slap. I'm going to charge you with selling the drugs. If either of those boys dies, I will charge you with murder—and this time, your folks won't get you out. Deputy Smith, hook them up."

An old dark blue Bronco rolled across the gravel and stopped behind Jordan's Jeep. Looking out the window, Maggie's head swiveled to see who else had arrived.

"It's that reporter," Bob said matter-of-factly.

"Thanks, Bob. I can see that. Great."

With a cardboard coffee carrier in one hand, Kyle Reeder scratched Maggie's head as he passed the Jeep and headed to the crowd assembled near the boats. The four swift water rescuers were loading the rubber boats onto the trailer racks. Claymore stood with the two teenagers, and Jean Smith stood beside Jordan.

"Coffee, Sheriff?" Reeder said and held out the tray. He then noticed that Smith had a cup of her own. "Good—one left for me."

"What are you doing here, Kyle?" Jordan asked.

"I heard the report about the campers. I was on this side of the county and came to see what was up. Are they okay?"

"No, they are not. Two are on the way to the hospital—drug overdoses. We are taking these two in for questioning."

Reeder saw the handcuffs, and he started to say something.

"Not now, Kyle. This could have been bad; they are lucky. These two"—she pointed—"are being arrested for drug dealing."

The boy with Lance yelled, "I don't know anything. I came to camp and fish."

"I suggest you keep quiet, Hank," Bob said.

"I didn't do anything," Hank yelled. "It was all Lance. He's the one with the drugs."

"Shut up," Lance yelled. "Just shut the fuck up."

"I'm not going to jail. Not for this, not because of you," Hank screamed and tried to walk away from Lance. Jean grabbed the link between the cuffs and jerked him back. He nearly fell.

"You will stay right here. We will sort it out later," Bob said as he took the boy's arm.

"Take them in separate cars, Bob. When you get to the office, keep them apart. I'll question them, and then we will charge them."

"Have they been read their rights?" Kyle asked.

"All in good time. I want this site cleared and the swift team ready to provide more assistance. Kyle, you and I will talk."

"When?" Reeder said.

"Right now. Follow me," Jordan said, walking toward her Jeep. Reeder followed.

She stood next to her Jeep and watched the swift water crew head up to the road above. Two minutes later, Claymore and Smith, with the boys, followed them. Jordan let Maggie out to do her business.

"So, what's the story?" Reeder asked; he held a notepad.

Jordan let the question hang in the air as she watched Maggie stroll around the gravel landing area of the park, doing what dogs do after being cooped up in a vehicle for an hour. "Mags, come." The dog bounded over to her.

"She's good for you, and you are good for her," Kyle said.

"I can't disagree. Sometimes, I think she is smarter than all of us."

"So, what's the story?"

For the next ten minutes, she told Reeder what had happened and the rescue. She told him about the previous run-in with Lance Collins and his involvement with his friends. She also remarked about the fentanyl plaguing the county.

"And this is connected to Suarez and that Chinese massacre?" he asked.

"Looks like it. Just one more instance of the bad shit they bring. The kids are lucky. An hour more, and they would be dead."

"What are you doing about it?"

"Everything I can to find and bring a rabid dog to ground."

* * *

Jordan spent the afternoon interviewing Collins and Hank Winston. An hour into the conversation, their parents showed up. This time, the Collinses had a lawyer in tow. Being a holiday, he was charging a lot, she thought. However, if Lance Collins had kept up this line of work, they would have saved a fortune in college fees and room and board. His next few years would be at the expense of the citizens of Montana.

She had Hank Winston in another interview room. His parents were with him.

"Hank's truck is still parked where he was rescued," Jordan said, sliding the keys across the table to the father. "I wouldn't leave it there overnight. I'm holding your son overnight while we sort this out. He is hanging around with some bad guys. You need to watch who his friends are."

"I told you, Dale, that Collins kid was trouble, and here we are," Doris Winston said.

"How much trouble is Hank in?" Dale Winston asked. He was frightened, scared to death frightened.

"Could be a lot or a little. His friends came within an hour of dying," Jordan said. "Lance has been here before. Hank can help me help him."

"How so?" Dale asked, then looked at his son. "What do you know?'

* * *

Jordan took the night off. She had two vehicles helping the Livingston police with the Fourth of July traffic management. The kiddie rodeo and barrel racing, usually scheduled around the Fourth of July at the fairgrounds, was pushed back a week to allow the grounds to dry out. The flooding wasn't too bad, but bad enough. The usual four nights of fireworks were also delayed until the following week; nevertheless, the town decided to put on the Fourth of July display.

Jordan, Louise, and Victor sat on folding chairs on the driveway and watched the fireworks from their front yard. Popcorn and Cokes were served, followed by chocolate chip cookies. Jordan was glad she didn't have to deal with the traffic. Unlike many dogs, Maggie did not have a problem with the pyrotechnics. Jordan watched her as she studied the explosions and the cascade of sparkling lights. She could see them reflected in the dog's big eyes. Dogs see in black and white; it was sad she was missing so much. Maggie was a stalwart friend; they had been through a lot together over the past five years, and Jordan guessed her to be eight. As she sat on the grass watching, Jordan wondered, like most dog lovers, what was going on in that head of hers. With her ancient heritage, Jordan believed she was a little different than most dogs, those purebred, long-lineage breeds bred for a purpose: herding, retrieving, hunting, tracking, and pleasing. A Carolina mountain dog, Maggie was traced back to those adventurous Paleo-Indians who crossed the frozen Bering Sea tens of thousands of years ago and slowly marched south until they reached Tierra del Fuego in South America. How many thousands of generations produced Maggie? All the traits found in dozens of breeds seemed to be found in the Carolina dog. Jordan knew Maggie was special and was glad she was her buddy.

Her father had drifted off. His eyes were closed; even the *pop-pop-pop* of the fireworks didn't wake him. His breathing was slow and regular; for all intents, she saw nothing that betrayed the slow nightmare growing in the man she most loved. Victor had been her rock, her friend, even confidant. When things got confusing in high school, and she had lost her way with the wrong friends and attitudes, he was there to steer her back gently and set her straight. Their friendship grew even after she went off to college and eventually the National Guard. He was her biggest supporter when she applied for the deputy sheriff. He always looked to the future and half-jokingly said, "Make sure they have a good pension plan and strong health benefits." Victor had been a union man his whole life, driving trucks for the Montana Department of Transportation.

She glanced at her mother, who was also watching Victor. A tear sat on her cheek, reflecting the shooting stars of the fireworks. She smiled at Jordan, breathed a deep soul-drowning sigh, and took Victor's hand. What was coming like an impending storm beyond the horizon could only be guessed.

Chapter 27

The information that Hank Winston offered up during his interview helped shine more light on the drugs available in the county. Hank was with Lance Collins when he bought the drugs from a guy in Billings. He texted a message and got a reply as to where and the price. The two friends who nearly died on the island each gave Lance fifty dollars for the pills and dope. Lance paid the dealer sixty dollars for the drugs and kept the rest to fill his Maverick with gas. Hank said the fellow was a Mexican, or more politically correct, a Latino.

"If he was Mexican, he was Mexican," Jordan said. "Can you describe the guy?"

"Medium height, mustache, straw cowboy hat, dirty checked shirt, and bad teeth. His boots were peculiar, shiny, clean, and sported a touch of silver on the toes. I didn't leave the truck, but you couldn't miss them as we pulled up. It was near Home Depot; guys were standing around, day labor. He fit in."

"This is where Lance always got his drugs?"

"I think so, but I don't know for sure. He handed the guy the money, and the guy palmed him a couple of plastic bags with pills. We immediately left."

"No names?" Jordan asked.

"No names. Sheriff, this is the only time. I screwed up."

"Yes, you have, Hank. Yes you have."

Jordan called Sheriff Blake Duran of Yellowstone County and passed on the information. He was aware of the drug dealing and was working with the DEA out of Helena to put an end to this particular group of dealers.

"You arrest some, charge them, they walk," Sheriff Duran said. "Sometimes we deport them, but that doesn't always work. It's a game. There are always others to fill the spots on the corners."

"I understand. Does this guy with the silver toes ring any bells?"

"Yes, he's been interviewed a few times. When he's picked up, he never has drugs on him. Smart. We've tried to sting him with buys; he sends someone else."

"A name?"

"Goes by a few: Serge, Sergio, Moe, all ending in Molina. He has an Arizona driver's license and is up here to work during the summer. He claims to be an American citizen. His English is excellent. Hard to prove he's not."

"Thanks."

"Sorry about those kids. I know the pain. We lost a fourteen-year-old girl last week; she got into her father's stash to give it a try. She died before she was discovered in her room. The family was Crow; the mother was a nurse, and the father worked for a contractor. The mother went nuts and shot her husband, then killed herself. Three died because of drugs. If we pick up this guy, I'll call you."

"Thanks, Blake. You said you are working with the DEA?"

"Yes, Special Agent Will Brewster has been our contact. Strangely, we usually deal with his subordinates, but lately, it has been directly with Brewster. I give him information, like the tragedy with that family and the guy with the silver toes. Information on arrests, busts, you know. I have no idea what he does with it. You know him?"

"Yes, I do. Thanks. Say hi to Molly."

Special Agent Will Brewster walked into her office to end her Friday on a low note. Candy came in directly behind him, an exasperated look on her face.

"I tried to stop him," Candy said.

Brewster turned to the deputy, walked to the door, and pulled it shut. Candy stared at her boss through the glass, raised her hands in disbelief, and marched away.

"Brewster, you are an asshole," Jordan said.

"A finely tuned, well-trained, and government-salaried asshole. As such, I outrank you."

"The only thing you outrank me with is height. Other than that, I'll stick with my original assessment. Why are you here?"

"I am informed that there is a pow-pow between the Mexicans and the Chinese coming."

"Pow-wow? Cute. You going native?"

"This meeting is to split up the western US territories each will control. It is to set prices and begin the framework for peace."

"These guys are killers; they would shoot their sisters for a buck. Please, Brewster, tell me this is bullshit."

"It is what I've heard through my CIs. You needed to know. That's why I am here."

"Where is this summit meeting going to be held?"

"I don't know."

"You are worthless. Have you ever heard about or run into a dealer who wears expensive boots with silver toe tips? Goes by the name Sergio or Moe?"

Brewster thought for a moment. "No. Not that I remember."

* * *

Deputy Wells Courtwright walked through the rented double-wide intentionally messing up the place. He left plates of half-eaten food around, empty beer cans, girly magazines stacked near the couch, and a few ashtrays filled with half-finished doobies. The kitchen was a disaster. The finishing touches were two crack pipes he'd acquired during his earlier years undercover; these were given prominent locations in the kitchen and bathroom. He sported a week-old beard that had spots of gray and had shaved his head. He wore a checkered shirt and black jeans, old Lucchese boots, and a Glock 19 tucked in his back waistband under the shirt. He even burned some dope from a dispensary to add to the mood. He also had hidden, throughout the trailer, three handguns, two Winchesters, and a 12-gauge sawed-off room-clearer easily accessed on a shelf behind the couch.

He had no intention of inviting his customers

home to the double-wide. But he knew these people were about as paranoid a crowd as you could find. However, they might just look through the window, and he wanted it to come off as real. Diana, his wife of fourteen years, understood—it was part of his job—nevertheless, she hated it, and he knew it. And if she'd seen this place, she probably would divorce him for cause. He knew he was getting too old for this shit. He missed his two girls, Laura and June; luckily, they both had had their birthdays, and he wouldn't miss them. He called Jordan every night at 10:00 p.m. on a burner phone, one of six he'd bought in Bozeman at Walmart. An old outhouse was in the back of the property (the trailer was on a septic system). After a week's use, he'd drop the burner down the hole. Maybe an archeologist in a thousand years would get a kick out of digging it up.

His ultimate objective was to tease out the Mexicans to use him as one of their local distributors. He had money to buy the drugs, and he would tell the cartel people he had downstream connections in new locations, such as Yellowstone Park and north toward Great Falls. Supposedly, the cartel people never directly sold cocaine and fentanyl; they always used locals, especially the Indians. Courtwright knew the damage they caused. Some of the reservations, such as the Blackfeet and Crow, were impacted terribly, and tribal deaths were measured in dozens. Families were torn apart, and the ancient customs and legacies of these tribes were disappearing. The tribal leaders were overwhelmed; they needed money from the federal government for more police and judicial support. However, Washington had other uses for the money.

* * *

When Jordan left the office late in the afternoon, she called Louise. Although she was running late, her mother had gotten used to her chaotic schedule. If she were going to be too late, Jordan would always call.

"You keep your nose out of that bag, dog. There will be leftovers, but you wait." She could see tears in the dog's eyes and the start of drooling. "And don't drool over the seats; sometimes you are worse than a six-year-old." She swore the dog understood every word she said. Maggie moved to the front passenger seat and sat, and the bag remained unmolested on the back seat.

Her father was struggling, but the aftereffects of the stroke had mitigated—some. He was walking with his cane and could navigate through the house. If Louise laid out his clothes, he could dress himself, and the motor controls in his hands were good enough to feed himself, though one of the women cut his meat if needed. Jordan and Louise saw progress and were optimistic.

"I'm going to check on some of those in-home care services," Jordan said late in the evening after Victor had gone to bed. "You need some time off."

"I'm okay, and it's not so bad—and he's getting better," Louise said. There was optimism in her tone.

"But it is twenty-four hours a day; you need to get away for a few hours. When was the last time you went to see Delilah?"

"Does my hair look that bad?" Louise said and turned her head away from Jordan.

"No, Mom, it's fine, but you need time for yourself, and Delilah's salon has always been a good place for you to relax. Get your nails done and spend a few hours pampering yourself."

"I can't do that. He needs me."

"I need both of you to be healthy and able to care for yourselves, but right now, it's almost impossible. It's taking too much out of you. I'll make some calls."

"I know you, and you will pass it on to Candy."

Jordan smiled; her Mom was right, but Candy didn't mind. She had already asked Jordan a couple of times if there was anything she could do; making a few phone calls would help. Maybe find someone for a half-day in the afternoons, and then Louise would have a few hours to herself, shop for groceries, and maybe have coffee with one of her friends from her days working in the county office. It was also Jordan's dream, a few hours for herself.

Her dad's insurance and pension were good; combined with Medicare, his medical costs were covered. He'd worked for forty years. When he had his first stroke five years ago, he took disability, swearing that he would be back at the Montana Department of Transportation. Early retirement is what happened, and he and Louise were enjoying it until this latest setback. Jordan needed to find out how much home care would be covered, if at all, and how to cover the costs. As it was, her paycheck wasn't too bad as sheriff, and her living costs were about as low as they could be. Even though she dreamed of a house or a rental she could call her own, the folks were her roommates for the time being. It was nice to have the company, and the bonus was that her mom was a great cook.

She turned onto her street and slammed on the brakes, nearly sliding into the shallow drainage swale alongside the road. Maggie almost ended up in the footwell. Victor was standing in the middle of the road. He had a cane in his right hand and wore a Mariners baseball cap, shorts, a denim shirt, and house slippers. He looked surprised at the confrontation with the vehicle. He put his left hand up to his forehead, gripped the bill of the cap, and steadied himself with the cane.

Jordan carefully climbed from the Jeep; Maggie followed. The dog ran straight to Victor and nuzzled his left leg. The man lowered his arm and put it on the dog's head.

"That's a girl; I missed you. Where have you been?" Victor said to the dog. "Have you seen Mrs. Tynes? She is out here somewhere. Maybe you and I can find her."

"What's going on, Dad? Why are you out here?" Jordan said, knowing full well what was happening.

"I couldn't find Mother in the house; it was empty. I knew you and the kids were all at school, so I started looking for her." Victor looked up at his daughter and smiled. "How was school?"

Jordan was stunned by how much her father had changed in just a few weeks. Her heart pumped hard, and she took a long breath, trying to relax. There was no need to get on her father; from his confused perspective, he was doing what he needed to do—his wife was missing, and he needed to find her.

Maggie gently tugged at the man's hand, trying to pull him along.

"Good idea, Mags. Let's get him in the Jeep."

Minutes later, she parked in the drive; her Dad's Dodge truck was not in the driveway. She knew Louise had it, but why wasn't she here?

Louise pulled in behind her as she helped Victor

out of the Jeep.

"Where are you two off to?" Louise asked as she climbed out.

"I found him a few blocks away walking the street," Jordan said.

"Oh my God," her Mom said, more like a cry. "Is he all right?"

"He's fine but confused. He said he was looking for you."

"I went to pick up his prescription. He was asleep watching a baseball game. It would take me twenty minutes. You called and said you were coming home. The pharmacy was closing, so I had to get there." Louise walked over to Victor and hugged him.

"Sorry, Mom, got a call, then another," Jordan said as she took her father's hand.

"There you are. I have been looking for you," Victor said to Louise. "Jordan is home from school; she gave me a ride. I'm hungry."

Jordan and Louise looked at each other. Yes, a near miss, but would there be others? They had much to discuss, new rules to understand, and a promise not to blame the other. They had a whirlwind in a bottle, and she knew it.

Chapter 28

Monday morning, sitting at her desk, Jordan asked Candy to join her.

"Shut the door," she said.

Candy placed a cup of coffee on the desk and took a seat.

"How's Victor?'" Candy asked.

Jordan wasn't surprised. Candy had a sixth sense about these things, which is one of the reasons she was the best part of the sheriff's office. She knew when things needed to be done and when follow-ups were required.

"We need to find daycare for Dad. I found him wandering the neighborhood Saturday night. His memory is worse, and so is his confusion. And Louise . . ."

"Needs some time to herself, I get it. There's a lot on the Tyneses plate."

"I got some Apple Airs Tags from the phone store last night. Seem invasive, but I can't worry that he'll wander off; I can see he is home and safe."

"I understand and wholly concur. Good idea. There is a woman I know who retired from teaching. She's helping a friend with a similar problem. It's her mother, dementia. Mary comes in and assists for a few hours and lets Fred get some time for himself. He has breakfast or lunch with his buddies. Do you want me to ask if she has some time?"

Jordan smiled and sipped the coffee. "Yes, that's what we need."

"Her name is Mary Soft Feather; she's Crow but lives here in Livingston with her husband, Arthur Strong Bow. He works at the hardware store. You know him?"

"Of course, nice guy—knows his hardware. Arthur Goodman," Jordan said.

"They've taken on their tribal names—good people. She taught grade school in the Indian school in Big Timber. Took early retirement. I'll make the call."

"Thanks."

Candy placed two notes on the desk. "The top one is from Mike; he has news about the Mexicans. He's on the road."

The dark and evil of the world outside was just a phone call away. The Mexicans. Jordan pursed her lips and exhaled. "He didn't say why?"

"No. He was heading to Bozeman, then here. Asked about lunch."

"I'll call him. The other?"

"That DEA guy, Brewster, called twice. He asked questions, ones I didn't have answers to. I don't know why he bothers me, but he does. There is something hinky about that guy, fancy suits and all."

"All last week during the flooding, he called. I

put him off. Then, the other day, he drops by, sniffing around. Offers information for a price. The questions?"

"Where you were and the schedules of our people, subtle yet way too curious for my taste. I deferred and told him to talk to you."

"What's his story? We still have a meeting tomorrow, right?" Jordan asked.

"Right. Ten tomorrow morning—here. I've heard from the FBI, Mike, and Brewster."

"He can wait. I have enough going on."

"I know I shouldn't ask, but . . ."

"Go on."

"How's Wells doing?"

Jordan kept everyone in the dark about Courtwright and his operation. Candy knew a little, but she also knew everything went through her boss. "He's okay. Is that enough?"

Candy stood. "Yes, that's enough. But I am concerned about all our people."

"So am I. I'll fill you in when the time is right."

"Thanks, I understand. I'll call Mary, and maybe we can get Louise the help she needs."

Jordan called Mike.

"Hi, Sheriff," Mike answered. The tone was official.

"Bozeman? What's happening?"

"The word on the street is that the Chinese are here and in strength. Some vehicles were ID'd from license plates crossing in from Canada, and Sheriff Rodgers has info he wants me to see—and he wants to keep it close, just me for now. Ever since that execution squad took out the house in Bozeman, he's watched for anything out of the ordinary. Can you do lunch?"

"Yes. Where?"

"The usual, along the river. Can you pick up some sandwiches? I'll meet you at the turnaround on View Vista. Wait, did that get flooded?"

"Yes, but it's good now. See you at one."

"Got it—one o'clock."

Mike didn't want to be seen in Livingston, and she got that. Again, the Chinese and the Mexicans. Something was happening, and it was not good.

She had talked to Wells Courtwright the previous night. She sat at the picnic table in their backyard. Dad was asleep in bed, and Mom was watching TV.

"You okay?" she asked.

"I'm good," Wells said. "One of my contacts says there is trouble coming. The word on the reservation is that Suarez is still in the area and is pushing the dealers hard, especially on the reservations. They are holding back product, and when it arrives, the cost is doubled. And I'm close to a meet with one of the cartel hombres."

"And they cut the coke and meth with fentanyl. Damn them. Anything more specific?"

"This guy also tells him that soon he will no longer have to deal with the Chinese—war is coming. What the hell does that mean?"

"The war has started. That Bozeman house fire and the unidentified dead were Chinese, and Suarez did it. And now the Chinese are coming in to eliminate the Mexicans. Damn, we don't need this. We're still cleaning up from the flooding. The deputies are stretched thin, now the Indians. Were you flooded?"

"The water came right up to the trailer. I was stuck

on the east side, but you know that."

"All good?"

"Yes, good, but two floods in two years. Maybe this global warming crap is real," Wells said with a laugh.

"One more thing to worry about."

"Let it sit for a day or two." There was a pause. "I should be there."

"No, right now, I need your eyes and ears where they are. I will call you when this changes. DEA Agent Brewster is bugging me about schedules and personnel. Have you heard anything about him?"

"Brewster? No, not a word. What's up?"

"Just a feeling, and not a good one. Candy's radar is pinging."

"I'll ask around. Are you good? How's your dad?" Wells asked.

"He's showing signs of confusion, and I'm trying to find help."

There was a pause. "He is in my prayers. You take care."

"Thanks, Wells. We will talk tomorrow."

* * *

When Jordan arrived, Special Agent Mike Cardona was sitting on the picnic table overlooking the access ramp to the Yellowstone River. The river was still muddy from the storm; she guessed it might be unfishable and unusable for boaters for most of the summer. She smiled at the thought as she walked to Mike: *When it rains, it pours.* Maggie ran ahead.

Jordan climbed up on the table, set a soft cooler on the bench seat, and slid close to Mike. She took a deep breath and watched a massive log, with roots still intact, pass in the swift current; she slowly let the air out.

"Such a sigh. Comes with the job, I guess."

"More like clearing my mind, a Zen thing. What is it with that son of a bitch, Suarez?"

"You had the chance to ask him—what do you think?"

"He likes the game and the killing—he's a sadistic psychopath. The rest is secondary; the money means nothing—he gets off on the killing, the winning. I saw it when we reviewed the tapes from the gas station. He walked around, not caring that we would see him. He even cleaned up his appearance for his chance to be seen. He tried it with me on the mountain, never admitted who he was, and played the game of being the innocent guy when arrested."

Cardona handed Jordan a manila envelope. "Information on the dead Bozeman Chinese—FBI wanted you to get it off the record. They believe, like we do, there's something else going on. None carried identifications; they were chased down through fingerprints and facial recognition. The government can move fast when it wants to. We also confirmed the identification of one of the bodies: Lawrence Hang Chow. He was the grandnephew of the head of the Hong Kong Hang Chow Group. The leader is George Hang Chow, grandson of the Chow Group's founder after World War II; there's no nastier syndicate in southern China. Our Chinese sources have them connected to the PLA, the People's Liberation Army. They launder money for the Mexican cartels and sell them raw materials—the PLA siphons off a percentage. The Army also supplies logistic support when it suits their needs. The others were listed as illegals who had overstayed their student visas, and two were from Vancouver. All assumed Triad members."

"How nice. Great. We aren't just facing thugs and gangsters, but governments as well. And they did not do well against the Mexicans."

She took a can of Coke from the cooler bag and gave one to Mike. Then, she poured water from a plastic bottle into a paper dish for Maggie and placed it on the bench seat. She turned back to Mike.

"I'm exhausted, Mike. Pop is not doing well, and Mom is a wreck. My brother and sister are doing what they can, but I'm the one who signed up for this. And it's summer, and I have a sadistic killer wandering the mountains, murdering Chinese gangsters, and feeding drugs to teenagers and tourists who want the great Western experience. I got a report from Billings that they found a family dead from the effects of fentanyl—overdose, murder, and suicide."

"That's them, not you—you are doing just fine. Nonetheless, your compadres in Gallatin, Lewis and Clark, and Yellowstone Counties are just as tired and pissed. This is dragging all of them down—and it is happening all over the country. Dozens dead every day, hundreds every month, a hundred thousand last year, twice the number killed than in automobile accidents. It is more than a tragedy—it is a disgrace."

A drift boar appeared with two anglers and their guide. They quickly passed them.

"They won't catch anything," Jordan said. "The water is unfishable."

"There are fishermen, and there are optimists; they are one and the same."

"Some kind of angling humor?"

"It was something my uncle, a cop, told me when I

was a kid, and it stuck with me. Cops are optimists; we must be. The job is tough enough; not believing what we do is right would eat us alive—optimists. See?" Mike pointed.

The fisherman on the bow had a fish; his rod bent in an arc that pointed to the river, the line flared in the sunshine—and for the briefest moment, the angler and the fish were one. A dance began; the guide moved the boat across the swifter river, and the second fisherman, net in hand, patiently waited; the fisherman slowly and deliberately raised his rod and led the fish to the side of the boat. A moment later, the fish was netted and, not a moment later, released.

Almost absent-mindedly, Jordan said, "You better believe I won't let that son of a bitch go."

Chapter 29

Diego Suarez leaned back against the front hood of the Dodge Charger, waiting. Beccara and Carrillo faced him and rested against the gray panel of the Ford van. Garza and Molina, carrying AK-47s, took positions behind the van; there was cover and protection if required. There was also easy access to the rear cargo area for the heavier weapons if needed. All wore sidearms. The two additional cartel vehicles, both stolen, a white Camry and a metallic green pickup, were parked across the highway from the El Pinatas Loco restaurant on Highway 89 on the south side of Livingston. The overpass for Interstate 90 was a few hundred yards farther south, and the noise from the traffic provided a buzz in the relatively quiet Monday morning. The sounds of diesel trucks beginning their climb out of the valley vibrated the still air. The restaurant building and the evergreen hedge of trees along the north property line hid the six men from curious eyes on the highway. To anyone passing by, they were friends just having a conversation.

It was the week after the Fourth of July, and the morning tourist traffic heading to Yellowstone Park's northern gate, sixty-five miles to the south, was building. Dozens of camper trailers, recreational vehicles, SUVs, and assorted cars and trucks were falling in line to enter the park early before the significant traffic flow began in earnest in midafternoon.

For Suarez, it was all irrelevant. He placed his people where they could best control the outcome of the meeting. He remembered a few other summits, or *reunión de pandillas*, where conflicts between other cartels had been resolved. Some went well, others not so much. In those instances, it was over territory, profit sharing, perceptions of respect or lack thereof, or mutual aid when the government got too close. They had common Mexican interests and culture, though they hated each other. These *pendejos*, these Chinks, they had nothing in common with the cartel. His people wanted money, simple. Sell a product—make money; the biggest problem was converting cash to digits. He believed the Chinese were in it not only for the money but were also agents of the Chinese government, useful idiots to serve the masters in Beijing—just one more tool to break the United States. He didn't care; he wanted an end to the confusion they caused. They brought more attention to his business by the US federal government. He wanted them gone, and they wanted to negotiate—fuck them. What the hell was he paying Brewster for? He was sure the man was playing both sides; he would take care of him later. Money bought only so much loyalty; he learned that twenty years earlier. He expected total loyalty from his people, nothing less. Even friendships were tested, and Luis Gambuzza had failed.

His watch read 10:03. Less than twenty-four hours had passed since the conversation with John Wang to set this meeting. He used a number given by Brewster. He played nice, knowing that the Triad was enraged over his actions in Bozeman. He didn't care.

"We need to talk," Suarez said.

"I don't meet with men without honor," Wang answered.

"Then I'm guessing you are a lonely son of a bitch, considering the company you keep."

"What do you want?"

"There are many things to discuss: territories, re-engagement with raw materials suppliers, and money transfers and laundering. There are also the issues of the boundaries between what we do and what you do. So, there is much for both of us."

There was a pause; Suarez waited. There was a muffled conversation in Chinese, then Wang said, "Tomorrow. Where do you suggest?"

"Is there somewhere you would prefer, Señor Wang?"

Another pause. "I don't know the territory, where it's safe or where police are. But I want it public."

It was Suarez's turn. He waited and then said, "There is a Mexican restaurant on the south side of Livingston. We will have privacy, and I will guarantee security. The food is good. I will text you the address."

"I hate Mexican food; it's too greasy. Ten o'clock. I will have four people with me."

"Excellent. I am sure, Señor Wang, that we can come to a mutual understanding."

The line went dead.

"I do not trust them," Jose Carrillo said. He monitored the conversation.

"I never trusted them," Suarez said. "Tomorrow, we will eliminate these cockroaches and prepare for a less complicated and more profitable future. This is what I want you to do."

At 10:10, two black SUVs turned off Highway 89 into the restaurant's parking lot. They passed Suarez and his vehicles and backed into parking stalls. Suarez patiently waited while two men, all carrying AK-47s, exited the rear passenger seats of the SUVs. They took positions at the front of the vehicles, and their eyes never left the Mexicans. Suarez walked into the parking lot aisle and waited, his hand hovering over his pistol.

From the lead vehicle, a man exited and walked past his soldiers. Suarez thought the man was tall for a Chinese, easily six feet. He wore a black sports coat, white dress shirt, dark slacks, and polished black shoes. Suarez thought of an accountant. Suarez walked to the man, stopped, and then extended his hand.

"Señor Wang, it is a pleasure to meet you," Surez said as he shook the man's hand. The man smiled and nodded. "Please follow me."

Suarez turned and walked to the door at the back of the restaurant. He heard car doors open in the SUVs and turned back to see two men join Wang. None carried weapons—they slowly pirouetted with open jackets to show they were unarmed. He waved to Carrillo and Beccara; both men laid their pistols on the hood of the Charger and joined Suarez. The six men entered the restaurant; Beccara led the way.

The Chinese followed Suarez into the restaurant. A

table had been set up in the front window. Two women, dressed in colorful traditional Mexican blouses and skirts, stood off to one side. Both looked scared, and neither smiled. Another table held trays of food and pitchers of ice water.

"Shall we sit?" Suarez said.

Wang said something in Chinese, and his two men looked at each other. They took seats at one end of the table. Suarez's men did the same at the opposite end; the two leaders sat at each end of the table, and their men flanked them.

"I was surprised by your invitation," Wang said in English. "It took balls, especially after what happened. That will cost you dearly."

"An unfortunate incident—my people got ahead of themselves. And, if necessary, we can make a settlement," Suarez said. "They have been disciplined. I did not want that to happen; we have much to gain and too much to lose."

"You should control your people better; I would not allow that among my people."

"I understand and agree. Discipline is critical." Suarez slowly moved his hand to his leather jacket. The three Chinese tensed. Smiling, he removed a cell phone and placed it on the table. His fingers hovered an inch over the phone. He studied Wang and his jaw clenched when he saw the earpiece buried in the man's left ear. A glance confirmed the others also with black earpieces. Without hesitation, he tapped the screen.

From the parking lot came the deafening concussions of grenades and gunfire. Then, from the street, another black SUV squealed through the traffic line and into the parking lot. Two men jumped out and began firing at Suarez's men. One of Wang's men busted through the back door of the restaurant, a rifle in his hands. The Chinese jumped to their feet as the women tossed pistols, hidden under their skirts, to Suarez and his men. The Chinaman at the back door fired, hitting one of the women. Outside, a gray van pulled to the front window; the panel door slid open. The Mexicans dropped to the floor as automatic weapons fired from inside the van, shattering the glass and knocking down two of the Chinese. Suarez swung his pistol to the hallway, fired, and shot the man. The van pulled away. Suarez fired at Wang, hitting him in the face.

The man dropped to the floor where his two associates lay writhing. Suarez hurriedly administered coup de grâce shots to each of the men. The five went to the rear door, more gunfire. Then another explosion. They quickly left the restaurant and walked to the vehicles; Trina, one of the women in the restaurant, helped the woman who had been wounded, her white blouse now crimson from the shoulder wound. Wang's men lay in the parking lot, and so did two of Suarez's men. The Chinese SUVs were stopped in the driveway, windshields were shattered, and bodies lay in the front seats.

The Camry and the pickup were blocking each entry in the parking lot. The Chinese were unable to escape, and they died. The van came around the restaurant's corner, and two of Suarez's men jumped out.

"*Jefe*, we need to go. There will be more," Carrillo said.

"The fuckers, no honor, no fucking honor," Suarez said.

The wounded and dead Mexicans were placed in the van; sirens wailed in the distance. They left the parking lot, drove through openings in the line of un-suspecting tourists, and headed to the on-ramp of the interstate.

* * *

Sheriff Jordan Tynes carefully walked through the scene of the massacre. Nine dead Chinese littered the parking lot and the interior of the restaurant. Blood pools suggested that others were shot but escaped. She was furious. This did not happen in her county; this should not happen in Montana.

The first call came in at 10:19: reports of explo-sions and gunfire. Within minutes, there were more calls, all frantic and confused. The Livingston police were the first on the scene. Deputies Claymore and Dolan were the earliest of her people to arrive. At 10:29, Candy burst into the ten o'clock meeting with the feds and told her to take the call from Claymore. He was agitated and told her what they'd found. The phones were ringing all over the office; she could hear the calls to the Livingston police department through the walls. A coincidence, she thought not. Ten min-utes later, three people in the meeting reconvened at the restaurant. Brewster told Jordan that he had a call from Helena and needed to head back to the office, and besides, "One more federal agent won't make a difference," he said. "It's a police matter now."

The carnage was beyond anything Jordan had seen, even in Iraq. Courtwright, responding to the "all hands" and Candy's call, arrived thirty minutes after she ar-rived. Jordan had Courtwright follow her and Cardona around the property, taking photos with his phone; the Livingston police detective and the crime scene people would take more detailed photos. FBI Special Agent

Morris was visibly upset. His people would arrive in two hours. Jordan assumed that they would take over the scene and the investigation. She smiled when Mike told Morris, "In for a penny, in for a pound."

"We should have stopped this, Mike," she said. "We knew this would happen." She turned to Courtwright and Claymore. "Suarez did this to make a point, to jam this in my face, on my streets. I want this man."

"We will get them," Claymore said. "We have witness reports that at least three vehicles raced from the scene and headed west on the interstate. I've contacted the Highway Patrol; they are setting up roadblocks."

"Tell them: extreme caution. Make sure they know."

"Done and done," Claymore said. "Between Bozeman and here, that's seventeen dead—all Chinese. What the Mexican count is is only a guess. They took the injured with them. Damn it, these people are bastards."

"This is cruel. He lured them here; they were naive—I don't get it," Jordan said.

"It looks like the Chinese knew something was going to happen," Mike said. He pointed.

"There are three vehicles here, five dead Chinese inside two of them, the others there and there, and three inside," Jordan said. "Sure, Suarez planned this; he was here. I'll bet he put the last bullet in their heads—but he just missed getting taken out by the Triad. The fools walked into this; they knew this was coming but weren't completely surprised. Something or someone put them at ease, and it got them killed. I want whoever that was, and I want Suarez."

"In the back of the black SUVs—they were the Chinese vehicles—there were AK-47s, pistols, ballistic vests, and a few grenades," Mike said. "I'm guessing the Mexicans beat the Chinese to the draw."

"Yeah, all-out war? What now?" Wells added. "Most of the Chinese Triad in this part of the western United States are lying in the parking lot, the restaurant, or the Bozeman morgue."

"Likely, but for how long? That's a choice to be made in Vancouver or Hong Kong."

"I want that son of a bitch," Jordan said.

"We will get him." It was becoming a mantra.

The FBI arrived in the early afternoon. Three vehicles and six agents pulled to the curb outside the immediate crime scene and reported to Special Agent Morris, who took charge. In some respects, Jordan was glad she would take a back seat to this shit show. She had enough problems, the least being the complete shutdown of Highway 89 that led to the north entrance to Yellowstone Park. Traffic was backed up east and west on the interstate, and her people and the police had their hands full handling the traffic. It got worse when the TV stations from Bozeman, Billings, and Helena arrived and set up their live broadcasts. She gave the unenviable job as public liaison to Deputy Jean Smith. "I owe you one," she told Jean. "Sorry."

"Comes with the territory. I'll do what I can," Jean said.

"Deflect, be vague, and point to the feds; it's their party."

"Yes, boss."

Chapter 30

They headed west on the interstate. Suarez checked his watch; it was time.

"We must get off this fucking highway; they will be setting roadblocks," he said. "Jose, call the others and tell them to split up and head to the Bozeman house; we are going to the Boulder River trailer. All vehicles in the barn—I want no one outside for the rest of the day."

Suarez watched the countryside as they drove west through the mountains. The fight was a disaster. Whatever Brewster told the Chinese to put them at ease had failed. They were ready and tricked him. Even though his people were prepared for the ambush, they were down four good friends. Culiacan would not be pleased. If the Chinese learned about Brewster, they would track him down and cut him into small pieces. In time, the man would need to be eliminated; he was a loose end that needed killing.

Four of his people were dead; his old friend Juan

Carrillo died in the van, shot in the stomach. One of the women, Margo Sanchez, died in the restaurant, and his men Gustavo Garza and Enrico Lapas were killed in the parking lot. They buried them behind the barn. They stayed inside the trailer for three days. The radio and television news described the chaos and confusion brought by the road closures and vehicle searches. Traffic throughout central Montana was a mess. The press conference by the governor blaming illegal Chinese who entered the state to sell drugs brought out Chinese rights groups and pro-drug demonstrators to the capital. Suarez smiled; the Americans blamed their government for the drug problem. People must be allowed to do what they want; it was the essence of being an American—all the cartels were doing was filling a need that was already there. It wasn't his problem. After all, the pharmaceutical companies were getting the American public hooked on their drugs; all he was doing was providing cheaper alternatives.

"How are we going to get out of here, *jefe*?" Jose Beccara asked. "I'm running short on cigarettes."

"I told you to quit, *mi amigo*," Suarez said, patting the man on the shoulder. "I have a plan, and it includes the sheriff. I will make a few calls."

He tried to reach Brewster, but his calls went to voicemail, and he began to wonder how loyal the man was. His calls to Billings and the three who remained behind also went unanswered—were they compromised, arrested, or dead? His paranoia grew daily, and now the cartel's operations were stopped. The business needed to restart, or he would lose the territory they had spent years building. It came to a head that evening when he called Culiacan on the satellite phone.

"You fucked this up, Diego," his boss said. "Now, you must make it right. Our so-called friends in China have shut us down. I'm sending you help; they will be there in a week. Sit tight."

"I can handle it," Suarez said. For the first time in his life, he was pleading to regain what was lost—he also knew he was pleading for his life. "With the Chinese eliminated, I can rebuild our operations better, stronger." He waited for an answer, then the phone went dead.

Beccara approached him. "*Jefe*, what are we going to do?"

"We need leverage and a way out of here. We are going north to Canada. Here is what we will do."

* * *

Jordan's first stop after leaving the scene of the massacre was the hospital. While she'd walked through the blood and gore in the restaurant, waiting for the FBI, Bob Claymore asked her, "What happened to the wounded guy? The EMTs took him straight to the hospital."

"What wounded guy?" Jordan asked. "There is a survivor?"

"Not sure. When we arrived, the Livingston police were overwhelmed. We did what we could; bodies were everywhere, evidence, shell casings, footprints, what a mess."

"A survivor, Bob?"

"Yes, one of the EMTs, Jack Scott, you know him, was triaging who he could; all were dead. Then, inside the restaurant, he found a man who had crawled under a table. He had a bad head wound, blood everywhere. Jack saw him move. They put him on a gurney and got him out of there. I thought you knew."

"I did not. Any name?"

"No, but he was Chinese."

Now, she stood in the hallway outside the emergency room, talking to a nurse she knew, Jeanne Corin.

"What do you know, Jeanne?" Jordan asked.

"Chinese, late thirties, maybe early forties, healthy except for the bullet in his back and the bloody track left by a head wound. Came a half inch away from being dead."

"He awake?"

"Doctor Larkin put him under, sedated him—he lost a lot of blood; he will be out for at least twenty-four hours, assuming he doesn't die. The bullet in his back is lodged near his heart and punctured his right lung. They are doing what they can."

"Did you find any identification?"

"One sec." Nurse Corin walked down the hallway into the room with the shooting victim; a moment later, she returned holding a plastic Ziploc bag. She gave it to Jordan. "That's all we have; we cut away his clothes—nice material, well-made suit. I know my cloth, do some sewing myself."

Jordan held up the bag. Inside was a wallet, a leather passport case, some loose change, and a gold Omega Speedmaster. The watch was probably pricey, but she didn't know one designer watch from the other. She wore a Casio military-style watch, which was cheap and durable. This guy's watch looked expensive.

She went to the break room, slipped on blue nitrile gloves, and carefully removed the wallet and passport. A couple of credit cards, a gas card and red Visa from Wells Fargo, a black American Express card, a stack of American bills, twenties, fifties, and hundreds, and a driver's license: the name on it John Lewis Wang, Seattle address, age thirty-nine. The American passport matched the name, place of birth was Hong Kong, China. The passport was three years old. She would match the photo to the face in the emergency room.

"Your deputy outside the emergency room said you came here," Mike said. "What's up?" After she abruptly left the meeting at her office when the first reports of the shooting came over the phone, she forgot about the ATF, FBI, and DEA. She held up the wallet and passport.

"I need you to chase down this guy." She held up the passport. "You can do it quicker, and maybe I can keep him away from the FBI for a few hours."

"Whose 'this guy'?" Mike asked

"A survivor from the restaurant. Chinese, born in Hong Kong, lives in Seattle. Body shot and head wound, sedated—he was there to meet Suarez, I'm sure of it. He was ambushed and may help us with our insider problem."

"That's a lot of hope. We don't even know if he's one of the Triad leaders."

She held up the watch. "Is this expensive?"

Mike looked closely at the watch as she slowly rotated it in the bag. He smiled. "Soldiers don't wear fifty-thousand-dollar watches. Yeah, he's one of the leaders. I will do what I can; it will give us a few hours before the FBI chases down our EMTs and the hospital people. I'll make a few calls." He took his phone and photographed the driver's license and the passport. "You heading back to the office?"

"I wanted to talk to the survivor; they are keeping

him under for the next twenty-four hours. So, yes, back to the office. Suarez is somewhere in the county; I'm sure of it. I've got a kid arrested for dealing bad stuff and nearly killed two of his friends. I'm interviewing him. Besides, Morris and his people will be all over this; I'm trying to stay out of the way."

"Not immediately telling the FBI about Wang there . . . that's NOT staying out of the way."

"Maybe I can trade him for something."

"Be careful; the FBI isn't like me. They play rough."

Jordan smiled. "See what you can turn up and give me a call, tough guy."

* * *

According to Courtwright's sources, drugs were re-appearing, the prices were dropping, and overdose cases were on the rise in Butte and Billings. Arrests were made, but the fear in the dealers was palpable; they would rather spend a month in a county jail than be suspected of informing on the cartel or even the now-neutered Chinese. It was turning into a free market—one that killed people.

Lance Collins had been sequestered in a jail cell for the past week. The attorney the family hired was having a fit. She leaned heavily on the kid when she finally pressed him; his parents sat in the room while she laid out the kid's life moving forward, a life that made him forty before he saw a free sun overhead. The arrogance was still there, and he didn't say a word. *What is it with these kids?* she thought. Did he believe that Daddy would wave a magic lawyer in the air and all would be good? Mom would make some deal, and he could return to being the cute and irresponsible kid they'd made. It was only when she spread the photos of the mutilated Indians hanging from the barn rafters that she saw a spark of fear. The mother quickly flipped the photos, trying to hide them from her son, but the damage was done. Jordan saw the nervous sweat, the clenching fingers, the unease as he sat in the chair. Even a tough guy would pale at the sight of such viciousness, cruelty, and sadism.

"Do you want to end up like this, Lance?" she said, tapping the photos. "This is where you are headed; your parents can't stop it. This man, this animal, also butchered a Wyoming family and seventeen Chinese drug dealers to make a point." She looked at the parents and the attorney, their attention on the two remaining photos still facing up. "These two believed they were in control, but this animal proved them wrong. You all talk. I will be back." She left after turning back all the photos face up,

She didn't know what was said in the holding room, but Beth Collins tapped on the door to her office twenty minutes later.

"Has your boy found some sense?" Jordan asked.

"I hope to God he has," Beth said as she sat in the chair across from Jordan. "Lance has it all: smarts, good looks, an easy manner, and more than anything, the ability to sway people to his side—and to buy his drugs."

"He sounds like the makings of a salesman or politician," Jordan said.

Beth looked at Sheriff Jordan, not grasping the comparison. "Robb and I never knew. We found twenty thousand dollars hidden in his room, twenties and fifties. Sheriff, he's a good boy; I know we can set him right."

"Your son has cost this county a lot of money and put the lives of my people at risk. Because of his drug business, I will not accept a slap on the wrist. I want him to spend some time in juvie. Luckily, he's just under the age limit. He's an adult a few months from now, and my hands are tied. I will talk to the county attorney and see what can be done. However, I need something. I want the names of all his contacts and dealers he's been working with, and the county attorney will want the money. Can you get that for me?"

Beth slowly stood. "I will get what you want. Thank you." She left and walked down the hall to her husband outside the interrogation room. Candy appeared at the door.

"This is a tough one," Candy said.

"They are all tough, Deputy. It's just that some are tougher than others, especially those built on arrogance and stupidity. Sometimes, this job is more like a school principal than a law officer. I want Bob to finish the interview and get names and whatever else the kid will give up; he's ripe. What do you have?"

"You need to call DEA Special Agent Brewster; he is insistent."

She called. "What can I do for you, Agent Brewster?" she said.

"I get the impression you are avoiding me, Sheriff," Brewster said, his manner folksy.

She wasn't going to do folksy. "What do you know about what happened at the Livingston restaurant? You took off when the first reports came in. Do you know something I need to know?"

"I had to get back to Helena; I had an important meeting—it couldn't be put off."

"Ten dead wasn't important—all drug dealers and Chinese? And you are the head of the DEA around here? And there's evidence that suggests some of Suarez's people were wounded or worse. They took the injured and left. Nobody has shown up at hospitals. What do you know?"

"I swear, I know nothing. I am insulted by your implications."

"You will get over it, but if you had anything to do with this . . ."

"Fuck you, Sheriff." The line went dead.

Her next call was to Mike Cardona. "It's Brewster. I'm sure of it, Mike."

"I understand. It's complicated. I'll talk with Agent Morris and get his take. We need evidence. Anything that man touched is infected; we need to be careful."

"*We?* You think I'm right?"

"It all points to the son of a bitch. I will get back to you."

She looked at the address the Collins kid had written down—a house in Billings, a hundred miles away. Then, she called the sheriff of Yellowstone County.

Chapter 31

Jordan's world was the office, her Jeep, and home after the disasters of the flood, the cleanup, and the massacre at the Mexican restaurant. The sheriff's office was back to full speed; she had good people, and they knew what needed to be done. Her father was improving, though a lot slower than the previous stroke, and with this developing dementia, it was distressing, especially for her mother. After fifty years together, Victor had been the rock the family was built on. While not physically near, Jordan's brother and sister were as close to Jordan as they were to her parents' hearts. One night, she found her mother sitting alone in the backyard, watching the stars and silently crying. Jordan held her hand and said nothing; touch has a way of saying love and understanding louder than a whisper.

The bastard Diego Suarez was never far from her thoughts; she hoped he was back in Mexico and someone else's problem. Maybe he was one of the wounded or dead, yet somehow, she knew she wouldn't be that lucky. The massacre at the restaurant told one undeniable story: *We are here to stay, and you will not stop us.* The man was as elusive as a wolf in the high country; you could see the signs but never the beast, and when he appeared, you were never ready. Her time with him on the mountain after the crash was more than enough evidence of the man's psychotic and brutal nature.

The call alerting the Yellowstone County sheriff wasn't a bust. When they raided the house, they found three Mexican nationals with improper papers and a quarter of a million dollars' worth of coke, weed, oxy, and fentanyl. Added to the pile were four handguns, five long rifles, and fifty thousand in cash. All claimed they had never heard of Diego Suarez. The sheriff told her they were scared out of their minds when he pressed them about Suarez. He was positive it was one of the Culiacan distribution houses. Unfortunately, they found no other addresses or helpful information about *El Martillo*.

The hospital called at ten the next morning. Her John Doe was coming out of the sedation; Jordan had asked that the man's name not be made public or put on the hospital records. One of her rookies, Terry Morgan, stood guard through the night. She didn't want an execution in the halls of the hospital. She stood behind Doctor Larkin and two nurses hovering over the man. Bandages wrapped his head. As the man gradually regained his senses, she saw confusion and then awareness. His head jerked from one side to the other. Jordan had secured both his arms to the hospital bed rails. He stopped and glared at her.

"There you are. Welcome back from the dead, Mr. Wang," Jordan said.

Wang mumbled something in Chinese.

"I didn't understand you," Jordan said. She turned to the doctor. "Doc, could you step out for a minute? I need to talk with this man." She looked past the medical staff to the deputy at the door. "Hold tight, Terry."

"We will be right outside," Doctor Larkin said, leaving the room.

She turned her attention to the man in the hospital bed. "You were lucky, Mr. Wang. Very lucky. If not for someone's bad aim, you would be in the morgue with the other nine members of your gang. You are the only survivor. How is this going to sit in Hong Kong?" She took the ball and ran, making stuff up with plausible assumptions and the files Mike had sent her. "You are John Lewis Wang, from Seattle. The Hang Chow Group employs you, a criminal organization headquartered in Hong Kong. Your job is to oversee the drug and illegal immigrant operations in the western United States. Am I right? You can shake your head."

Mike Cardona had come through with pages of information about the group and the man. He emailed her the information at six that morning. Why the feds hadn't arrested this bastard and sent him home amazed her. She saw a slight tightening around Wang's eyes, maybe even a twitch in his cheeks. He understood her.

"And somehow you got yourself and your people caught in an ambush with the Mexicans and Diego Suarez, am I right?"

The glare returned.

"Yes, right, good. We are on the same page. Well, Mr. Wang, you are safe here—nothing to worry about. Our prison system hasn't lost a Chinese drug dealer to a Mexican execution squad in a while." She leaned in.

"Where is Diego Suarez? I want him. I can help you if you help me. Who set the meeting up? Was it you or Suarez? You wounded some of his people, maybe even killed them. You want to pay back what he did to you. I can help. Where is he?"

Wang pulled against his cuffs, and they rattled. He glared at her; his face reddened. "I don't know where he is, but I know someone who does," Wang said hoarsely; his oxygen nose prongs gave it a nasal buzz. "I want a deal, in writing."

"You a lawyer or something?"

Wang smiled. "A deal, in writing. You want the fish; you need a net. I can get him for you."

* * *

Twenty additional Federal Bureau of Investigation agents landed in Livingston by the end of the day of the massacre. There wasn't a motel room in town with the travelers, tourists, and now federal agents. Some agents bitched that they had to commute from Bozeman.

Agent Morris was demonstrably upset when he learned of John Wang in the hospital, more so because Sheriff Tynes did not immediately inform him. What Jordan learned from Mike Cardona about Wang was helpful. When Morris learned about the Billings raid, he turned a brilliant hue of Irish red as he berated her in her office about federal procedures and practices.

It was her county, her state, and she smiled when he said, "We have a partnership here, Sheriff. It's a two-way street: You help me, and I help you."

"You might start by stopping the drugs from coming into the country before they get to Montana," she said. "I have enough problems with tourists."

At the request of FBI Special Agent Morris, the US Attorney for the District of Montana personally handled the paperwork for what amounted to a get-out-of-jail card for John Lewis Wang. What it was was a plane ticket back to Hong Kong after they were through squeezing him of every piece of information they could.

The nine dead were all Chinese nationals (most illegally here in the United States and entered through Canada). Three died from shrapnel from grenades, the others from 9mm and 7.62mm bullets. The assumptions were AK-47s and pistols. At least fourteen guns were recovered: a mixture of 9mm pistols, AR15s, and Chinese QBZ-97 machine pistols—most illegally modified to fire automatically.

Blood samples pointed to at least four others injured; the DNAs did not match any of the Chinese dead. The bodies were not recovered at the scene. Three, possibly four, vehicles left the scene: a gray van, a dark blue sedan, a white compact sedan, and maybe a green pickup truck. No license plate numbers were recorded. Witness reports agreed that all vehicles headed east on Interstate 90. Traffic cameras twenty miles east of Livingston did not photograph the vehicles.

Jordan was positive they had left the interstate and were still in her county. She had her staff collect any video footage from cameras that might have captured the vehicles.

The day she left Wang at the hospital, she drove east on Highway 89 to access Interstate 90. She passed a large corporation yard with businesses and storage facilities. From the interstate, she saw at least four cameras mounted on the one-story metal buildings.

Two hours later, she was reviewing videos from two of the businesses of the traffic on the interstate. At precisely 10:23:30, the morning of the massacre, four vehicles closely following each other passed the camera and continued east. One more confirmation, or lack of confirmation, was footage from a security camera mounted on a storage building on the east side of Big Timber. These vehicles did not pass through Big Timber. The state traffic cameras along the interstate were not live but cycled at fifteen-minute intervals.

The logical conclusion was that these vehicles left the interstate and disappeared somewhere in the thirty miles between Livingston and Big Timber. There were over two hundred square miles of rugged foothills, washes, canyons, and abandoned farms—all worthless information other than confirming that they were most likely still in the area.

The vehicle descriptions were listed in a statewide APB. Nothing materialized from the Interstate 90, Highway 89, and Highway 298 roadblocks. They had gone to hiding before the roadblocks were set up. She hated the idea, but they would have to wait for Suarez to make the next move.

Chapter 32

Saturday night supper was Louise's venison stew. She made enough for two more dinners. Jordan helped her father to the table; he insisted on sitting with his girls, he said. It was his way of helping as best as he could. She held the napkin to his chin and ensured he didn't choke. He could at least drink his Diet Coke through a straw.

After dinner, she helped him back to his chair and put on the Mariners game. The Air Tag clipped to his suspenders caught on his shirt; she unclipped it and placed it on the table next to his Coke. It was the fifth inning. Maggie took her spot on the dog bed, and Jordan returned to the kitchen.

"He is doing better, Mom. I can see it."

"I can, too, honey. But he's frustrated—first one thing, then another. I wish I could wave a wand over all this and make him whole. Victor deserves better than this—if there was a just God—"

"You stop right there, Mom. God didn't do this; it's not part of a plan, not a test. Dad had a stroke, two of them, and he's getting the best care, and he is better. That is more than enough right now. There is no one to blame. We will all get better." She leaned over and kissed her mother on the cheek.

"Thanks, honey." Louise took a deep breath. "There is one thing I do know: The laundry will not wash itself. I'll put some things in the machine and then join you and Dad. Do you have anything?"

The Mariners scored two runs in the bottom of the sixth and tied the Angels. Jordan sat on her usual spot on the couch. She smiled, watching her father nod as he tried to stay awake.

When someone approached the front door, Jordan's head turned to the alarm from the door camera. She looked at Maggie, who was standing and staring at the front hallway.

"Relax, Mags," she said and looked at her phone, which had also chimed when the front door rang. There was nothing on the screen; it was black, no view of the front porch. The doorbell rang again.

Louise was in the back bedroom, putting away laundered clothes. Victor was in his chair, his cane leaning against the wall nearby.

"You expect someone from the office?" he asked, the vowels still jumbled.

"No," Jordan said as she walked to the living room window and looked out on the street. Nothing out of the normal. It was getting dark. A single streetlight washed the corner a half block down. Porch lights glowed on the front porches of most houses, and cars and trucks sat in most of the driveways. Her Jeep sat on the driveway to the side of the house. The family Ford F-150 was in the garage where her mother had parked it. Quiet as a church an hour before services.

Maggie, still standing, stiffened and growled.

"What's your problem, dog?" Jordan said. As if triggered, the front door crashed open and slammed against the wall. Two men wearing cowboy hats and rough canvas jackets, their faces hidden behind bandanas, swung pistols up and aimed them at Jordan and Victor. Maggie began to bark and prepared to jump.

"Maggie, no! Down," Jordan screamed.

The dog froze, caught between instinct and obedience. Jordan screamed again as the man pointed the pistol at the dog. She knew the man.

"No. God damn you, Suarez. No!"

The man turned to Jordan, his eyes betraying the smile under the bandana. The other man slipped his pistol into his holster and swung up the AK-47 slung over his back. His eyes, black and sunken, scanned the room for a target.

"If that fucking dog moves, she's dead. Do you understand me, Sheriff?" Suarez yelled, the cloth muffling his voice. "I thought I killed her once."

"Down, Maggie, down." Jordan slowly raised her hand and then lowered it toward the floor. Maggie followed the hand and then sat on her haunches. Jordan could tell she wasn't happy; she was tense and ready to spring. Jordan desperately hoped that she would stay.

"Who the hell are you?" Victor said from his chair. Immobilized, he couldn't stand or even sit up without help. His speech was garbled.

"What did you say, old man?" Suarez laughed. "So, this is the geezer with the stroke? He's the reason why we rushed back from Wyoming—why we crashed? Maybe I should just shoot him and put him out of his misery." He swung the pistol toward her father.

"No, damn it. Stop. He can't do anything. Leave him be." She looked at Maggie, who looked like a snake ready to strike. "What do you want? You want something, or you would have shot us by now. You only solve your problems with a gun or a knife. What is it?" Jordan, unarmed, stood in the center of the room; she had placed herself between her father and Suarez, giving some protection.

"Insurance. I need insurance. You have us cornered. The Chinese are dead and neutralized. We need to get out. So, insurance."

"The only insurance I can offer is your arrest. Simple: Give up and live. Run and die."

"Not going to happen. Tell your mother to come out. I know she is here. Do it now."

From the hallway that led to the bedrooms, Louise slowly walked into the room, her hands low but up, palms out. "Please, don't—I'll do what you say."

"Stand right there. Sheriff, she is going with me. She is my insurance."

"Like hell she is; stay right there, Mom. Suarez, take me. Leave them out of this."

"No, no, no, Sheriff," Suarez said. "I need you out there pointing in the wrong direction and giving the wrong instructions. I need your mother to ensure you do what I tell you. If you try anything, like send in the fucking feds or state cops, I'll know, and she will die. If I see anything causing me problems, she dies. Once we leave, I want you to guarantee we are not caught—simple, right? *No problema.*"

"Take me, Suarez. I will guarantee you everything."

Victor mumbled something from his chair. When

Jordan turned to face her father, he stood, his cane high, trying to walk toward Suarez.

"No," Jordan screamed.

The man behind Suarez turned to her father, swinging up the rifle; Maggie leaped like a hound from hell directly at Suarez. The man fired, but the dog's momentum carried her into Suarez, knocking him to the floor. The deafening sound of the AK-47 on automatic roared and stitched holes across the ceiling. Victor fell to the floor; the side table fell, spilling his Coke across the floor; plaster dust and the smell of gunpowder filled the room. Louise screamed and went to her husband. Suarez pushed the motionless dog away as he slowly stood; his man covered them. Jordan tried to move toward her parents.

"No, Señora, you move, and you die," the man with the silver toes said and waved the weapon.

"This did not have to happen; this is all on you. What the hell was the old man thinking?" Suarez looked at Molina. "*Coge a esa mujer, nos vamos de aquí.*"

The man crossed the room to Louise, grabbed her arm, and pulled her from the floor. She screamed again and scratched the man across the face as she tried to pull away. He slammed the barrel of the rifle against Louise's face, cutting it. Jordan turned to grab her mother.

"You do that, and you are dead," Suarez yelled, his pistol pointed at her. "I will still take your mother, shoot your father, and you will have nothing."

"I'll be okay," Louise said as she stumbled across the room. "Take care of your father; he's still alive. Get help. I love you. I know you will find me."

Suarez's man pulled her roughly through the room

and toward the front door. Suarez jerked the bandana from his face, revealing a ghoulish smile. "*¡Para! Dame el celular de la mujer.*"

Holding Louise at arm's length, the gunman yelled: "*Teléfono, celular.*" His free hand was out. Louise reached into her jeans, removed the cell phone, and handed it to the man.

"*Pásame el teléfono,*" Suarez said.

The man tossed the phone to his boss. "Now yours," Suarez said to Jordan. She handed him her phone. Suarez looked at Louise's phone, then walked over to the woman and held it to her face. The phone opened. He expertly ran his thumb across the glass. "It seems your mother has been busy; two calls two minutes ago. I assume one is to the police, and I don't know the other. But in either case, we are leaving." He then repeatedly slammed both phones on the edge of the hallway table until they nearly snapped in two. He pitched them to Jordan. "Now take care of your father—if he's not dead. Sorry about the dog, again."

Molina provided cover. Preceding him, Suarez pushed Louise out the door. Jordan wanted to run to her father, but first, through the front window, she watched a gray van pull in behind her yellow Jeep, then another dark sedan pulled up behind the van. Suarez, her mother, and the gunman climbed into the van and left.

The sounds of sirens filled the quiet night as Jordan tried to staunch the blood flowing from the wound to Victor's shoulder. She looked at Maggie and, for a fleeting moment, was stricken by intense, almost paralyzing grief. Then Maggie's front legs moved, and she tried to stand before collapsing on the bloody floor.

"Stay there; lie down. I'll be right there." She turned back to her father.

* * *

For an hour, all was chaos and confusion. An ambulance arrived within minutes of Deputy Claymore's and Deputy Courtwright's separate arrivals. Then came Deputies Bob Dolan and Jean Smith. The ambulance took Jordan and her father to the hospital; Jean followed in her SUV with Maggie carefully laid in the rear. Jordan left an order with Bob to lock down the entire fucking state (her language shocked them all). "I want every blue van from Butte to Billings stopped and searched; probable cause is a kidnapping, attempted murder. Approach with extreme caution. I will be at the hospital." She said nothing about the other car.

A half hour later, Jordan stood in the now all too familiar hallway of the hospital. Doctors and nurses raced in and out of the emergency trauma room. Down the hall, Jean Smith stood outside a door where Maggie was cared for. Rookie Deputy Morgan came down from his station outside John Wang's room, one floor up. He ran into his boss's anger.

"What the hell are you doing, Terry? I want you in Wang's room. I want you on alert. Shit is going to happen."

Stunned by the rebuke, Deputy Morgan tried to tell the sheriff he was there to help; she would have none of it.

"Get back to your goddamn station," she said and turned back to Jean.

Jordan could only wonder about the strength of that hound. She had to be part mountain lion, nine lives and all. Yes, a mountain lion: same color, same intense eyes, and same unwavering focus, and those catlike lives. Shaking her head—what, five lives to go, now.

"She's tough," Deputy Smith said. "She will be okay."

The lie she told Claymore more than troubled her; it was enough to demand her resignation. Rationalization? Bullshit! She intentionally gave false information. It was a gray van, but she told Bob it was blue. Two vehicles—she described only the van. It was a simple thing, yet now, every driver in Montana in a blue van was in jeopardy. It was wrong, and she knew it.

"How's Victor?" Mike asked, handing Jordan a cup of coffee.

"Stable, but the damage is bad. The bullet was a large caliber and nearly blew out his shoulder. The trauma is intense, and with the blood thinners he's taking, it is like a dam broke. He's lost so much blood. They are doing everything."

"He's tough," Mike added.

"We all are until we are not."

"Maggie?"

"She's with Jean; I can't be at both places; my heart can't take it. But Mags is strong; the bullet somehow missed just below her ear, and she was attacking Suarez. A long wound along the side of the face knocked her out; it was the same bullet that struck Dad."

"What was your father thinking?"

"I don't know. Protecting us? It's all too crazy, Mike. Suarez must be stopped. If Dad dies and I can't get Mom back . . ."

"Don't think like that. We will get her back."

"God, Mike, I don't know what to do."

Chapter 33

A dozen roadblocks across the major highways of southern Montana shut the state down. Tourists in two blue vans were particularly upset when the Highway Patrol pulled them to the side of the interstate. Nervous officers approached with guns drawn. Both were close calls. When word got to Jordan at the hospital about the stops and the reactions, she knew she was wrong. Somebody was going to get injured or worse. She walked out the emergency room doors to the parking lot. Mike followed her.

"I've really fucked up, Mike. It was wrong; somebody will get hurt," she said.

"What the hell are you talking about?" Mike said.

After a moment, she turned to Mike. "Suarez told me to order our people in the wrong direction and give false information. If I didn't, he would kill my mom. I told Bob it was a blue van and that there was only one vehicle—there were two. Somebody will get hurt. I need to stop this, correct this."

"I'll fix it, don't worry. I will keep you out of it."

"It was a gray van; the other vehicle was a sedan, maybe a blue Dodge Charger. I should have told him."

"I will correct the APB. You get back to your father; he needs you."

The corrected report went out, and nothing more was said. Updates always followed initial reports, and witnesses remembered new information. Mike's new report was clear and precise. The APB was updated, and the roadblocks remained.

Candy Middleton handed Jordan another cup of coffee. "How's Victor doing?" she asked.

Jordan looked at the two cups of coffee and then at Candy. "What are you doing here?"

"Taking a break, boss. I've been up twenty-four hours, and I was on my way home. I knew you needed coffee. The office is good—your dad, how is he?"

"They put him in an induced coma after pumping pints of blood into him. He's on the edge. His shoulder will need reconstructive surgery if he lives . . ." Jordan stopped and took Candy's arm. "Dear God, what will I do?"

"He's tough, and so are you; there's an army of your friends out there looking for Louise; they will find her."

Jordan looked down the corridor; a ball of tan fur carefully walked out of a room and looked both ways. When Maggie saw Jordan, she limped quickly toward her. Jordan dropped to her knee and hugged the hound.

"See, she's good," Candy said.

Maggie nuzzled Jordan and then looked around, almost sensing something was wrong.

"He'll be okay, Mags; thanks for trying," Jordan

said.

Doctor Larkin emerged from the room where her father lay. He tilted his head toward an empty waiting room. Jordan followed; Maggie was close to her hand. Doctor John Larkin was the head of the hospital and a close friend.

"Jordan, I'll be honest, it's touch and go," Doctor Larkin said. "Time will tell. It may be days before we can make a full assessment. Where is Louise?"

Jordan told the doctor what had happened; he was stunned. "There is little you can do here. He is in excellent hands. Right now, take a breath and see what you can do to find the son of a bitch and bring Louise home."

"Thank you." Jordan walked out of the room and into the corridor. Mike and Candy were standing there. Her phone buzzed.

"Who is on dispatch?" Jordan asked.

"One of the rookies," Candy answered.

"Sheriff Tynes here." She listened as the report came in.

"Shit." She turned to Mike. "You're with me, Special Agent Cardona."

* * *

Jordan stood next to one of her sheriff's vehicles; it sat crossways on the asphalt, its front tires flat. The Interceptor's windshield and passenger-side windows were blown out, shattered by gunfire from Suarez's men. Nearby, another sheriff's vehicle, a pickup, had rolled halfway down the Highway 89 embankment. The pickup was Wells Courtwright's Ford 150; Deputy Bob Claymore had been driving it. He sat on the grassy shoulder above the truck, looking down at the Shields

River. He shook from the adrenaline rushing through his system. Mike Cardona was on a knee next to him.

Jordan and Mike had passed the EMTs and their van as she neared the site of the ambush—lights and sirens. Two of her deputies, Corporal Dan Mecklenburg and Deputy Jean Smith, were inside the emergency van. The report was they had been shot in the legs, but the wounds were not life-threatening. They were headed to Livingston Hospital, where she and Cardona had just left. Like Claymore, her anger shook her. She cautiously walked over to her deputy.

"You okay, Bob?" she asked as she stood behind him.

"I'm going to kill those assholes," he said. He tried to stand, but Mike pushed him back down. "And Wells will be pissed I trashed his ride."

"I'll try and get you the first crack; besides, Wells didn't own it; the county did." She took a knee next to Claymore and Cardona. Maggie sat next to her. "What happened?"

She waited while Claymore composed himself; she didn't hurry him. She looked up the highway and remembered that, four years earlier, she had found Mike Cardona's Porsche submerged under a highway bridge a few miles north.

"We set the roadblock there," Claymore started. His voice was low and deliberate. He pointed to a spot about a quarter mile south toward I-90. "It was around the curve. We used two vehicles; it was a V-shaped block. There were steep banks on each side of the road. We had already let a couple of cars through, tourists. We had the update on the van: gray, not blue. Then, two vehicles came at us at high speed:

a gray panel van and a blue Dodge Charger. They blew through, firing automatic weapons out the side doors; they hit Jean's Interceptor. We stood our ground, but I yelled 'no shooting'; your mom may have been inside. None of us were hit. We took off after them. It was here, just after that blind curve, they slammed on their brakes and blocked the road; three got out and started shooting like it was Main Street in Fallujah. Jean and Meck were hit and stopped where the Interceptor sits; I passed them and headed straight at the shooters. Then my truck exploded; steam and glass flew into the cab and blinded me. I caught the road's soft shoulder and flipped. God damn them. I ended up here. What happened after that is all a blur. Blood was in my eyes; I was blind and on my side; it felt like my shoulder was dislocated. I managed to get out somehow and climb to the road. Jean and Meck were on the pavement. Both took rounds in the legs. I called it in."

Jordan stood, looked at the scene, and reimagined what Bob had just described. Her people were lucky, damn lucky. The pavement a hundred feet ahead was littered with brass cartridges.

"They took off?"

"Yes, north. When I reached the road, they were gone. Shit, they could have just shot us all. I put a tourniquet on Jean's leg. Meck was nicked but bleeding. They were both fucking lucky. It took ten minutes for the ambulance to get here."

Nearby, three civilian vehicles had pulled to the side of the road. This time of year, even in the early morning, Highway 89 saw a lot of traffic. It was a decent north–south road, extending from Helena and Great Falls, 120 miles to the north, to Livingston and

Yellowstone Park, 120 miles to the south. Canada was another 120 miles beyond Great Falls.

"Do you need help, Sheriff?" a voice yelled. Two civilians stood on the highway. Maggie looked toward the voice; she barked.

"Can you help control the traffic?" she yelled. "We are okay, banged up, but good. I will be right there."

"What do you need, Bob?" she asked, gently touching his shoulder.

"Help me up. I'm good but need a few minutes. The scene is all messed up; at least two RVs have passed through, and the assholes didn't even stop. They scattered the casings."

Jordan turned to the approaching traffic, which was backing up. The two cowboys directed the traffic, parking their pickups on the opposite side of the road. They managed the flow as the vehicles slowly passed the scene.

"Thanks, fellas. I'm Sheriff Tynes."

"There're bullet casings all over the road. Jesus Christ. Ain't seen anything like this since Iraq; what the hell happened?" one of the men asked as he waved an RV past.

"We were trying to stop some drug dealers," Jordan said. "That's all I can say."

"They had serious firepower, I can see that. I saw the ambulance turn onto I-90; they your people?" the other man asked.

"Yes, they wounded two of my deputies."

"They okay?" The man pointed to Claymore and Cardona.

"Are you good, Bob?" she asked.

"I'm good, and yes, it was like Iraq," Claymore said,

coming up to Jordan. "You have a camera?"

"Yes, it's in the back." She clicked her key fob, and the back door of her Jeep popped open.

"I'll shoot the scene and get as much as possible before the traffic messes it all up," Bob said. "It's almost impossible to shut this road down. There's no alternative for fifty miles."

"I called the Highway Patrol," Jordan said. "They will start roadblocks further north, but they are stretched thin—and there is a lot of country between here and Great Falls."

"Canada is two hundred and fifty miles away," Mike said. "There is a hell of a lot of Montana between there and here."

"How is your father?" Bob asked.

Jordan told him what she could, but the chaos of the past twelve hours was catching up to her.

"Jordan, I want you in your Jeep," Mike said. "You take a few minutes, try and relax. We got this."

Chapter 34

Thirty minutes after breaking through the roadblock, Suarez, his two men, and Louise Tynes were thirty-five miles away on Highway 86, heading back toward the house in Bozeman. It was imperative to hide the vehicles and lie low for a few days. In less than an hour, the Highway Patrol would have roadblocks on every major highway for a hundred miles in every direction of the ambushed roadblock—he had to dump the van. At the Brackett Creek Trailhead parking lot, they moved the guns to the Dodge and abandoned the gray van. Other trucks and horse trailers were in the gravel lot; he parked the van behind the largest rig, hiding it from the highway. Luckily, no hikers or horsemen were in the lot to see them move Louise to the Charger. Five minutes later, they were heading into Bozeman.

Beccara drove, Sergio Molina sat in the front passenger seat, and Suarez in the back seat with Louise. He was on the phone speaking Spanish. The smells of sweat and two days on the run filled the Dodge.

"We will be there in twenty minutes; make sure the garage door is open . . . *Si, si, muchos problemas*—the whole fucking state of Montana is looking for us." He clicked off the phone.

"That guy is an idiot. Why do you work with him?" Beccara said.

"We need him, at least for now. He is our eyes and ears," Suarez said.

"So he says. He worked for the Chinese—I don't trust him."

"You don't trust anyone."

"That's why I am still alive, *jefe*."

Louise Tynes said nothing; she told Suarez she wouldn't scream if they didn't gag her. Her hands were secured with a zip tie. She didn't speak Spanish and did not understand what the men were saying.

Beccara carefully drove through Bozeman to a house on the southwest side.

"Boss, isn't this near where we shot up the Chinks a few weeks back?" Molina said.

"Yes, that way, about two miles." Suarez pointed out the side window. "They never knew we had a house so close."

They drove down a gravel road to a low ranch house buried in a grove of old trees. A detached garage with an open garage door sat to one side. In front of the house sat a white Ford Explorer. Suarez, Louise, and Molina exited the vehicle and headed to the house. Beccara pulled the Dodge into the garage next to a black Ford Expedition. Another of Suarez's men stood on the house's porch, carrying an AK-47. Standing next to the Explorer was DEA Special Agent Will Brewster.

"Nice ride, fits you—so suburban. Screams federal officer," Suarez said as he confronted Brewster.

"You really fucked this up, amigo," Brewster answered.

Suarez swung up a chrome revolver and put it in the face of the agent. "Don't ever talk to me like that, ever. *Entender . . . amigo?* Inside."

In the doorway to the house stood Trina Duarte. She had arrived with the others after the Chinese shoot-out. She held Louise Tynes by the arm and a black pistol close to her long right leg. She wore a denim shirt, blue jeans, sunglasses, and western boots and was accessorized with silver earrings and a silver belt buckle.

Brewster preceded them. Suarez kissed the woman on her cheek as he passed her. Two more of his men were in the living room, and another woman was handing out beers.

"Who the hell is she?" Brewster said, pointing to Louise.

"Insurance. The mother of the sheriff. She will help us get out of Montana," Suarez said.

"You took her? The mother of the sheriff? Goddamn. Insurance? What kind of insurance can that old woman provide?"

"I'm not old, sir, just experienced," Louise said, her face turned to Suarez.

Everyone looked at her; she hadn't said a word for hours. "My daughter will find me and kill all of you for shooting my husband—her father. I hope I am alive when she does it." A chill passed over the room.

Suarez stared at Louise and smiled. He turned to Brewster and his people.

"*Amigos, relájense. Tengo que hablar con un pedazo de mierda.*" Suarez pointed to the door that led to the backyard. "Mr. DEA, outside."

"I speak Spanish, you asshole—I'm a piece of shit?" Brewster said. "Show more respect."

"Yes, Mr. DEA man, you are a piece of shit. When I cut you to pieces, I will do it a little faster—out of respect."

Suarez removed a cigar from his coat pocket and lit it. He didn't offer Brewster one.

"They are locking down the state; you trust your people?" Brewster said.

"Yes, I trust them. They are family; that bond is stronger than a government paycheck or a bribe, amigo."

"The information was good, wasn't it?" Brewster said. "Everything I told you about the Chinese was right, their numbers, the guns. They were shocked, right? It was me who set them up. However, you left one of them alive. He's talking."

"I know about you, Brewster. I know you have been talking to the Chinese—my boss told me. We have people in Hong Kong. You put me in an impossible situation. I lost four people when you told me they wanted to make a deal; two were cousins of my boss, and one was Trina's sister. My boss does not accept mistakes."

"I wasn't working with them."

"Don't lie to me—of course you were. One of the Chinese is alive? I would think you would be the one who has a problem. He'll sell you out for an eggroll."

"His word against mine," Brewster said.

"Si, maybe for now." Suarez took a long drag on

his cigar and blew the smoke in the agent's direction. Brewster waved off the cloud.

"And the field is now clear, right? You own the market," Brewster said. "No competition. I helped with that; that was what we talked about. That was the deal, and it's all yours."

"In this business, the field, as you call it, is never clear. Someone always wants a piece, and the Chinese are not going away. This is a setback for them. What do you know about Chicago and New York?"

"New York is sending in a truckload of product. They have a distributor here, a new guy from Missoula. He wants a piece of the tourist and university trade."

"Nature hates a vacuum."

"What?"

"Nothing." Suarez walked away and studied the Gallatin Mountains to the south. Trina walked out of the house and handed him a beer. She glared at Brewster; she didn't offer the agent one. "I do not trust anyone, amigo, understand? I especially don't trust those who will turn on their own to make a dollar, particularly one to whom I have paid ten million dollars."

"All my information was good and has been these last two years. You are here because of me and the interference and information I have provided."

"Money is the root of all evil."

"What are we doing here, Diego? Having a pithy aphorism contest?"

"The enemy of my enemy is my friend? Not today."

"Fuck you. You needed the information. I got inside their camp and gave them to you on a platter. If my boss found out, I'd spend the rest of my life in prison."

"Be very careful, Mr. DEA. Your life in prison won't last that long. It is best that you do not get discovered. I need the name of this new guy, as you put it. Where is he? And I want to know if his loyalties can be changed."

"His name is Frank Lee Matthews, and he goes by Frankie. He's in it for the money; I've never met the guy, but the word is out. He's picked up a few Chinese dealers; yours are next. Or at least those that aren't scared to death of you. I'll try and find him."

"Don't just try; do."

"Jesus, a fucking Yoda philosopher. I'll get you the location. He's somewhere in Paradise Valley."

"How appropriate, and one more thing: I do not like double agents or even triple agents. If this even smells like a setup, I will find you and kill you; then I will find your family and kill them. Do you understand?"

"Yeah, I get it. An eye for an eye, tooth for a tooth."

Trina moved up from behind Brewster and, with a swift, experienced move, cut the Special Agent's throat from ear to ear, nearly severing his head. Wide-eyed, he stared at Suarez for a moment, then dropped to the ground, his head at an obscene angle. Suarez looked back at the house and, through the window, saw Louise Tynes staring at him.

* * *

Jordan was beside herself; almost twenty-four hours had passed since the kidnapping and ten hours since the roadblock shoot-out. Suarez told her to point her troops away from where he would be—now he could be anywhere. Mike understood, but that hardly helped.

It was her decision, and it would be her orders that might get somebody injured or killed.

"There's a phone call for you," Candy said. "No name, a woman's voice."

"Take the name, get the information, and I'll call back."

"She said she is calling for Diego."

She looked at the phone's blinking light, her hand hovering over the receiver. "Sheriff Tynes here."

"One moment for Diego," the voice said.

"Good afternoon, Sheriff. I need your help to clear up a problem I have. There's a dealer in Paradise Valley I want to be arrested and removed. Your actions will go a long way in helping your mother. How is your father? I'm sorry about the shooting—it was your dog's fault."

"You son of a bitch. I want to talk to my mother. I want to know if she is okay."

"Take my word for it, she is fine."

"Your word. I'd believe the devil first."

A muffled voice came to the phone. "Honey, it's me. I'm fine. How is Victor?"

"Dad is in serious condition and has lost a lot of blood. They are keeping him in a coma for now, hoping to stabilize him."

"That's good; at least you know where he is with his tag. They murdered him, a man he called Mr. DEA. I wish I could help . . ."

"That's enough," Suarez said. "See, Sheriff, she is okay. I keep my promises."

"Who was she talking about? Who was murdered?"

"I cleared up a problem for you, one less federal agent. So, here are your orders. We are going north, and I want you to send your people south. Simple."

Jordan paused, thinking about what Louise said. "When? I need to know when."

"Soon. You will get a text message. What is your phone number?"

"You busted my phone; I haven't had time to get a replacement."

"Get one; I will send you the information. Your mother has the number, right, Señora Tynes? I will text you." Suarez hung up.

She had forgotten about her phone; it was in pieces in evidence bags—both hers and her mother's. All communications were with department phones and radios. The clock read 4:15.

"Candy, what time does the phone store on Park close?"

"I'll check," Candy replied.

A minute later, Candy stood at the door. "Five o'clock. I told them it was you and you needed a replacement for a broken phone. They started telling me about all the deals. I told them you would be there in five minutes, so scoot."

She left Maggie in the Jeep and walked into the phone store. A young man held up an Apple phone and said, "Hi, Sheriff. This is the latest. I can offer you a special deal and even throw in an Apple watch."

She looked at his team name badge. "Gary, here is what I need from you. This is a matter of life and death. I need that iPhone in your hand synced with my phone number and account. I need that done now. We can talk about deals and watches some other time. Can you do that for me, Gary?"

"My boss—"

"Your boss will be thrilled to know that you helped the sheriff. So, please, Gary, make it happen now."

Fifteen minutes later, Jordan sat in the Jeep's front seat, scrolling through text messages; none were from Suarez. She knew one would come, but the wait was unbearable. Then a note popped on the screen: *Victor's Tag* and a map of Bozeman. She flashed on her mother's cryptic non sequitur on the phone call: "At least you know where he is with his tag." She remembered unclipping the tag with its key chain holder from his suspenders and setting it on the table. Then, after the shooting, her mother was on the floor next to her husband. He was in a hospital bed in Livingston, not Bozeman. She called Candy, Mike Cardona, and the Gallatin County sheriff.

Chapter 35

After the calls to the Gallatin sheriff and Mike Cardona, Jordan called Wells Courtwright. "We need to shut it down, Wells. Suarez knows about you; he murdered DEA Special Agent Brewster. Brewster told them everything and gave you up. You need to get out."

"And leave this palace I've created?"

"Yes. I need you here. I know where my mother is."

"Thirty minutes."

She was short-staffed. She should have called in Courtwright immediately after the shootings at the roadblock; that was moot now. Two of her people were in the hospital, both okay, but Jean Smith needed to stay at least a week before her release. Bob Claymore was banged up. She looked up. Bob was at his desk—she'd told him to go home. He said he would stay in the office and sleep on the couch. Deputy Candy Middleton was being Candy; she would leave when this was over. The rest of her staff and deputies were on the road.

Her call to the Gallatin sheriff, Cliff Rodgers, was to ask him to check out the location of Victor's Apple Air Tag. Its location was a house in the county on the southwest side of Bozeman. She told him why and that it was connected to the massacre of the Chinese drug dealers three weeks earlier and to the shoot-out in Livingston the previous Monday.

"What the hell is going on, Jordan?" he said. "This is it, right? The war? Are we in the middle of a drug war?"

"Yes, Cliff, over drugs and money. When they kidnapped my mother, she took my dad's Air Tag. I pray she and the disk are together. And they may have killed DEA Special Agent Will Brewster."

"Damn. I saw Brewster a few days ago. He asked about the Chinese and the Mexicans—wanted addresses, anything I had. Was he fishing?"

"It is possible."

"Shit," Rodgers said. "I will get my team together, full SWAT—I want no mistakes or injuries. These assholes have proved that they will shoot first. I need two hours, then we will find your mother. Are you coming over?"

"I'll be there. Are you calling in the feds?"

"That's your call, Jordan. I'll chase down a warrant and get my people together. Be careful. If Brewster is dead, the DEA will be a mess, and the FBI will take over."

"I understand, and you be careful."

An hour later, Mike Cardona joined Jordan for the thirty-minute ride to Bozeman. A quarter moon and a million stars hung above the Gallatin Mountains as they crossed over the pass and dropped down into Bozeman. She was surprised when they arrived at the sheriff's office; one vehicle was in front of the building. A young deputy stood next to the cruiser.

"Sheriff Tynes, Deputy Madigan. Sheriff Rodgers has taken his team to the location you sent him, and he wants you to meet him there."

"Why didn't he call?" Jordan said.

"I don't know, Sheriff. They left forty-five minutes ago. I will lead you there."

Jordan looked at Mike and raised both hands in frustration. They followed the deputy through Bozeman, past the university, and along a gravel road for two miles. At the Air Tag location, they found fire trucks and a half dozen city police and sheriff vehicles. The coroner's van sat in the middle of the flashing lights.

Sheriff Rodgers was with a group in SWAT gear; everyone appeared relaxed. Jordan and Mike walked over to the sheriff.

"It was a bust, Jordan. No one here," Sheriff Rodgers said. "We got calls about a house fire here at the location; that's why the jump start. The house was burning. We found one deceased Latino lying on a bed in rigor in one of the bedrooms. He was dead at least twenty-four hours from a gunshot wound. There was a gray van and a dark blue Dodge in the garage. When we opened the garage door, an incendiary device exploded. The vehicles are a loss."

"You could have waited, Sheriff," Cardona said, getting into the face of Rodgers.

"I knew the importance, the kidnapping, the shootings, and the murder. I got the warrant, then the fire—I moved. What's your problem, Cardona?"

"Did you find the tag?" Jordan asked.

The sheriff held up a plastic bag. Inside was a silver dollar–sized disk, and a piece of paper was in another bag.

"Your Air Tag, etched with the name Victor Tynes and a phone number. The note is addressed to you."

She washed her flashlight over the note.

Sheriff,

Your mother is smart and resourceful, so much so it nearly killed her. I changed my mind about the direction. You guess where we will be going.

El Martillo

"Where was this found?" Jordan asked.

"He placed it and the note on the dining room table where no one could miss it," Rodgers said. "Do you know where he is going?"

"No. The man likes to poke bears. I am very tired of him."

A deputy approached. "Sir, we have another body in the back."

With flashlights, they followed the deputy behind one of the metal outbuildings. There, half under a plastic drop cloth, lay a body. The smell of vomit hung in the still air.

"Who got sick?" Sheriff Rodgers said. "You didn't contaminate the site?"

"No, sir," came a quick response from someone in the dark. "Sorry, sir."

Mike Cardona washed his flashlight over the body. The pale and ghastly face of Special Agent Will Brewster lay twisted to one side, blood and gore covering his upper body. His eyes were wide open. Jordan believed she saw surprise. The deputy turned, wretched, and walked away.

"That looks like DEA Special Agent Brewster?" Sheriff Rodgers asked.

"Yes, that's him," Mike said. "Shitty way to die."

"Can't think of many good ones, Agent Cardona," Rodgers said. "What the hell was he doing here?"

"That is under investigation, Sheriff. He was part of the task force hunting these people."

"The FBI will be involved," Rodgers added.

"They already are. They will be here in the morning; sorry to add to your problems," Jordan said.

"The body count is bad," Rodgers said.

"More than twenty," Jordan said. Her phone pinged another text.

Send your people south to Yellowstone Park. I assume you are in Bozeman. Brewster was a shit. Be respectful of Luis Fuentes; he was a friend, and the Chinks killed him. Your mother is safe for now.

She showed the text to Mike.

"The balls on that guy. So, he's going north?"

"Looks that way."

"Who is going north? Was that Suarez? Is he sending you text messages?" Sheriff Rodgers said.

Jordan looked at Mike.

"A text from her office in Livingston," Mike said. "We need to get back. Sorry about the FBI."

"It is what it is, Cardona. Find this son of a bitch."

"Copy that."

* * *

When Jordan and Mike returned to the office, exhausted, Maggie greeted her. She had stayed with Candy in the office during the sheriff's trip to Bozeman. Mike got some sleep in his truck; Jordan crashed on the couch in her office. At dawn, she was in the hospital visiting her father, Corporal Dan Mecklenburg, Deputy Jean Smith, and John Wang. Her father was still in an induced coma but stable. He'd had a peaceful night, and there was no change.

Meck was watching the morning news. The house fire, the death of the federal agent, and the discovery of a second body were the top stories. A reporter with a microphone in the face of Sheriff Rodgers asked him if this was linked to the shootings over the last few weeks. Was it safe for residents? Was this about drugs? Who were the dead?

"You there last night?" Meck asked, putting the TV on mute.

"Yes, awful," Jordan said. "We found it using one of those Apple Air Tags. My mother had it; it was my dad's. They escaped."

"I saw that reporter Kyle Reeder. He was on screen for a second. Did you talk to him?"

"Fortunately, no. We left soon after we arrived. Too much here going on. Gallatin had it handled, and the FBI was on its way."

"Suarez can't be that good. He will make a mistake. Have you seen Jean?" Meck asked.

"I'm headed that way. Do you need anything?"

"Freedom—the doc says I can leave here this afternoon. The wounds were to my calves. Lucky, nothing was broken. Jerry is picking me up."

"How's she handling this?"

"When we married, she knew I wanted to be a cop—nothing has changed. I know she's having a tough time. We will get through it, boss. The kids are home for the summer—there's a lot to keep them busy."

"You take the time to heal. Be with your family," Jordan ordered.

In the next room, Jean Smith was asleep. Her wounds were worse than Mecklenburg's. Two bullets that ricocheted off the pavement shattered and severely damaged her left quadricep and another piece was lodged in her abdomen. Healing would take time, and they wanted to be sure about ancillary damages, especially to her uterus and bladder.

Jordan was drinking bad hospital coffee in the empty waiting room when Mike handed her a cup of coffee from Dotties.

"They okay?" he asked.

"All good, all lucky—including dad. Jean got the worst of it, but she is fortunate. It's Mom I can't shake. I'm powerless. She needs to be here, and Dad needs her. I need her."

"She'll be okay; I know it," Mike said.

"I know. I believe it, but that man is a monster. They are all monsters. I don't understand them. I understand the money, the greed, but their absolute lack of humanity and the brutality—all for what?"

"They can't go far. All the roads are either watched or blocked. The burned vehicles were what we had been looking for. The van was gray, like the one they used when they took Louise. It is registered with a Mexican restaurant in Billings. They didn't know anything about it, and they had never seen it at the business. We are chasing down the possibility that the restaurant is a front. The Dodge was stolen in Rapid City, and the plates were changed to stolen Montana plates. The FBI is working with Rodgers to determine how they escaped the house."

"They found the Air Tag, then took off." Jordan sipped her coffee, then asked, "What was Brewster driving? Did he have a DEA pool vehicle, or was it his?"

"Give me a minute."

Jordan stood in her father's room's doorway, watching the greatest person she'd ever known lie there with tubes and wires everywhere. Their lives together flashed by: Her helping him paint her room, her learning to drive, the night they sat down and talked about the Army, and then a few years later, joining the sheriff's office. Family camping trips, Disneyland, seeing the ocean, waiting all night for him to come home during snowstorms, her first prom, his love for his family. How would she cope if he died?

"Brewster drove a 2022 white Ford Explorer, a DEA vehicle, with no exterior ID and white government plates. I put out an APB."

"Does it have a LoJack or other location device?" Jordan asked.

"They are called telematics devices and mandated on all government vehicles. I'll start the process. The problem is authorization. With Brewster's murder, there is a temporary issue with hierarchy and chain of command. Helena is working on it."

"They likely changed out the plates. I'll check with the Gallatin sheriff to see if either of the burnout cars is missing plates. At least a place to start."

John Wang, his left wrist handcuffed to the bed's railing, gave Jordan and Mike a Cheshire cat–like grin.

A federal marshal sat on a folding chair outside the door.

"Good morning, Sheriff. He's eating breakfast," the marshal said.

"Thanks, Tim," Jordan said. "I need a few minutes."

"No problem."

Jordan and Mike walked into the room.

"Big-time fuckup last night. You just missed the asshole." He pointed to the muted TV. "And this food is crap."

"Get used to it, Wang," Mike said. "It is worse in prison, fried rice on Fridays only."

"They killed DEA Special Agent Brewster," Jordan said. "Was he working with you?"

Wang twisted his mouth and repressed a smile. "That man had no honor. I paid him a lot of money, and he set us up. He's responsible for the meeting at the restaurant. He assured me that this was all legit. I lost friends because of his shit. I'm not surprised that he is dead—you fuck with the devil, and the devil will get his due."

"Where is Suarez?"

"I wish I knew; I'd give him to you on a plate. We didn't know about that cartel house in Bozeman, and it was just a couple of miles away from the one they burned. He knew about us; Brewster told him. I would kill him again if I could."

"He kidnapped my mother," Jordan said. "Anything to help would be a plus in your column."

There was a pause as Wang closed his eyes and considered her words. "Before we were to meet Suarez, I got a call from my boss. Culiacan told him that

Suarez went off-script. Suarez was sent to do a job: remove people who wanted to go their own way—make an example of them."

"The Indians? Is that who you are talking about?"

"Yes, the Indians. Killing my people has upset his boss in Mexico; he went beyond his orders. One of the murdered men at the Bozeman house was a cousin of my boss. We have arrangements with the cartels over materials, technologies, and financials. His excesses have destroyed those arrangements. Order must be restored."

"All nice and businesslike—considering the deaths involved," Mike said.

"If that were a legitimate measure of business, cars would be outlawed due to the million deaths worldwide and tens of millions of injuries. Too much money, too many jobs, and political interference confuses everything. Free will—people will do what they enjoy."

"You get them addicted, families are ruined. Maybe you should get lobbyists in Washington."

"And there is the liquor business, marketing liquor on TV programs, and now the sports leagues are involved in gambling. And lobbyists? How are we any worse?"

Jordan looked at the man. "This conversation on ethics is for some other time. Why do we care if Suarez's boss in Mexico is upset?"

"Because with one phone call, I can find out where Suarez is, and you can eliminate him. If I do that, I want immunity, a plane ticket, and my friends' bodies returned to China. I will miss Seattle, but Hong Kong is nice."

Chapter 36

Diego Suarez, Jose Beccara, Sergio Molina, and Trina Duarte sat in the cold living room of the trailer along the Boulder River. He sent the others to Billings; he wished them well. Louise Tynes, hands bound with zip ties, sat on an uncomfortable chair in the small dining room off the small kitchen. Suarez and Jose sat in the cramped living room while Trina opened cans of food.

Five hours earlier, in Bozeman, after the short phone conversation with Sheriff Tynes, Suarez had Trina thoroughly searched the hostage; she found a silver dollar–sized metal disk in the woman's jeans pocket but had no idea what it was. Louise said it was a good luck token. Trina showed it to Diego and Jose, and all Suarez could say was, "Fuck."

"We leave in five minutes," Suarez said. "Burn the cars. I want no evidence left. Burn the house."

"What is that thing?" Trina asked.

"A locator device that uses an app for Apple phones. When the sheriff checks the application, they know where we are—we leave right now—go, go."

"We take her?" Beccara said.

"Yes. Load her in the agent's SUV. We are heading east. I need to make one call." He looked at the last two survivors of the Culiacan Cartel in Montana. "Go. I will be right there."

The satellite call was to Culiacan. He waited for five minutes while they found his boss.

"Where are you?" The question was sharp.

"The Bozeman safe house; it's been compromised. We are leaving."

"You fucked up again, Diego. You are a liability."

"We need to get out. I want a plane—there's a small airstrip near a town called Ringling. There's a church across the street. The airstrip is next to it; it's grass. I checked it out a few weeks back. They can fly in from Canada, just over two hours away. It's on the maps, near Ringling on Highway 89."

"And the kidnapped woman? What are you going to do with her?"

"How do you know about the woman?"

"You have your sources, and I have mine. Kill her. I will call you back."

Suarez climbed into the front seat of the Explorer, and Beccara drove east. Louise was in the back seat next to Trina and Molina. He looked at the woman.

"Who are you staring at, psycho?" she said with a smile.

"Where to, *jefe*?" Beccara said.

"Back to the safehouse east of Livingston along the river. Then, tomorrow morning, we fly home."

An hour later, after they arrived at the house, Trina made a simple dinner from cans of Mexican foods that

Suarez had his people stock months earlier. No one complained.

Louise refused to eat. "Let me go, cut the ties, and just open the door. By the time I'm found, you will be miles away. One less problem."

"I could shoot you, and then there would be one less problem," Suarez said.

"You could have done that hours ago, and I'm still alive. You need me—why, I don't know. My daughter should have left you on the top of that mountain, but she couldn't. Morality is tough; the eternal question of what is right over what is wrong. I'm sure, as a psychopath, you don't understand."

"Challenging me? Is this a game? Psycho, psychopath? Certainly not a way to make me let you go."

"Maybe this is a reason. I worked in the county clerk's office for years, and my husband worked for the state highway department."

"I hope this isn't a long story," Suarez said.

"My husband had a second stroke, and then you had that man shoot him." She pointed to Molina. "For all I know, he is dead, and I have every right for vengeance." She paused and glared at Suarez. "Park County staff is small; we talk among ourselves. Victor said the new trucks and vehicles come with a GPS location device. I assume that the feds are ahead of us in outfitting their cars. That SUV is the murdered man's, right? It is a good bet it has GPS. I would say you have hours until you are caught. They could drop a bomb on us. Let me go, and I'll put in a good word."

"Let me shut her up," Trina said, setting a knife on the table beside her chair.

"Is she right, *jefe*?" Beccara said. "Is there a device

on that *vagón?*"

"Check it out. Look in the engine near the battery, glove box, under the seats."

Molina left. Trina sat quietly, studying Louise, spider to a butterfly. Early morning light began filling the windows.

Five minutes later, Molina returned, a small plastic box in his hand and wires hanging loose from one end.

"They know where we are. What are you going to do?"

* * *

Mike placed his laptop on Jordan's desk. "The application that monitors the GPS location device on Brewster's Explorer places the device here." He pointed to a map on the screen. "This is the path the device took over the last five days. We could backtrack further. Why Brewster didn't disable the thing, I don't know."

"Maybe he didn't know about it?" Jordan said. "Or if he did, suspicion would begin if it were disabled."

"Maybe. We may never know," Mike said. "Right now, that is where the SUV is, and we can assume that is where Suarez is. It is out in the middle of nowhere. It has been sitting there for six hours, just before we hit the Bozeman house." The signal was a flashing dot on the screen, then the dot disappeared.

"What happened?" Jordan asked.

"I'm guessing the device was just discovered. We need people there right now. They will be leaving."

"That location is over the county line with Sweet Grass. It will take twice as long for their people to get there. I will call the sheriff and let him know what is happening. It is about twenty miles from here, where Swingley Road and Boulder Road intersect. I'll call the

Highway Patrol to see what they can do. If we cut him off here and here"—she pointed to the county map on the wall behind her desk—"we can stop him." Jordan walked to the door. "Candy, who is on the board this morning?"

"You, Courtwright, Claymore, and Dolan."

"Wells is here?"

"He came in early and said something about his entrepreneurial days being over. No clue what that meant."

"Get them in here," she said. "I also want the Sweet Grass County sheriff and the district head of the Highway Patrol in Belgrade. I can't remember his name."

"Rick Seldon."

"Right. Call him, please."

As the deputy sheriffs arrived and sat in her office, she talked to the Sweet Grass sheriff. He had two people on the road; they were at the county's north end, more than an hour away from the GPS location. He had one vehicle he could spare; she asked him to set up a roadblock on Main Boulder Road near the Big Timber airport. She told him about the white Ford Explorer and the possibility of a hostage. He said he was sorry he couldn't provide more. Belgrade Highway Patrol was pulling a team together, but Jordan could tell that after three weeks of this cat-and-mouse circus with the drug cartels, assistance was wearing thin. "Sheriff, it is the peak of our season. I don't have to tell you that. We have allocated resources, but we keep bumping into the feds. I'll do what I can, but from what you said, I think they are gone."

"Thanks, Rick. Deputy Claymore will contact your

people and let them know what's happening."

She looked at her staff; after five years, they were her deputies and friends. She pointed again to the map. "Wells, riding single, will come in from the west on Swingley. Mike and I will follow you in my Jeep. Bob, you and John will come in from the north from the interstate and be ready to block the road."

Candy would monitor cell phones, and due to cell problems in the canyons, she would radio information if needed. They mounted up. Maggie climbed into the back seat of the Jeep, and Mike took the front passenger seat.

* * *

They were headed north five minutes after Molina walked into the house carrying the disconnected GPS device. Beccara drove, and Suarez, carrying an AK-47 in the front passenger seat, concentrated on the road ahead. Molina, Trina, and Louise Tynes sat in the back seat. Trina also cradled an AK-47. They passed one vehicle as they drove north fifteen miles on Main Boulder Road to the interstate.

Suarez knew their world had shrunk to nothing more than this SUV and time. Would the next curve bring them to a stop and a roadblock? Would they make the interstate? Then what? Head east or west? They were as exposed as crows on a wire. He was never asked if Montana was a good market; he was never included in those cartel conversations. Looking around this countryside, there were few people, not enough to spend the capital to develop the market. He liked the big cities; a vehicle like this would disappear in the traffic. Right now, the Explorer screamed: *look at me*.

They were all tired. They had been up for almost

three days straight. The short nap at the safe house barely took the edge off.

"Jose, when we reach the interstate, go west. Then, at the first exit, get off and head north to the river. We can hide in the trees. We need sleep. I will contact Culiacan and set up the time for the plane."

"You are sure, *jefe*? We can be in Billings in less than an hour and a half," Beccara said.

"We are too exposed; they will have aircraft up. We must hide, and then we will head north tonight. The plane will pick us up in the morning."

There were no roadblocks. When they reached the interstate, they headed west. At the next exit, Beccara pulled off the highway and drove on gravel roads to the Yellowstone River. It was obvious where the flooding, from just ten days earlier, had washed through the basin. Temporary ponds of water still filled the low areas along the channel. There were no trucks or trailers for fishermen and driftboats; the river was still too muddy to fish. Beccara found a parking spot under a thick grove of cottonwoods. Trina passed around energy bars and bottles of water. During the whole time, Louise Tynes said nothing.

Louise bided her time; adrenaline pumped through her. Trina's eyes glared at her for a while, and then, like the two in the front seat, she fell asleep. Louise tried to pull the wrist tie apart, but it was too strong. Through the trees, she saw a driftboat working down the river; three people were in the boat. She took the chance, pulled hard on the door handle, twisted herself out, and fell to the gravel. Then, standing, she ran toward the river, expecting any moment to feel the impact of a bullet. She pushed through the brush, reached the riverbank, and fell three feet down to the river. She yelled at the boat; then the water was to her knees; she kept yelling and fell face down into the current. The water was cold. She twisted and rolled onto her back. Spitting out water, she yelled again for help and hoped the men in the boat heard her.

Confused, Suarez pushed open his door, pulled out the rifle, and tried to regain his senses. Trina was beside him. Her rifle was up, and she aimed it at the woman standing in the thicket of shrubbery along the riverbank. The woman then disappeared.

"Stop, she's gone," Suarez said. "We need to leave. There is no time to find her."

In the morning light, Beccara drove out from under the trees, and they continued west. At the Highway 89 exit, they headed north, thus completing a murderous circle that had started two days earlier when they blew through the roadblock. Six miles north of the Park County line, a half hour later, they turned right onto a gravel road. A single building stood on a hill overlooking the wide valley; the sign read ST. JOHN'S CATHOLIC CHURCH. To the east rose the Crazy Mountains, the snow on its peaks faintly visible. On the opposite side of the highway was a scattering of houses and outbuildings with lights visible through windows. A sign on Highway 89 read RINGLING. The old, weathered, and classic church design appeared abandoned.

"Where is this airport, *jefe*? I don't see anything," Molina said.

"To the right, in that flat area near the highway, Jose. The pilot will know."

"It doesn't look good; I don't know. Maybe in the morning, it will look better."

Beccara parked behind the church, hidden from the highway. Suarez was unsure if anyone had seen them park from the small community of Ringling below.

Chapter 37

Thirty minutes after the Explorer hid in the trees along the river, Deputies Claymore and Dolan unknowingly drove past the location on I-90. Twenty minutes later, the deputies reached the last location of the Explorer's GPS tracker on Main Boulder Road near the intersection of the two county roads. They arrived fifteen minutes before Jordan, Mike, and Wells. The others took the slower gravel road east through the mountains from Livingston. They crossed the one-lane bridge over the Boulder River and waited until Jordan and her team arrived. The broken-down trailer was hidden behind a grove of cottonwoods along the creek bank. The remains of a burnt house were off to the side of the trailer. Behind the trailer sat two metal buildings. Jordan joined Bob and John on the far side of the river; she kept Maggie in the Jeep. After cautiously reconnoitering the house and property, Jordan admitted they had missed them.

The dust on the gravel drive showed tire treads.

Wells said they were recent, just hours old. Empty cans of food, all freshly opened, were on the kitchen's countertop. A cigar was crushed in an ashtray in the kitchen, and the smell still hung in the air. Next to the ashtray lay a fist-sized plastic electronics box with wires extended from one end.

"The GPS unit," Wells said. "Two hours at most, boss. We just missed them. Do you want us to search . . ."

"For my mother, yes."

Five minutes later, John Dolan said, "You must see this, Sheriff. Behind the garage."

She saw four fresh grave sites or what she assumed were graves: four narrow piles of dirt, wildflowers laid on the surface, and simple crosses driven into the ground. Jordan nearly collapsed, not sure what she was seeing.

"Get the coroner here," Jordan said.

"They can't be far," Bob said.

"Two hours? They could be halfway to Wyoming or North Dakota."

Jordan stared at the graves, scared of what she didn't want to think about. Her phone began to buzz.

"Tynes here," she said.

"Honey, is that you?" The woman's voice was strong and reassuring.

"Mom, is this you? Are you okay?"

"I'm cold and wet, but I'm fine. I'm with some fishermen—they pulled me from the river. I escaped. I'm okay. You need to talk with Matt; he's one of the fellows that rescued me. I'm using his phone." Then, a pause. "How is Victor? Is your father still alive?"

Thirty minutes later, as dusk settled along the Yellowstone River, Jordan and Mike parked near a boat landing. An aluminum driftboat was pulled to the gravel shore. Wrapped in a long coat, Louise walked around a campfire. Introductions were made, and thanks were offered. After hugging her daughter, Louise knelt on the gravel and cuddled Maggie.

Jordan stood with the three fishermen. "It was a slow day, Sheriff. Louise was all we caught. She is lucky we were there," Matt said with a smile.

"Thank you, thank you all," Jordan said as she hugged her mother again. "Where were you going to pull out?"

"Another landing a few miles downriver, near Big Timber. We parked the trailer there this morning. The usual leapfrog back and forth from put-in to landing."

Wells pulled into the parking lot. Introductions were made, and Jordan offered to have Wells drive one of the fishermen to his trailer so they could load up here. It would save them a few hours in the dark. They appreciated the offer.

Wells reported that the coroner was on his way to the house on Boulder River. A forensics team was being assembled to open the graves in the morning.

Jordan was relieved beyond words over the rescue of Louise. Her fear that one of the graves held her mother disappeared. They headed straight to the hospital. Jordan called Candy and asked her to stop by the Tyneses' house, tell her sister what happened, and have LeeAnn help her pick up a few things for Louise to change from her damp clothes. In the chaos, Jordan didn't ask questions about Suarez or what happened; she let her mother rest. Maggie lay on the back seat, her head in Louise's lap.

"Victor is okay, alive?" Louise asked. It was almost a whisper.

"He is in a coma, Mom. He lost a lot of blood, and the transfusions have taken their toll. According to Dr. Larkin, they wanted him to be calm and quiet; this is the best thing. But it is not good."

"Doc Larkin knows what to do." She looked out the window; night had fallen, and it was black with occasional headlights flashing by. "I know where they are going, or at least a good idea," Louise said.

"Suarez and his people?" Mike turned in his seat. "Did you overhear them?"

"They thought I was asleep. They spoke Spanish. I caught words: *Aeroplano, Canada, manana, iglesia, Ringling.*"

"Ringling, on Highway 89," Jordan said.

"*Iglesia* is 'church,'" Mike said. "Is there a church in Ringling?"

"St. Johns—it's a landmark on Highway 89," Jordan said. "And there's an old airport there from the railroad days."

"There are four of them. Suarez, the man who shot Dad, another man, and a woman. She's the one who murdered the DEA agent. She cut his throat; it was awful. They are in a white SUV, maybe a Ford. They have rifles and pistols."

Mike made a couple of calls and passed on the information.

At the hospital, LeeAnn was waiting in Victor's room. She was in tears when she embraced her mother. She had driven down from Helena the day after the kidnapping and was staying at the house. Her husband, Tim, remained in Helena and cared for their twin girls.

She helped Candy select clothes for Louise. An hour later, after a cursory check of her vitals and placing a bandage on the cut on her cheek from the rifle butt, Louise fell asleep in the chair next to her husband.

* * *

It was 3:00 a.m. Jordan was in her office, and Mike Cardona sat on the couch watching—this was not his show. Maggie lay on her bed. Jordan was short two deputies, Danny Mecklenburg and Jean Smith. Jordan talked to Jean for a few minutes in the hospital before she headed to the office. She called in Wells, Bob Claymore, John Dolan, and rookies Sandy Bullock and Terry Morgan. Deputy Candy Middleton leaned against the doorway in case there were phone calls.

The Sweet Grass sheriff and his people covered the scene at the Boulder River house. The Park County coroner's morgue was full of murdered Chinese and had no room for the four bodies they assumed were buried at the Boulder River trailer. The Sweet Grass County coroner would assume control later in the morning. The state medical examiner's hands were full; his deputies would assist Gallatin, Park, and Sweet Grass Counties sort out the deaths and notifications. Jordan knew that now that a federal agent had been murdered, the FBI would be investigating and that the prosecutions would most likely become federal. She didn't care; she wanted this son of a bitch.

Jordan did not tell her deputies where the source of the information came from. Mike knew and agreed to keep her mother out of the conversation. Jordan laid out the operation.

"We have a reliable source that places Suarez and three others at St. John's Church in Ringling. You all know it and have driven by it a hundred times. There is a plane coming in to collect them in the morning."

"They going to use that old Higgins Brothers Airport?" Bob Claymore said. "Hardly call it an airport. It's a cow pasture complete with cow shit. When the railroad ran through Ringling forty years ago, that may have been the last time a plane landed."

"We will find out in the morning. They did not get further north; the Highway Patrol blocked 89 at Highway 12 and 294. They also have 89 covered here at the south end. This is our show."

She rotated her computer so that it faced her deputies; she pointed to the screen. "The church is here, and there's an outbuilding behind it. It is isolated and away from people in Ringling. The Meagher County sheriff will handle the town and quietly notify everyone to stay inside. We will set up here to the south on this road. Sandy, you and Terry will take a position here at the airport. You will deter any landings; park one of our vehicles in the middle of whatever airstrip you find. The terrain south of the church will hide us. We will meet here." She pointed. "When I give them the signal, the Highway Patrol will collapse their roadblock two miles south and north. That will reduce civilian traffic."

"Maybe they will give up?" Dolan said.

"It's possible but not likely. They know what and who they are facing," Wells said. "In nine hours, the FBI will be all over this. We can't keep them out of the loop too long. This is our operation; our people were wounded. We need to settle this now."

Jordan looked at her people. "This is why we are here; this is our job. Gear up. We leave in twenty minutes. First light is at five, and sunrise is at ten to six."

She turned to Wells. "Do you still have that toy?"

"It is not a toy; it is a thermal imaging drone with a high-def camera," Wells said, "that I bought with my own money, boss."

"Where is it?"

"Trunk of my car. So, yes, I permit you to give it a try." He smiled. "If you break it, you will buy it. Right?"

* * *

The four vehicles headed north on Highway 89. Jordan was in the lead (Maggie stayed with Candy in the office; she was unhappy about it—Candy, not Maggie). Mike was with Jordan. Next was Wells Courtwright with the rookies Bullock and Morgan. Then Sergeant Claymore was in his Interceptor, and Corporal Dolan was in the pickup.

Wells would operate the drone and reconnoiter the areas around the church and adjacent roads from a position south of the problematic airport. According to Wells, the drone had an effective range of about two miles. Due to the terrain, they would not be visible from the church while they surveilled the location. Once they knew what the situation on the ground was, they would finalize their attack.

It was still dark when they reached Ringling. Five minutes earlier, they passed the Highway Patrol roadblock two miles south. The night was Montana clear. Stars filled the sky, and the air was still, almost expectant. Bob drove past the church and noted that there were no lights, and no white Explorer was visible from the highway. He turned around and headed back to the rally point. Everyone was geared up in ballistic vests and tactical belts. The drone was up and hovering twenty feet over the vehicles.

"Wells, take a look," Jordan said.

The laptop was on the fold-down tailgate table of her Jeep. The monitor displayed the digital image from the camera of the deputies; even in the morning darkness, the image was remarkably bright. Wells walked away from the group and flew the drone toward the church. He positioned the drone two hundred feet above the building and slowly circled it. The white Explorer sat in the back of the building, hidden from the highway. He switched to the infrared camera. Four glowing forms popped up; two were in the vehicle, and two stood outside. As the camera zoomed in, the man looked up.

"Likely, he's heard the drone," Wells said. "I sure wish we had some wind to cover the sound. You can hear a cricket from a hundred feet out here."

The man continued looking, and then what he heard dawned on him.

Jordan pulled out her phone and dialed.

It rang twice, and then Suarez answered. "*Hola*, Sheriff. I should have killed that woman; they wanted me to, but I owed you a debt—that has been paid."

"This is over, Suarez. Give up, walk down the road to the highway, hands in the air. You are surrounded. The plane will never land."

"How many of your people do you want to die today? I can guarantee that somebody will be hurt. We are all dead here; we know it. We will not be going to jail."

The image sent by the drone grew brighter as the morning began. Jordan stood and looked around. Sunlight streamed from the east. The jagged shadow of the Crazy Mountains appeared in the backlight of the sunrise. The white Explorer, caught in the sun, was almost blinding in the video feed. Three others had joined Suarez. All carried rifles; all looked up at the drone as it hovered above.

"It does not have to end this way," Jordan said.

"Of course it does. There are no options, and this is our job. You will have to come and get us."

"They have the high ground, and if they get into the church, they can use the steeple," Wells said. "I do not relish the thought of a shoot-out; we know the outcome, and we don't want to damage the church."

"Agreed," Jordan said. "They have two options: stay or try to escape."

"We can wait them out," Bob offered. "They will have to give up sooner than later."

"They are making their move," Wells said. He had returned to the group. On the screen, they watched as four people climbed back into the Explorer.

"They are making a run for it. Bob, call the Highway Patrol and let them know what's happening. John, you and Bob head north and block the road. Go now. Wells and I will come in from the south. They can't make the highway."

From above, the buzz of an airplane's motor filled the silence.

"You two go and block the runway, now. Go, go."

Jordan and Mike followed Dolan as they sped up the highway to the driveway from the church. The white Explorer appeared on the rise, heading to the highway. Above, the plane made a low pass and suddenly banked hard and away from the converging vehicles. Jordan prayed they weren't trying to make a strafing run to give Suarez cover. It banked again and then turned to the east into the rising sun. In a moment, it was gone.

All the vehicles converged on the highway. Halfway down the hill, the Explorer slid to a stop. The sheriff's vehicles blocked the exit. Sheriff Jordan Tynes and her deputies exited and took cover behind their trucks; Jordan aimed with her Winchester. The doors of the Explorer opened, and four people got out and commenced shooting. The deputies returned fire and riddled the Explorer and the people standing behind the doors; in a moment, it was over.

"Anyone hit?" Jordan yelled.

A moment passed, and "All good" was yelled back.

Bob and John remained behind, providing cover if needed. Jordan, Mike, and Wells cautiously advanced up the road to the vehicle. Steam and smoke rose from the perforated SUV; four bloody bodies lay on the ground.

Chapter 38

The aftermath of the Ringling shoot-out was complicated and inquisitorial. The Park County sheriff, along with her deputies, wrote their reports. The FBI and the DEA demanded answers and wanted to know why they were not involved in apprehending the criminals; they added, with the usual yelling and fist pounding, that it was a federal case. Jordan told them there was oversight by the ATF and Special Agent Michael Cardona. Due to the exigencies of the kidnapping, the murders, and the overall safety of the community during the pursuit of the escaped prisoner, Diego Suarez, and other artel members, haste was required.

Jordan was on the phone with her sister when the TV reporters appeared at the scene.

LeeAnn said their brother had arrived.

"It's good that Bob is there," Jordan said.

Jordan looked at the three reporters, one of whom was Kyle Reeder, and raised her index finger, telling them to give her a minute. "I will be there as soon as

I can."

"I heard you killed the son of a bitch who shot Dad and kidnapped Mom," LeeAnn said.

"He confronted us and shot first. They are all dead—hold off telling Mom for now. I will talk to her later."

"I will. You are one seriously badass sister."

She walked over to the reporters and three microphones. She thanked them for being there. She then described the pursuit across four counties, the cooperation between the sheriffs of those counties, and the final resolution of that pursuit when they fired first and the killing of the suspects.

"These were bad people," Sheriff Tynes said. "Diego Suarez was an executioner for the Culiacan Cartel in Mexico. He was directly involved in the deaths of at least twenty-one people across two states and numerous jurisdictions. These drug cartels have poisoned our youth, ravaged the reservations, and brought international terrorism to our country and the state of Montana. The federal agencies have been helpful, but it is our duty as Montana sheriffs to ensure the safety and welfare of our residents and visitors."

"I understand that your family was directly involved. Could you explain?" one of the reporters asked.

"Before I answer that, I want to acknowledge the brave men and women who serve this county and put their lives on the line. Two of my deputies, Sergeant Dennis Mecklenburg and Corporal Jean Smith, were wounded by Suarez while manning a roadblock. Thank God both are doing well. We were lucky this morning; they had high-powered automatic weapons, and none of our deputies were injured."

"We are glad to hear that, and our prayers are with them. And your family?" another asked.

"Suarez broke into my family's house, shot my dog, and wounded my father; then they kidnapped my mother—all in front of me. Until it was too late, Suarez didn't realize my mother was a tough Montana woman. A day later, she escaped. It was her statements, after being rescued by locals, that led directly to the discovery and elimination of the Suarez gang. My father is still in serious condition, my mother is with my father at the hospital, and"—she smiled—"my dog is doing well. I will have more after seeing my people and my family in the hospital."

Jordan quickly turned away and walked to her Jeep. Mike Cardona leaned against the hood.

"Thanks for not mentioning me. I'm probably in a lot of hot water. I'll find out soon enough. The inquiry into Brewster's actions and connections will involve dozens of agents and at least four agencies, including the DOJ and the FBI. I've been told that Brewster's activities go deep into the system. He took vacations during the last three years to Mexico and Hong Kong. This may be just the tip of the proverbial iceberg. A lot of people are wondering how he could hide all this. Supposedly, there are safeguards and checks to prevent this."

"Obviously, not enough. These people have more money than many of the countries they are killing with their drugs. Bribery is easy when they offer enough."

Kyle Reeder walked over to the pair. "Some morning. This has been a tough couple of weeks. I'm glad that your folks are doing okay."

"Thanks. Dad is still in a coma; I just talked with my sister. Not sure what is happening. It is day to day."

"And the agencies, there's a lot of crap going down. There is a rumor of a traitor, an agency guy," Kyle said, looking at Mike.

"Do you want the cynical answer or the optimistic answer?"

"This is all off the record. I'll ask for a formal interview later. That work for you?"

"Works fine for me," Mike said. "This is Sheriff Tynes's show. I'm here from the government to help." He smiled. "I will give my optimistic answer, Kyle. We were lucky; the sheriff mentioned that more than twenty-two are dead; if you include those four, that's twenty-six. All were involved in the drug business; all prayed on decent folks, and children were involved, so they will not be missed. Sadly, there is too much money involved. People take drugs and support these scumbags. You can't kill these drug dealers fast enough. They are terrorists, plain and simple, and should be treated as such."

"We will talk. Jordan?"

"I'm going to the hospital. I am needed there more than here. Deputies Courtwright and Claymore are handling this. The Highway Patrol is here, and it won't be long before the feds show up." She caught Bob's eye, pointed to her Jeep, and then south. He gave her a thumbs-up.

"Do you need a ride, Mike?"

"You were my date, so yeah, I need a ride."

* * *

Jordan spent an hour talking with Deputy Jean Smith bringing her up to date on Suarez and the outcome of the confrontation. Smith was pleased. "I'm glad you got the son of a bitch, he was evil. And I even happier for your mother and her escape." The nurse said that Jean could be going home in a few days. She wished she could talk to Jimmy Belvedere and tell him what had happened, but he had been transferred to the hospital in Bozeman, where he could get the neurological treatment he needed. He was doing well, but therapy would be needed.

As she walked the corridor to her father's room, it occurred to Jordan that it had been three years since the family had all been together. It was a happier time; she had just won the election as sheriff. The post-election party had hot dogs, hamburgers, beer and wine, and dozens of her supporters at the house. She discovered a few empty Jack Daniel's bottles in the trash the next day. She didn't drink, and she couldn't remember the last time she saw her parents drink. But she also knew her friends weren't teetotalers. Those were good days then; Dad was well, and her folks were planning on traveling. Even an RV was mentioned. Now, an evil cloud had settled over the family, some of it due to Suarez and some due to life's natural course. She wanted to blame it on someone; there must be a reason. And yet, sometimes, there is no one to blame.

Louise stood beside Victor; LeeAnn sat in a chair near the window, and her husband, Tim, stood behind her. Tall, now with a beard, Bob leaned against the wall, his wife, Mary, beside him. She was surprised to see Oscar, Victor's older brother, standing on the far side of the bed. She hated hospitals. She had spent too much time in them; between accidents and incidents, the hospital was a proxy for whatever was happening, good and bad, in the community: births and deaths, celebrations and pain, and healing and trauma.

"He's awake," Louise said when Jordan entered. "He has been drifting in and out."

The incessant beeping of the monitors was the most annoying of the dozens of noises a hospital generates. This was a heartbeat, plain and simple. *Thump*, *beep*, *thump*, *beep*—it continued until it didn't.

Dr. Larkin came to the door and tilted his head to the corridor. Jordan followed.

"I wasn't sure what you were doing or when you would arrive; you have been busy," Doc Larkin said. "I heard about the drug dealer; I can't say I'm sorry."

"We were lucky. Dad?"

"I talked to Louise and the family and told them about the reality behind Victor's condition. He is aware and comes in and out of consciousness; the blood loss was significant and has severely impacted the liver and kidneys. This is mostly due to a lack of oxygen carried by the blood. The blood thinners were there to protect the brain from further clots and strokes; unfortunately, the bullet to the upper chest and lung was catastrophic. We did what we could, but it was impossible to stop the bleeding no matter how much we transfused; he went into hypovolemic shock. I'm afraid he has lost his kidneys, and there is peripheral necrosis in his legs, and it is spreading."

Jordan turned and looked back to the room. She took a deep breath. "He is dying."

"Yes, Jordan, he is dying. There is nothing I can do to change the outcome. I will do what I can to keep him comfortable. There is no pain; if he begins to show any, we will take care of it. Your mother said he was showing signs of confusion. Is that what you saw?"

"Yes, between the strokes and the growing confusion, he was fading"—Jordan stopped and grabbed Doc Larkin's hand—"away."

Larkin squeezed Jordan's hand and led her back into the room.

Victor woke and talked to Louise. The conversation was slow and confusing, but Louise understood every word. She kissed him and held his hand. Just before midnight, the beeping stopped, and Victor William Tynes died. He was the fifth generation of the Tyneses in Montana; his father, William Tynes, who was born in Bozeman, died in 2003 at age eighty-five.

* * *

A month later, Jordan learned that John Wang had been released to Chinese officials to be tried in Hong Kong. It was a matter of international diplomacy. She also learned that the bodies of those Chinese killed at the Mexican restaurant and the house in Bozeman were returned to China. She was sure the trial would not be held. The bodies of the Mexicans, including those exhumed at the house along the Boulder River, were not claimed. Suarez and his gang members were interred in the cemetery near the state prison in Deer Lodge.

Investigations were underway to discover the owners of the various properties and houses where the killings had occurred and the bodies had been found. There was little incentive to pursue these owners; resolutions would take years. In time, the counties would step in and take them for back taxes. No one stood in their way.

Victor William Tynes's funeral was held in the

American Lutheran church. He was buried in the Mountain View Cemetery, next to his family. He was the twenty-second Tynes to be interred in the family plot. It was a short walk from the house to the cemetery for Jordan and Louise.

During the month since the end of the war and her father's death, Jordan and Louise talked for hours about the future. Three weeks later, Louise told Jordan she was moving to Helena to be with LeeAnn for the rest of the year. They had a large house, and she would have a bedroom with a bathroom. LeeAnn suggested the arrangement. They needed help with the girls—while beautiful children, two-year-old twins were a handful. Louise offered to babysit and cook—essentially work for her room and board. Tim and LeeAnn Grayson were thrilled. Louise thought she was getting the better part of the deal: time with her grandchildren.

Jordan took on the job of managing the house, as she put it. It was empty and made noises she hadn't heard before when her parents were roommates. But there they were, the squeaks and clatters that every house has. They seemed louder. And finally, she had a place she could call her own. She also redecorated her bedroom.

Special Agent Mike Cardona frequently visited Livingston. The federal investigations were underway, and the Drug Enforcement Administration was the focus. Most of the hearings and meetings were held in Washington, DC, behind closed doors. The theory of one bad apple governed. Mike traveled to Washington twice for meetings and interviews. He could not discuss this testimony with Jordan. But he did confess, in his usual cynical way, that time squashes all, and apple sauce will result.

Maggie recovered from her injuries. Her get-a-long had a little hitch, but Jordan was sure her age was catching up to her, not so much the recent traumas. Maggie seemed down and confused and missed Victor and Louise. She moped around the house for a few weeks and even spent evenings in Victor's chair. It is hard to explain these changes to dogs. Jordan tried to tell her, but it took time for Maggie to adjust to the new housing arrangements.

Jordan's escape was her office; it was the nerve center of her life. Five years as both acting and elected sheriff changes you. New habits are formed, your staff are both employees and friends, and you realize you are part of a web of law enforcement and camaraderie across the state. Mutual aid is more than just sending people; it provides support and help. It was a man's world, this sheriffing business, she joked; sometimes those boys need to understand a different point of view.

She was also reminded that an election was coming in the fall. Josiah Potts and Russell Pike took her to lunch to strategize, and they offered her their total support. This coming election was like a storm pushing across the horizon—a Montana storm full of thunder and lightning, boiling black clouds, and driving rain. She could not wait.

The End

A Note from the Author

Gregory C. Randall was born in Traverse City, Michigan. He grew up in the Southside suburbs of Chicago. Greg has never forgotten his Midwestern roots. Mr. Randall makes his home in Northern California.

Mr. Randall is the author of fiction and nonfiction works available through the usual outlets.

For more information about the other books that Mr. Randall has written and planned sequels, please visit and connect with Greg online:

www.gregorycrandall.info
www.windsorhillpublishing.com

See his occasional blog:

http://www.writing4death.blogspot.com

Other books by Mr. Randall:
Fiction

The Cherry Pickers
White Rabbit
Wars Amongst Lovers
Four Women Named July
The Marigold Gang, The Mystery of the Four Bodies in the Freezer
Sector 73

The Sharon O'Mara Chronicles

Land Swap For Death

Containers For Death
Toulouse For Death
12ᵗʰ Man For Death
Diamonds For Death
Limerick For Death

The Alex Polonia Thrillers
Venice Black
Saigon Red
St. Petersburg White

The Tony Alfano Thrillers
Chicago Swing
Chicago Jazz
Chicago Fix
Chicago Boogie Woogoe
Chicago Back Beat

The Max Adler World War II Thrillers
This Face of Evil
Pawns in an Ancient Game

The Deputy Sheriff Jordan Tynes Modern Westerns
One Yellow Dog
The Killings in Paradise Valley
Blood in the Yellowstone

Nonfiction
America's Original GI Town, Park Forest, Illinois

Additional copies can be purchased through Amazon.com.